WHEN MURDER CALLS

Daisy answered her phone and saw that Trevor was calling. *Her* instead of Tessa? She remembered when he'd called her before out of the blue. A shiver of foreboding made the hairs on the back of her neck prick up.

She answered, "Hey, Trevor. Does Tessa have her phone turned off?"

"No, I wanted to talk to you. She told me you went out to Wilhelm Rumple's place to buy a birthday present for Jonas."

"I did."

He went on, "And I know Jonas volunteers at Four Paws Animal Shelter."

"He does," she responded warily.

She heard Trevor let out a breath and braced herself for what was coming.

"There was a death at Four Paws. Wilhelm Rumple was found dead in a dog run."

Daisy swallowed hard. "Did he die from natural causes?"

This time, Trevor didn't hesitate. "I'm afraid not. Someone bashed him in the head . . ."

Books by Karen Rose Smith

Caprice De Luca Mysteries
STAGED TO DEATH
DEADLY DÉCOR
GILT BY ASSOCIATION
DRAPE EXPECTATIONS
SILENCE OF THE LAMPS
SHADES OF WRATH
SLAY BELLS RING
CUT TO THE CHAISE

Daisy's Tea Garden Mysteries
MURDER WITH LEMON TEA CAKES
MURDER WITH CINNAMON SCONES
MURDER WITH CUCUMBER SANDWICHES
MURDER WITH CHERRY TARTS
MURDER WITH CLOTTED CREAM
MURDER WITH OOLONG TEA
MURDER WITH ORANGE PEKOE TEA
MURDER WITH DARJEELING TEA

Published by Kensington Publishing Corp.

Murder with Darjeeling Tea

KAREN ROSE SMITH

Kensington Publishing Corp.
www.kensingtonbooks.com

First Printing: June 2022
ISBN: 978-1-4967-3398-6

ISBN: 978-1-4967-3400-6 (ebook)

10 9 8 7 6 5 4 3 2 1

Printed in the United States of America

To the men and women involved in animal rescue.
You make this world a kinder place.

ACKNOWLEDGMENTS

I would like to thank Officer Greg Berry, my law enforcement consultant, who so patiently answers all my questions. His input is invaluable.

CHAPTER ONE

Daisy Swanson and her son-in-law, Foster Cranshaw, stood on a rural road outside the more bustling tourist area of Willow Creek, Pennsylvania. The small town was nestled deep in Lancaster County Amish country. Together, they faced a stone cottage that looked like something out of a fairy tale. With its red shutters, gabled roof, and arched wooden front door, it gave off a quaint air.

The September breeze, with notes of cooler days ahead, lifted Daisy's blond hair and tossed it away from her face. Scents from the pine forest near the eastern side of the cottage lingered, wafting toward her.

"Have you ever met Mr. Rumple?" Foster asked as they headed toward the fence to the side of the house with its sign RUMPLE'S STATUARY.

"I don't think he's ever visited the tea garden, but so

many of my clients have bought statuary here. They tell me he's a little odd. I'm not sure what that means."

"We're about to find out," Foster warned as the gate on the fence opened.

A dog trotted out. Daisy had seen photos of canines like this one. It was a Plott hound, probably weighing in at about fifty pounds. His brown coat was brindled—striped with tan.

Foster's elbow nudged Daisy's. "Stand perfectly still."

They did, but Daisy soon realized there was no need for that.

After the hound stopped about three feet from them, a short man exited the backyard and smiled as he approached.

Foster leaned toward Daisy's shoulder and murmured for her ears only. "He looks like a troll."

"Foster," Daisy chastised, though looking at the little man, she had to admit there was some truth in Foster's description.

Wilhelm Rumple was a stumpy man with unusual features. His brown hair was curly, fuzzy, and stuck out around his head. His nose was large and his mouth wide. His ears were more pronounced because of the style of his hair. He wore red overalls with a long-sleeved black T-shirt underneath. His feet were bare as he stood on the concrete walkway that led into his backyard.

"Mrs. Swanson?" he asked with a tilt of his head and a smile, as he extended his hand to her. The dog stood at his side.

"Yes." Daisy glanced at the dog who seemed stoic. "We spoke on the phone yesterday when I called to ask about your hours."

"I never forget a potential sale," he assured her with a wink. "This time of year, I don't have many customers stopping by, so private appointments are good to make sure I'm around."

Daisy introduced Foster, and he too shook Mr. Rumple's hand. "I'm the manpower," Foster said in a kidding tone. "In case whatever Daisy buys is heavy."

"Come on into the backyard," Mr. Rumple invited. "Hans, here, won't bother you. I already told him you're safe. Tell me what you're looking for."

Following Mr. Rumple and Hans, Daisy realized she'd had never seen so many concrete statues. There was a lion practically as huge as a real one. It was surrounded by smaller statues that were replicas of frogs, birds, toadstools, and children. They were lined up everywhere in no particular order.

When Foster gave her a wide-eyed look, she almost laughed. She answered the proprietor's question. "I'm looking for a statue for my boyfriend. He adopted a golden retriever. I thought a lawn ornament depicting one would be nice."

"I sell a lot of these," Mr. Rumple said, waving his hand over his backyard. "But I have a collection of dogs if you're considering a birthday gift for someone special."

"More expensive than these?" Foster guessed.

Mr. Rumple grinned. "Exactly. I keep them inside if you'd like to see them. Then you can decide if you want a collectible for a shelf or something larger for the outdoors."

Daisy wasn't exactly sure about going into a stranger's house, but Foster was with her, and after all, this was

Rumple's Statuary . . . a business. As she'd told Foster, many of her clients at the tea garden bought from Mr. Rumple and seemed pleased with their purchases.

Foster gave her a shrug as if this decision were up to her. She'd come to love this young man as she would a son. He and Vi, her older daughter, hadn't married under the best of circumstances because Vi had been pregnant. But they were doing their best to forge a life together.

The truth was that Daisy respected Foster more and more each day. His russet-brown hair had also been blown by the wind, and his rimless glasses were slipping down his nose. He was wearing jeans and a green windbreaker with the Millersville insignia—the college he attended. Like Daisy, he'd worn sneakers, not knowing where they'd be trekking.

"I'd like to see what you have," Daisy responded to the man, curious about the inside of the cottage. Even the back entrance had a storybook quality with its little red gable that protected the back door.

"Come on then," Mr. Rumple encouraged, leading them to the granite steps.

On her way, Daisy passed a four-foot alabaster statue of a boy with a fishing rod. Beside him was a two-foot concrete statue of a little boy reading to a dog. That one was cute. She didn't see any replicas of cats. Her two felines would be insulted. Maybe Mr. Rumple only liked dogs.

They entered a kitchen that was compact and tiny. However, it was up to date with stainless steel appliances and granite countertops. The knotty pine cupboards, somewhat like those in her own kitchen, gave this space an old-world air.

"This is an unusual cottage," she said to its owner. "When was it built?"

Rumple turned to them as he led them past a living room with a stone fireplace that had a wood stove insert and then into a room on the left. "The original house was built in 1934. When I bought it, I completely gutted and renovated it."

"The millwork around the doors is beautiful," Daisy noted.

"That's oak. I did that all myself. I also used it on the walls in my office."

In Wilhelm Rumple's office, she studied what looked like a floor-to-ceiling gun safe. The room wasn't large. There was a blond oak desk adorned with a small Tiffany lamp, but she noted the absence of a computer. Maybe there was a laptop in one of the drawers . . . or elsewhere.

Mr. Rumple's dog sniffed up and down the legs of Daisy's jeans. Mr. Rumple asked, "Do you mind?"

"Not at all," Daisy responded with a smile. "He probably smells my two cats."

The man wrinkled his broad nose as if the idea of cats wasn't attractive to him. Then he requested, "Can you and your son-in-law turn around while I open the safe?"

Now Daisy was intensely curious to see what was inside the appliance. From the interested expression on Foster's face, she could tell he was curious, too.

Daisy heard the *beep-beep-beep* as Mr. Rumple tapped in digits. She counted six.

There was another second or two until the man said, "Okay, you can look now." He set his thumb on a small square on the side of the digital pad. After another beep and a green light, he swung open the safe's door.

That was some secure safe!

As the Plott hound finished sniffing Daisy's legs and settled on the floor beside her sneakered foot, she peered into the safe. With a glance at Foster, she saw that his eyes behind his glass lenses were wide.

The shelves within the safe narrowed in height. There were six of them. Mr. Rumple began to explain what they were seeing. To that effect, he'd taken a pointer with a stiff felt tip from his desktop.

From her first glance at the dog figurines on the shelves, Daisy suspected they were all collectibles.

Mr. Rumple began with the lowest shelf, which was about five inches high. The first dog he pointed to looked to be primitive art.

"This is a paperweight," he explained. "As you can see in the casting, it's a Plymouth Foundry iron dog with the price of five hundred and fifty dollars." He gave Daisy a wink. "Everything, of course, is negotiable."

Daisy's gaze traveled to the next dog, a replica of a Dalmatian.

Mr. Rumple carefully pointed to that. "That's a Victorian bronze doorstopper. The price comes in at five hundred and ninety-five dollars."

Foster stooped closer to the floor. "How can that be a doorstopper when it's only as tall as a soda can?"

Mr. Rumple straightened to study Foster. "It's very heavy . . . small but mighty, and all that."

Foster straightened, too, and arched his brows at Daisy. "Which is the most expensive dog you're selling? Not that Daisy's interested. But I'm curious," Foster confessed.

Mr. Rumple didn't seem put off by Foster's question. "The priciest collectibles here are those." He pointed to a pair of blue dogs on the center shelf. "Four thousand for these. Herend Reserve Sapphire Blue Chrysanthemum Foo Dogs, porcelain, made in Hungary with twenty-four-karat gold accents. They only made a hundred pairs. The folklore says these dogs keep away evil spirits."

"They *should*, for that price," Foster muttered.

Mr. Rumple just gave a short, almost cackling laugh. "You'd be surprised what folks value. I have an eighteen-karat gold pug pin on the way to me that will sell for six thousand dollars."

Foster's eyes almost glazed over. "I hope you have security on this place."

"Oh, I do. And I don't just show anyone this collection. But speaking with your mother-in-law yesterday, I had the impression she might appreciate it."

"Oh, I do," Daisy responded. "But I really am searching for something simpler."

Mr. Rumple nodded. "Let me secure this, and we'll go look for something out back." Moments later, Mr. Rumple commanded his dog, "Outside, Hans."

The dog headed out of the room towards the back door.

As Mr. Rumple led them through the house once more, Foster leaned close to Daisy. "There weren't even any normal-looking dogs in that safe. Why would he think you were interested?"

"Maybe he thinks I'm a high roller," Daisy teased. "Or . . . I did mention I owned the tea garden. Maybe he thinks I'll spread the word."

Daisy again admired the stone fireplace and chimney as she walked through the living room. She preferred a real wood fire, and that's why she hadn't had a wood stove insert installed into her fireplace. But she supposed Mr. Rumple's method kept the house warmer.

Outside again, Mr. Rumple said, "Come on. I'll show you the section where I have the most dogs."

They walked down a gravel path, turned right at a concrete bench, and entered an area where statues stood in an assortment of heights. She spotted a greyhound right away. Another statue, about two feet high, resembled a cocker spaniel.

Suddenly, there was a yell from the gate where Daisy and Foster had entered the property. A man called, "Rumple, I need to talk to you."

Mr. Rumple didn't seem bothered by the intrusion. To Daisy and Foster, he said, "You just look around. I'll be right back." Hans trotted after his master.

When Daisy checked the fence again and studied the man who'd come into the sales yard, she thought she recognized him. She'd seen his face more than once in the *Willow Creek Messenger* and on the local news. Leaning closer to Foster, keeping her voice low, she asked, "Isn't that Stanley King?"

Foster took a look for himself. "You mean that CEO of the pet supplements company?"

"Yes, that's the one. He has that large farm over near Possum Road."

All at once, King's voice raised enough in volume that both she and Foster could hear him. "My son's wedding is costing me a *mint*. You're just going to have to wait for this month's payment."

She watched as Hans took a step closer to King, but she didn't hear him growl. Mr. Rumple nonchalantly kicked a stone at his foot, and it tumbled through the grass as he answered Stanley King. "No, I won't wait. You'll just have to scale down your flower order for the wedding."

Mr. King studied the dog and growled something that Daisy couldn't hear. Abruptly, he left the yard, slamming the wooden gate behind him.

As Mr. Rumple and Hans returned to the area where Daisy stood, she quickly turned back to Foster. They perused the statues once more. It wasn't long before Daisy found one she liked. It was a two-foot-high concrete statue of a golden retriever and looked just like Felix, the dog Jonas had adopted. It would be perfect for his townhouse's porch.

"Do you think he'll like this one?" she asked Foster.

"That looks like something Jonas would appreciate. Vi told me that you were spending all your free time together. Felix sure likes your place, too."

Daisy and Jonas Groft, who owned Woods—a furniture store down the street from Daisy's Tea Garden—had been dating seriously for months. They'd had bumpy times over those months, but the outcome of each challenge was that they'd grown closer. They were serious about their relationship. They'd both said *I love you*. They hadn't taken their relationship to a more intimate level, but Daisy was ready and expected that Jonas was, too. She was planning a surprise birthday party for him at a farm-to-table facility in an old barn. She was inviting friends and family, and she hoped he'd be pleased.

In the silence of the early evening, Daisy heard a car

angrily start up outside the property's gate. The car sounded angry because King revved the engine three times, and the tires squealed as he pulled away.

Mr. Rumple glanced in that direction but didn't seem particularly bothered by what he heard.

Daisy said, "I'll take this one," and pointed to the statue. The price tag was on it, and she thought it was fair.

Mr. Rumple said, "If you give me your credit card, I'll take care of it inside and then bring out your receipt."

"I'll carry it to the car for you," Foster offered. "It has weight to it."

After giving Mr. Rumple her card and making sure Foster didn't need help with the statue, she turned to watch Mr. Rumple walk under the red gable to the inside of his house. As he did, she wondered what his dispute with Stanley King was all about.

Daisy walked through the main tearoom at Daisy's Tea Garden early the next morning, making sure everything was ready for the first visitor. Daisy and her Aunt Iris had bought the old Victorian after a bakery had closed on the first floor. She and her aunt had renovated the downstairs into a tea, baked goods, soup, and salad business, and the upstairs into an apartment. Daisy's best friend Tessa from high school, who was her kitchen manager, lived upstairs now.

The main tearoom wasn't fussy like many tearooms, though it did have a subtle flower theme. She and her aunt had wanted men to feel comfortable here as well as women. They drew from the professional offices in Willow Creek and Lancaster, too, as well as from the tourist trade. Lancaster County Amish country was a popular getaway. The walk-in, be served, or buy-and-go room was welcoming with its oak glass-topped tables and mismatched, antique oak hand-carved chairs. The walls had been painted the palest green because Daisy believed the color promoted calming . . . as tea did.

The spillover tea area—where she was heading now carrying a tray with cups and saucers—was a more private room. The quaint qualities of the Victorian—a bay window, window seats, crown molding, and diamond-cut glass—characterized the area where the walls were painted the palest yellow. The tables here were pristine white, and each chair wore a seat cushion in blue, green, and yellow pinstripes. Iris and their staff took appointments for full-service tea customers in this room on specified days.

"I'm right behind you," Tessa announced, carrying another tray, this one with baked goods for their meeting. Daisy, Tessa, and Iris would be discussing the Storybook Tea, an event they were hosting in October.

Daisy glanced over her shoulder at Tessa. Her best friend's rich caramel hair was braided today. She'd paired her lime-green top with white slacks. She liked wearing smocks in lieu of the usual chef's coat.

Iris was already waiting at the table in front of the window where autumn sun flowed into the room. As Daisy set the tray with cups of Darjeeling tea on the table along with a pot of wildflower honey and thin slices of lemon, Iris sniffed the flavor in her teacup. "I do love Darjeeling."

Darjeeling tea was the tea garden's special of the month. The Darjeeling region in the Himalayan Mountains of West Bengal, India produced a black tea. Today,

Daisy was serving the group a first flush Darjeeling that was harvested in the region in mid-March. It had a light color and mild aroma.

Daisy smiled, seeing her aunt's pleasure at breathing in the scent of the brewed tea. Daisy and her Aunt Iris had always been close. Her aunt's short ash-brown curls bounced with enthusiasm as she arranged the tea service on the table for all of them. The sun glinted over Iris's shoulder. She'd already donned her Daisy's Tea Garden apron with its huge daisy logo on the yellow fabric. Under the apron, she was wearing a pale pink T and matching slacks with taupe and black sneakers. She took a cheese biscuit from the tiered tray Tessa had brought in, setting it on the dessert plate as Daisy and Tessa took their seats.

"I've already started the flyers for the Storybook Tea," Daisy explained. "At least, the text on them is finished. Foster will be able to set it up and then print them out when he arrives. Iris mentioned that the children should bring their favorite book, and that their parents should bring their favorite childhood book. If they don't have it, they should wear a name tag displaying the title. We'll provide the tags, of course."

Tessa added a spoonful of honey to her Darjeeling which had been poured into a porcelain cup with a fluted rim. The finish was pearlescent aqua. "Are we sure Ned Pachenko will be able to play and sing for the kids?"

Daisy added a cinnamon stick from a small crystal bowl to her cup of tea. She'd poured hers into a Royal Doulton cup with blue flowers and a silver trim. "I spoke with him yesterday, and he's assured me that he's ready. He said he even made up a few songs with children's book titles. He's going to put a placard in his store about the Storybook Tea, and we might gain some new customers. Foster will be advertising it on a few tea websites along with the newsletter that we send out. I'm hoping we'll sell all the tickets. There's no telling what the weather will be, or if we'll be able to serve at the outside tables."

The tea garden had a side entrance that led to a patio where they served customers in acceptable weather under yellow-and-white-striped umbrellas.

"We can always sell more tickets closer to the date," Iris suggested. She took a bite of the cheese biscuit that was still warm, flaky, and oozed cheesy goodness.

Studying the tiered tray, Daisy lifted a lemon teacake from it and set it on her plate.

From the other side of the silver serving stand, Tessa selected a mini-cherry tart. She popped it into her mouth, chewed, and then wiped her fingers on a napkin. "Did you find Jonas a birthday present last night?"

"I did. It was an interesting visit to Wilhelm Rumple's house and business. Jonas and I have passed that house many times on our bike rides." Jonas had bought the two of them bikes that one of his customers had been selling. They'd found one for Jazzi—Daisy's younger daughter—at Wheels, Willow Creek's bike shop, and the three of them often went bike riding together.

"In what way was it interesting?" Tessa asked with a side tilt of her head and a mischievous grin.

"Mr. Rumple is an unusual man." Daisy didn't know how else to say it. She explained how he'd invited her and Foster inside to see the expensive statues in a gun safe. "Afterward, while I was outside choosing a statue for Jonas, Stanley King stopped by."

"Stanley King?" Iris asked. "The one with all the

money, who always has his picture in the *Willow Creek Messenger*?"

"That's the one. And he didn't seem happy. I don't know exactly what he had to do with Mr. Rumple, but Mr. Rumple mentioned Mr. King's son's wedding."

Tessa lifted a snickerdoodle from the tiered tray and set it on her plate. She pointed to it. "I have more dough for these ready to go in the walk-in." Then, moving the conversation back to the discussion, she admitted, "I know all about the King–Miller wedding. Trevor is going to cover it for his *Pennsylvania Country* blog."

Tessa was dating Trevor Lundquist, a reporter for the *Willow Creek Messenger*. In recent months, though, he had expanded his career into blogging, hoping to earn more money from advertisers.

As Tessa continued, she smiled. "Talk about storybooks. The King–Miller wedding is a Cinderella story for Clancy Miller's daughter."

"How so?" Iris asked.

As a side thread, Daisy added, "Violet loves the croissants from that bakery."

After Tessa nodded in agreement, she answered Iris's question. "Miller's daughter Caroline works at Pastry Goods. She met King's son Andrew when he contracted with their bakery to deliver bread products to the King farm on Sunday mornings. Apparently, they have a family brunch every weekend."

"Is Clancy Miller related to you?" Iris asked.

"Not that I know of. He and his daughter moved to Willow Creek about three years ago. I suppose every Miller is related in some way from way back when.

"What type of statue did you buy Jonas?" Tessa asked, dropping the subject of a wedding.

"It's a sitting golden retriever, about two feet high. I hope he'll like it. I'm meeting him at the animal shelter this afternoon."

"Is he volunteering again?" Iris asked.

"He is. He makes time for it, like so many volunteers do. I wish I could help out."

"Not a good idea," Iris warned with a shake of her finger. "If you did, you'd convince all of us to adopt a dog."

Daisy laughed. Her Aunt Iris was probably right.

CHAPTER TWO

Daisy parked by the building that had once been an old schoolhouse. Four Paws Animal Shelter had originated as a farm family's dream. Noah Langston and his sister Serena had taken care of the farm animals on their mom and dad's Willow Creek farm. They'd also taken in strays and found them homes. Noah had become a veterinarian, and Serena had earned a business degree so they could partner in Four Paws—an endeavor they'd discussed since they were teens. Serena and Noah had given up their former lives which had helped them earn the seed funds for the nonprofit, no-kill shelter that relied on donations and fundraising to survive.

Since the old schoolhouse had practically been collapsing, they'd managed to buy it from the town for a pittance. The black door was decorated with four huge white paw prints.

Daisy walked up the two steps to the open front porch that was supported with two pillars. The structure, probably once clapboard, was now covered with red vinyl siding. The gabled roof was topped with a cupola.

Once inside, Daisy stepped onto the gray laminate flooring. The counter in the reception area had a glazed butcher-block top.

Serena Langston was seated behind the counter and welcomed Daisy with a warm smile. In her thirties, Serena was a pretty young woman who wore her dark brown hair in a distinctive braided corona around her head. Her constant companion, a black standard poodle, sat beside her and gazed up at Daisy with intelligent brown eyes as she approached.

"How are you doing today?" Serena asked.

"I'm doing well. I came to meet Jonas."

Serena motioned through the glass-paned door and down the hall. "He's cleaning kennels. He told me he left Felix with his original owner for a little visit."

"Yes, he did." Adele Gunnarson, Felix's original dog mom, lived in an assisted living facility. "She gets lonely sometimes for Felix, so he visits. It does them both good. We'll pick him up after Jonas is finished here and take him to my place where he can run to his heart's content."

Serena looked down at the poodle and fondly gave her a scratch behind her ears. "Bellamy here likes to run, too."

"When Jonas adopted Felix, Adele told us his name means *fortunate and happy*. And he is."

"Names are important. Bellamy means *fine friend*, and she certainly is."

Daisy could see the affection between the poodle and Serena. After a wave and *see you later*, Daisy went through the doors that led to where the dogs were housed. Jonas was standing in the hall, speaking to a woman who looked to be in her sixties. Her hair was brown and gray, parted in the center. There were bags under her eyes, and Daisy wondered if she hadn't slept well. She had a double chin and thin lips with no lipstick. Her uniform of choice said she was a volunteer, too. She was wearing a FOUR PAWS T-shirt and gray sweatpants with sneakers.

As soon as Jonas saw Daisy, his face lit up, the same way hers must have when she spotted him. When she reached him, he swung his arm around her. "Daisy, this is Hetta Armbruster."

"Hi, Hetta." Daisy extended her hand.

Hetta shook it and smiled back. "This might be our first meeting," Hetta said. "But I know who you are. My sister's one of your regular customers at the tea garden."

"Who's that?" Daisy asked, eager to know.

"Fiona Wilson. She loves your soup. She takes home enough for a week."

Daisy laughed. "Yes, she does. I told her that if she ever needs it to be delivered, we'll do that."

"Oh, I can always pick it up for her."

Daisy realized there must be at least a ten-year age difference between Hetta and Fiona, the older sister.

Jonas interjected, "Hetta volunteers here many more hours than I do."

"I love taking care of the pups," Hetta admitted. "I have a Yorkshire terrier who goes to work with me."

"Where do you work?" Daisy asked.

"I work at the local flower shop, Bouquets To Go. Winkie just sits on the counter and greets customers. My daughter loves dogs, too. She bakes dog treats and sells them at the farmers market and supplies the pet store with them."

Someone called to Jonas from the back door. Jonas said to the women, "I'll be right back. They might need help unloading bags of dog food."

After Jonas had exited the kennel area, Hetta said, "Jonas is one of those good guys."

"Yes, he is."

"He told me all about Felix. You like him, too?"

"Oh, I do, and so do my girls. My grandson has become friends with him."

Daisy engaged in conversation with Hetta while Jonas was gone. Soon Hetta returned to the subject of Jonas. She said, "It's obvious Jonas loves dogs. That's how you can tell he's a good guy."

Daisy mentioned, "Jonas's birthday is coming up. I bought him a golden retriever statue from Rumple's Statuary. I'm hoping he likes it."

At the mention of Rumple's business, a scowl crossed Hetta's face. However, like the sun coming out and changing the weather, it disappeared, and she smiled once more. "I know Mr. Rumple. He loves dogs as much as I do. He volunteers here, mostly at night to watch over the dogs that just arrived or need extra care. The thing is, he's much better with dogs than humans."

Daisy had no idea what that meant. She didn't have time to ask because at that moment, Jonas returned.

"I'm ready when you are," he said. "Adele is probably going to want us to share a cup of tea with her before we leave."

"I can catch up with her for a bit. Jazzi isn't expecting me home right away."

Jonas hung his arm around Daisy's shoulders and said to Hetta, "I'll probably see you the next time I'm here."

Hetta waved. "You two have a good evening."

After Daisy wished the woman the same, she and Jonas headed up the hallway to the lobby. Daisy didn't mention what Hetta had said about Wilhelm Rumple because she didn't want Jonas to know she'd been at the statuary site. After all, his birthday present was going to be a surprise.

The following evening, Daisy and Tessa stood at a long table with refreshments at the chamber of commerce meeting. Jonas came up beside Daisy and looked over the trays of snickerdoodles, whoopie pies, and small slices of shoofly pie. She had decided to simply serve hot tea tonight. There was an urn with Darjeeling brewed for anyone who wanted a cup. The plastic plates looked like glass and had a leaf design. White napkins were printed with foliage patterns. Daisy fanned them out along one end of the table.

"The setup looks good," Jonas said. "I think they're about to start. Let's grab our seats."

Daisy slipped her hand into Jonas's as they sat and watched the president of the chamber of commerce, Betty Furhman, come to the podium. She owned Wisps and Wicks, a candle shop. These meetings were held in the firehouse's social hall, and tonight they had a good attendance. That was probably because they had a special speaker, Dalton Ames.

As Betty introduced the man, Jonas leaned close to Daisy's shoulder. "Have you heard anything about him?"

"Not yet. No scuttlebutt. But I'm sure there will be some soon."

As the man stood at the podium, Daisy studied him. She had heard Dalton was in his mid-forties. He was handsome in a hipster kind of way. His black hair with a graying tint swept up from his forehead and back. There wasn't a crease in his forehead, and Daisy wondered if he'd had Botox. Sitting in the second row, she could tell that his eyes were hazel. He had high cheekbones, and his ears were close to his head. In a contemporary style, his mustache and beard were scraggly and so popular now. She estimated he was probably as tall as Jonas. Wearing a pale blue T-shirt under a navy sports jacket paired with navy slacks, Dalton obviously meant the outfit to be casually professional.

As he looked out over his audience, he caught Daisy's eye and smiled wider. What the heck was *that* about?

Dalton Ames was a professional fundraiser for the homeless shelter that Willow Creek wanted to build. Maybe he smiled like that at everyone.

She listened intently to the man. The homeless shelter had been controversial with many pros and many cons, but the town had decided to build it because they felt they needed it. This professional fundraiser was supposed to help the town meet their monetary goal by the end of the year. Whether that would happen or not, Daisy didn't know.

One by one, Dalton Ames laid out his strategies. He warned the business owners that the most important thing was to create a plan of action. They would set goals, choose the right strategies, and work the plan.

"I know the chamber of commerce and the town council will be involved with this," Dalton said. "I'll submit a list of ideas, and you will have to vote on the strategies you want to employ. That could include anything from a walkathon to individual businesses hosting donation parties to forming a comprehensive email list to reaching out to organizations farther afield from Willow Creek for their help."

Daisy was listening to Dalton, but at the same time, she was glancing around the room. The town council members were all sitting together in a back row. To her surprise, she spotted Wilhelm Rumple in the row in front of those members. She wasn't sure why she was surprised. Maybe because he just didn't seem the type to be a member of the chamber of commerce. But she shouldn't have made that judgment.

After Dalton finished his presentation, other business didn't take very long. Soon the people gathered were dispersing. Zeke Willet, a detective on the police force and a friend of Jonas's, came to sit with them. Dalton was still at the podium, speaking with the mayor and Daniel Copeland, who was the assistant manager of Willow Creek Community Bank and also a member of the town council.

Recently, another member of the town council had asked Zeke to look into Dalton Ames's background. Before Daisy could ask about it, Zeke leaned across Jonas and said to the two of them, "Obviously Ames checked out, or he wouldn't be up there. He has a divorce in his past, but there aren't any lawsuits against him. So I guess the town's going to let him raise all the money he can for this project."

"I have a feeling we're all going to be involved in raising the money," Daisy responded.

"You're probably right." Zeke sat back in his chair.

To her surprise, an Amish man came up the aisle. When Daisy caught a better look, she saw that it was Levi Fisher. His wife Rachel had been a childhood friend of hers. Daisy's parents owned Gallagher's Garden Corner. When they were opening their fledgling business, they were able to grow some of their trees, or at least start them, on Rachel's family property. Her family was New Order Amish, and their district's bishop wasn't opposed to Englischers the same way Old Order Amish could be. As Willow Creek grew, the Gallaghers and the Eshes had helped each other out. A by-product of that was Daisy's friendship with Rachel as they played on the Esh farm together, collected eggs from the chickens, and tomatoes from the garden. They'd stayed friends throughout the years. When Rachel had married, Levi Fisher had accepted Daisy as one of Rachel's friends.

He wore black trousers with black suspenders and a dark blue shirt. With his black felt hat in his hands and his beard signifying his marital status, he could have looked like any other Amish man in Willow Creek. Levi's face had always held warmth and friendship. He was a kind man, a good and loyal husband, and a wonderful father. Now, however, he looked somewhat upset.

Daisy rose to greet him. "Levi, is everything all right?"

"Rachel insisted I come to this meeting to see what the fundraising was all about. But she broke her arm this afternoon, and I wanted to stay home. When I saw you, I thought you might want to know."

"Of course, I want to know. Tell Rachel I'll be out to see her. What happened?"

"She had a fall. I'm sure she'll tell you all about it. She said she's sure feeling *fahuudelt*."

Levi lapsed into Pennsylvania Dutch when he was upset. She could tell he was worried about Rachel. *Fahuudelt* meant tangled and confused.

"Is there anything I can do? Anything I can bring?"

"*Danki*," Levi murmured. "Just your presence will help. I want to get back to her. You have a *gut nacht*."

Dalton and fundraising forgotten, Jonas asked Daisy, "Do you want to ride out to Rachel's tonight?"

After Daisy thought about it, she decided against it. If Rachel had been injured today, she had probably been at the hospital to get her arm set. "She's had enough disruption for today, I imagine. She'll have family around her. I'll stop tomorrow around midday and take her lunch."

"The weather's supposed to be perfect tomorrow for bike riding. Why don't you and Jazzi and I take our bikes out after supper?"

"And Felix?" Daisy asked with a grin.

"Do you think Vi and Sammy and Foster would like his company for an hour or so while we're gone? I don't want to impose on them, but Sammy seems to like being around Felix."

"Everyone likes being around Felix," Daisy assured him.

With that conclusion a certainty between them, Daisy and Jonas said goodbye to Zeke and headed out.

The following afternoon, Daisy drove to the Fisher farm. She parked on the gravel area and went to the back door. She'd been here many, many times since Rachel had married Levi.

When Daisy was a child, she and Rachel had run in

and out of the Esh house as if it was home to them both. Daisy had felt comfortable there, even without modern conveniences. She'd learned modern conveniences weren't as important as family, meals around the table, good smells in the kitchen, and playtime around the chicken coop or pond.

The Esh property where Daisy and Rachel had run through the fields of corn stalks was now run by Rachel's oldest brother and his wife. In this house, Levi's *grossmami*, his grandmother Mary, lived with him, Rachel, and the children.

Mary came to the door, and her smile brightened when she saw Daisy. "I'm so glad you're here."

Daisy carried a basket of baked goods, salads, and soups. She handed it to Mary. "I hope you can use this."

"I've been cooking, but I'll be glad for this, certain sure. Rachel insists she can cook, too, but with one arm, that's not so good an idea. *Ya?*"

"I'm sure Rachel would find a way."

"Don't encourage her," Mary warned. "She's sprained her ankle, too, and should be off it. But she'll tell you all about it. *Gott segen eich*," Mary said and lifted the basket Daisy had given her.

Daisy knew Mary had just said *God bless you*. Daisy responded with, "Rachel is my friend. I want to do anything I can to help."

After Mary moved into the kitchen, Daisy followed. There, Daisy could see that Mary had been slicing apples.

Mary saw her looking. "I'm going to cook them with cinnamon and butter. I'll stay here." She motioned Daisy into the living room. "You talk to Rachel."

Daisy found Rachel sitting in a chair by the window, quilting squares on her lap. Lots of the furniture had seen generations of Levi's family. Rachel was seated in a wood armchair, her leg propped up on a stool. Her heart *kapp* was a bit askew, which was unusual for her. She was wearing a lavender dress with her black apron.

Daisy warned quickly, "Don't you even try to get up."

Rachel gave her a weak smile. "I have heard that many times today."

"What can I do to help?" Daisy asked.

"Just talk to me," Rachel said. "Take my mind off everything I cannot do. Levi's brother is helping with the farm chores. Hannah's betrothed is, too. Her wedding is in a few weeks, and I'm afraid not everything will be done. The doctor says I need this cast for a month. A month!"

Daisy knew the kind of preparations that went into an Amish wedding. Everyone from the district would be invited. There would be cooking, cleaning, and Hannah's wedding dress to be made.

"Take my mind off the wedding," Rachel said with a pleading tone in her voice. "I'm not able to do what I usually do. Hannah and Sarah are running the store for me. As soon as my ankle feels better, at least I'll be able to go in there. I can check out customers if nothing else. How is Jonas?"

Daisy felt her cheeks pinken. "He's good. I'm trying to make final arrangements for a surprise birthday party for him. It's a farm-to-table dinner at The Farm Barn. You, your family, and Levi will come, won't you?"

"I'll speak with Levi about it. Did you find what you wanted for Jonas's birthday? You said you were looking for something special."

Daisy told Rachel about her visit to Wilhelm Rumple's.

"He does sound a little unusual. But it takes all kinds, *ya*? We know that, don't we?"

"Yes, we do. So how did you fall?" Daisy asked, seeing Rachel look a tad perkier than she had a few minutes before.

Rachel fingered a string on her *kapp*. "I was at the chicken coop. Two of the chickens skittered in front of me. I was carrying a basket of eggs and not watching where I was going. Besides the chickens, there was a dip in the ground, and down I went. I'm just thankful Luke was around doing morning chores. He heard the ruckus in the chicken coop and came to see what was happening. He called a driver to take me to the hospital."

Luke, Rachel's and Levi's son, was a responsible young man. "He could have called *me*," Daisy assured her.

"It was early, Daisy, and you had your own business to run."

When Amish needed to travel more than a few miles, they hired drivers. It was a common practice. Daisy knew Rachel had a list of three who were often available when they were needed. She was just glad her son had called one who had been available to help her. The Amish prided themselves on being self-sufficient, though community was everything to them. They rallied around each other when they were needed, but they didn't often like to go outside of that circle to find help.

Mary poked her head into the living room. "How about a cup of tea?"

"Only if you let me help you make it and serve it," Daisy said. "That's non-negotiable."

"Such long words you Englischers use," Mary said teasingly.

A burst of laughs all around brightened Rachel's face even more.

Daisy went to the kitchen to help Mary brew tea. She was sure a cup of tea, a bowl of soup, and a few snicker-doodles might cheer them all.

The maple trees seemed to be the first to turn every fall, coloring yellow. The oaks dripped with russet colors and stood in patchy groves that Daisy, Jonas, and Jazzi biked past down the country roads. Autumn was strikingly making its appearance. As they biked along farms both large and small, they didn't converse much, only commenting now and then when something caught their attention.

At one point, though, Jonas steered closer to Daisy and edged up beside her. "I might lose my store manager."

"Oh, no. Why does Tony want to leave?"

"That's the thing. I don't think he does."

Tony Fitz had been Jonas's manager since he opened the store.

Jazzi caught up to them from behind and asked, "Then why is he thinking about leaving?"

Their voices carried in the day-end country silence. Absent of noise and traffic—not even horses and buggies clopping past—they could hear each other easily. Ever since Jonas had helped Jazzi find her birth mother, the two of them had formed a bond. He didn't mind Jazzi being involved in his life. They were all involved in each other's lives now, and Daisy liked that. She liked that a lot.

Pedaling slowly, he included Jazzi in the conversation. "You might be able to understand it, Jazzi, more than some people I know. I imagine relationships are difficult in high school, too. But I think teenagers today talk about it more than older folks."

"You're not all that old," Jazzi asserted, making Jonas crack a wide smile.

"That means I'm not old either," Daisy interjected.

Jazzi ignored her mother's comment, even though she gave her an amused glance.

Jonas explained, "When Elijah and I had that sale this summer, I know that Tony was upset that he wasn't more involved."

Apparently eager to jump right in, Jazzi asked, "Tony doesn't make furniture, does he?"

"No, he doesn't. I think that's part of the issue," Jonas decided. "He feels left out while he manages the store. Elijah and I took care of the sale, set everything up in Elijah's barn, and then delivered the furniture to the customers who bought it. Tony kept the store running."

It seemed that Jazzi understood what Jonas was saying right away. "So he feels like he's on the fringes."

Daisy added, "He doesn't feel needed." She settled back on her seat more comfortably, letting the breeze whip her windbreaker a bit. "Are you going to talk to Elijah about Tony?"

Without giving Jonas the time to answer, Jazzi said, "That's not the right thing to do. You compared them to teenagers. Believe me, I know my friends."

"What do you suggest?" Jonas asked with genuine interest.

Without hesitation, Jazzi answered. "You know how you felt when Mom talked to Zeke instead of *you* talking to Zeke. Elijah and Tony need to figure this out without you stepping in."

Daisy didn't have a chance to hear what Jonas might comment because he glanced over his shoulder when the scream of a police siren sounded.

Daisy, Jonas, and Jazzi pulled over to stop as a police car with flashing lights zoomed past them. After it passed, the three of them climbed on their bikes and started pumping faster. Daisy knew they were headed past Wilhelm Rumple's property. Did that police car have something to do with him? Why was she even thinking that?

"Maybe we shouldn't be rushing toward that police car," Daisy said, out of breath as they pedaled harder.

Jazzi asked facetiously, "Do you want to turn around and go the other way?"

Daisy knew that wasn't in any of their natures.

After a half mile, they came upon Rumple's Statuary. She didn't want to tell Jonas that she'd stopped there the other night. She threw Jazzi a look. Jazzi nodded, knowing exactly what Daisy meant. They were both going to keep quiet.

Daisy knew that keeping her drive there with Foster a secret was possible, unless Rumple was in his front yard, and he recognized her. She'd have to stay out of his sight.

A second police car, without its siren blaring, was also parked at the property. Both Jonas and Daisy knew Bart Cosner, an officer who was standing at the edge of the yard as if he were guarding it. Mr. Rumple didn't seem to be around, and Daisy wondered if he was inside.

"What's going on?" Jonas asked Bart.

"It's an attempted break-in," Bart said to Jonas, not thinking twice about it. "It's over."

Jonas pounced on the word *attempted*. "You're sure it was only *attempted*?" he asked.

Bart nodded. "The owner has a sophisticated security system that surrounds the property. It's underground."

At that, Daisy could feel her eyes widen. She supposed that made sense, with the large statues in the open and expensive ones inside.

"He has a dog, too," Bart added.

"Is it a watchdog?" Jonas asked.

"Might be, but not a very ferocious one." Bart was holding his mobile phone in his hand. "Tommy's behind the fence. When he checked in with me, he said he was petting the pooch."

"Maybe the trespasser was a kid trying to steal a statue," Jonas commented.

Apparently, Jonas knew what business Rumple had here.

"Could be," Bart said. "After Tommy makes his report, I think we'll be leaving. No harm, no foul."

Daisy was glad about that. She just hoped *no harm, no foul* would be the final conclusion.

CHAPTER THREE

Daisy loved her home. It was a barn that had been turned into something a lot more. The building had been made over, outside and in. The outside had been covered with barn-red siding, and the gray, brown, and white stone base had been repointed and cleaned. Pristine white trimmed the windows as well as the dormers. Her deceased husband's insurance money had made her new life in Willow Creek possible. She'd always be grateful for that.

The inside now looked like anything but a barn. The second floor had been divided into two bedrooms with a bath in between that had suited her daughters perfectly. The downstairs had been renovated for practicality as well as coziness. There was an open stairway to the rear of the living room that led from the upstairs to down. A huge wagon-wheel chandelier glowed in the living room that opened into the dining area and kitchen. A floor-to-ceiling stone fireplace was the focal point in that dining area on the east wall. Daisy's bedroom was behind the living room, with a short hall that led into the kitchen. A small powder room was located under the stairs, and the laundry room was also along that wall—tiny but workable.

Daisy loved her home the most when her family was in it. Right now, Foster and Vi perched on the blue, cream, and green upholstered sofa. The blue armchair, as well as the coffee table, sat on the braided blue and rust rug that had been woven by a local Amish woman. Sammy was crawling on it with Marjoram watching from a distance.

Marjoram was a tortoiseshell feline with unique markings. One side of her face was mottled in tan, brown, and black. Her other side was completely dark brown. Various colors, including ginger and cream, spotted her back and sides while her chest was a creamy tan and rust with an almost straight line down the middle. Pepper, Daisy's other feline who was black with white fluffy spots on her chest, sat on the back of the sofa on an afghan. Pepper was calmer than Marjoram and took almost everything in stride, meowing when she approved or didn't approve. At the kitchen island, Jazzi sat, filling out applications for college.

Suddenly she got up, went to a knotty pine cupboard, and pulled down a mug. She called into the living room, "Does anyone else want hot chocolate?"

"I'll take some," Foster called back.

"Do you want me to make it?" Daisy asked from the dining area where she was putting the table to rights after they had eaten. The dining area pedestal table was oak with a distressed wood finish. She ran her hand over one of the chairs. It was an antique. She'd found them all at a flea market and refinished them herself. All of that activity had been part of her rehabilitation from grief when she'd decided to start over. For the most part, it had worked.

Daisy watched Sammy with a grandmother's pride. He was dressed today in corduroy navy overalls with a blue T-shirt underneath. He crawled almost as fast as Marjoram could run. He was pulling himself up these days and soon would be walking. Daisy watched him as he took hold of the top of the coffee table and tried to stand. He seemed frustrated, his mouth turned down, and Daisy was afraid he was going to start crying. She hurried over to him, scooped him up, and tickled his belly. He giggled and then reached to her to put his arms around her neck. She loved holding him. She loved being around him.

"How about milk in a sippy cup for you?" she asked.

He seemed to like that idea and patted her cheek with a smile on his face.

"Mom, can you sit and talk to us?" Vi asked with a serious expression on her face.

"Of course, I can." She sat with Sammy in the armchair. As soon as she did, he squiggled around, turned on his tummy, and slid down onto the floor.

Foster said, "I'll get his blocks. That should keep him occupied for a little while."

If Foster wanted Sammy to be occupied, and Daisy's attention on *them*, a frisson of nervousness went up her spine. Just what were they going to talk about?

Daisy kept a basket of books and toys handy so they could reach for them easily whenever Sammy visited.

Foster pulled out about a dozen wood blocks in many colors from the basket and sat them on the rug beside Sammy. Daisy had bought them at the farmers market at a stand run by an Amish friend of Rachel's who made wooden toys. She wanted Sammy to know the wonders of simple things as well as busy boxes with their flashing lights and music.

Jazzi, always the openly honest one around, asked, "Do you want me to go upstairs when you have this conversation?"

Vi exchanged a look with Foster. Then she called back to Jazzi, "No, you can stay."

Daisy studied her older daughter. Vi had started highlighting her honey-blond hair again. Some strands were golden while others were lighter blond. She'd gotten her hair cut recently, and it curved around her face. Daisy remembered she'd worn it that way when she'd first gone to college. Her college experience had been cut short by an unexpected pregnancy. At first, Daisy had been dismayed when Vi and Foster had decided to marry. She had been married young herself and knew how difficult it was when a couple was young and idealistic.

After Sammy had been born, Vi had been plagued with postpartum depression. It had been a rough time for them all. But with the right support, both medically and emotionally, Vi had come through it. She, Foster, and Sammy all appeared to be happy now, but they also looked nervous. That made Daisy nervous.

"What did you want to talk about?" she asked.

"You told us we could live in the apartment rent-free for a year. It's been a year, and we're thinking about moving out."

Daisy's major worry was that they wouldn't be able to afford rent somewhere else. "I know you're tight on space, but I'm worried that you won't be able to afford an apartment elsewhere," she said honestly.

"I'm picking up more and more website business," Foster said. "I'll be handling the PR for the homeless shelter and all the Internet hours that will go with that."

A shop owner who had volunteered to do the PR for free had bungled it. Foster had applied to the town council for the project, and they'd accepted his offer. "Foster, you have so much going on—working at the tea garden, going to class, and now the websites. That PR is going to take lots of hours."

"I know it is, but with Vi working more hours at Pirated Treasures, I think we'll be okay. Dad's still covering college."

Vi's part-time work for Otis Murdock at his antiques shop, Pirated Treasures, had been a godsend. "Let me ask you something. How many hours a week do you think you'll have for Sammy and Vi with all that going on? When Sammy starts to walk, I don't think you'll be able to take him to Otis's shop. The way it is now, you put him in a playpen for an hour or so while you work there. But a child who is walking can get into everything. Are you going to use day care? And if you are, how will you pay for that?"

"Aunt Iris and Gram said they'll babysit in the evenings for me. I can work at Pirated Treasures then," Vi said hopefully.

Daisy thought about her mother and her aunt who spent long days working. Her mother and her dad were fully involved at Gallagher's Garden Corner and were seasonally busy at the nursery. Iris worked six days a week at the tea garden. They both loved Sammy, and they *would* help out.

"I want you to think about something," Daisy advised. "Foster will be graduating in the spring. After graduation, he'll probably be working full-time. What if you stayed in the apartment over the garage until then? That will probably be about another nine months. But if you feel you want to start paying me, we can do that or use some kind of a sliding scale. Whatever you don't spend on rent and expenses, you can save. You wanted to buy another vehicle. I'm not sure if Foster wants to ride that motorcycle in the snow."

Sammy had stacked a few blocks on top of one another. Now he batted them all down and giggled.

Jazzi brought a tray with hot chocolate in mugs and a sippy cup for Sammy into the living room and set it on the coffee table. "You ought to listen to Mom," she said to Vi. "I think she's right about this. Why make your life harder than you have to?"

"The truth is—I like having you so close," Daisy confessed. "I know there will come a time when you won't be."

Vi looked at her mom with her eyes wide. "Don't you think we should have to work out our life on our own?"

Daisy nodded. "Yes, I do. Eventually. But I don't think you should rush it."

Foster picked up a mug of hot chocolate. "Let us think about it."

Daisy knew she had to say, "If you really want to move out, I'm okay with that, too."

But she wasn't okay with it. She liked having her family around her and nearby. After this senior year of high school, Jazzi would be going off to college. Daisy knew she was going to have to deal with an empty nest eventually, but the longer she could put it off, the happier she would be.

At one time, Daisy hadn't looked forward to dinner at her parents' house. These days, it was usually a comforting experience. For years, Daisy and her mom had navigated a relationship that had become worn and tattered all because of a secret that her mother had kept. Her mother had experienced postpartum depression after Daisy was born. It had changed her for that year that Daisy was an infant. Daisy's Aunt Iris and her dad had stepped up to make her feel loved and nurtured. However, as time went on, her mother gravitated toward Camellia, Daisy's older sister. Daisy had confided in her aunt more than her mother. There had been division and resentment and bitterness and guilt that they were just now compensating for.

Daisy's mom Rose listened more than she used to. She tried to stay tuned in to Daisy's life and her feelings.

This Sunday evening, Rose had made her famous chicken potpie. Daisy's aunt had brought a broccoli casserole. Daisy baked the cheese biscuits that were going over so well·at the tea garden, while Vi had put together an apple-walnut salad. Jazzi had brought a snack mix that they could eat while sitting around and talking. The meal wasn't really about the food. It was about connecting with each other, catching up, and understanding what was happening in each person's life. It was about spreading love around.

Foster began talking to Rose about the garden center

and what plants they could use at the tea garden to liven it up through the winter. Daisy's mom suggested small shrubs in pots and making them artistic arrangements with cattails and maybe vintage glass ornaments. Small evergreen plants would survive the winter along with the ornaments, and Foster could change the decorations for fall, Christmas, and then the beginning of spring.

Daisy overheard some of the conversation, and she liked the idea. Jonas and her dad had gone to the living room to be out of the way. Daisy heard the name Dalton Ames and wondered if they were talking about the fundraising for the homeless shelter.

As she and her mom spoke about the farmers market and other things happening around town, Rose asked her, "Rachel's daughter is getting married soon, isn't she?"

"In October."

"Amish weddings are as special as any other weddings," her mother said, "even though they're done quite differently."

Daisy knew the service itself would take a few hours, concluding with the wedding vows for the couple. Afterward, there would be a dinner for the whole district. No wonder Rachel was worried about readying everything in time. The wedding was held during the week, and the couple usually spent their first night in the bride's mother's home. It was just part of the tradition.

As if both Daisy and her mom were thinking about the details of the wedding, Rose said, "I'm sure Hannah and Daniel's wedding will be very much different from the Miller–King wedding."

While Foster carried the warming pot that held the potpie to the table, Rose said, "It's going to take place on the King farm. I guess you can't exactly call it a farm. It's

probably an estate. We're going to be handling the greenery, and Bouquets To Go will be handling the flowers."

"What type of greenery?" Daisy asked, curious about
what the Kings would choose.

"They put in orders for palms, peace lilies, and dief-
fenbachia to decorate the property."

"Speaking of decorating . . ." Daisy leaned closer to
her mother. "I bought Jonas a present for his birthday—a
statue of a golden retriever."

"One of those concrete ones?" her mom asked.

"Yes, exactly. I found it at Rumple's Statuary. Do you
know Mr. Rumple?"

"Yes, we do," her mother revealed. "When we landscape large gardens, clients want statuary. I've got to
admit, Wilhelm is a shrewd, funny little man. I always
have to bargain with him as if it's a game."

"A game?" Daisy asked.

"You know what I mean. Like going to a flea market.
Everyone knows the price on an object isn't what that
person will take. Wilhelm is like that with his statues."

"He wasn't like that with me."

"Did you offer less than what the statue was priced?"
Rose asked.

"No, it never occurred to me. I wanted that statue,
there was a price tag on it, and that was that."

Her mother laughed, but then she sobered. "I'm sorry I
laughed. If you thought it was a fair price, then it was a
fair price. I think some of Wilhelm's grander statuary is
marked up so the price can be negotiated down. I believe
he thinks it's just part of doing business. I hope Jonas
likes his birthday present. Did you make all the arrangements at The Farm Barn?"

"I did. I'm going to send out the invitations this week."

"Let me know if you need me to do anything to help."

"I will. Thanks, Mom."

"For what?"

Daisy waved her hand around the kitchen and living room. "For all of this. Vi and Foster are thinking about moving from the apartment above the garage, and Jazzi will be going to college eventually. I appreciate having everybody around while we can."

Out of nowhere, her mother gave her a hug.

Daisy felt loved and content. She hoped that feeling would never end.

Four Paws Animal Shelter was becoming a welcoming presence in Daisy's life. She'd decided to meet Jonas there on Monday evening, and then they would drive into Lancaster to have a dinner for two.

After she opened the black front door with its four white paws, she was surprised to see no one was sitting at the reception counter. She wasn't exactly sure where Jonas would be, though he was usually cleaning out the kennels or in the dog runs. She spotted someone behind the glass door where the kennels were located.

She was about to head that way when she heard a voice coming from the hall behind the reception desk. Serena had her back to Daisy. Her poodle was sitting beside her, looking up at her face as if the dog was concerned. No one else stood in the hall, and Daisy realized Serena was on her phone.

She was saying, "I can't do that. I simply can't. My

schedule doesn't allow it. Maybe when you come in
tonight, we can talk."

Maybe she was talking to her brother, Noah. An argument between them? Serena sounded upset.

Daisy's attention had been focused on Serena. She
hadn't heard Jonas come in the back door of Four Paws
and down the aisle between the Plexiglas rooms, until he
opened the door into the lobby area.

Serena must have heard him, too, because she said into
the phone, "I've got to go." When she came out to the
desk, her poodle trotting beside her, she looked pale and
shaken.

Daisy couldn't help but ask, "Is everything okay?"

Serena seemed to rally. "Oh, sure. No problem. Just a
mix-up in the schedules. You know how that can be, I
imagine."

Daisy could. Every week when she sat down to set up
schedules for shifts and any requests for time off, it was
like putting puzzle pieces together. When someone called
in that they couldn't make it, she had to quickly scramble
to see who else could. She imagined that happened here,
too. However, something alerted Daisy that Serena's
problem wasn't about schedules.

Serena had leaned down and was clutching the top of
her dog's head, sliding her fingers through Bellamy's fur.
At first, it seemed to give Serena comfort.

When she straightened, she asked Jonas, "Are the dog
runs all washed down?"

"They are," he said.

He was carrying his jeans over his arm, his sneakers in
the other hand. He'd obviously changed for their date,
probably in the break room. His claret-colored Henley

shirt looked good with his black slacks. But then, Jonas would look good in anything. His black hair had grown a little longer over the past month, and it dipped down his neck in the back. The scar on his cheek was barely visible. Daisy guessed he'd shaved before he'd come in to do his volunteer work because there wasn't any beard stubble on his face. She liked his dark five-o'clock shadow when it grew in, and she didn't know if she'd ever told him that.

Serena's complexion seemed less pale as she asked, "Are you two going on a date?"

"We are," Jonas answered. "Felix is with Daisy's daughter and her grandson. Sammy has a new game of tossing him a ball, and then Felix brings it back to him. It keeps them both busy."

"You'll have to bring Sammy to the adoption parade," Serena suggested. "I'm sure he'll like that."

Daisy knew the shelter was having a fundraising event the first Saturday in October that they called an adoption parade. They had even obtained a permit to walk down the center of a few blocks of Market Street so everyone could come out and watch them. It should be a lot of fun. She was sure most of her family would be coming to watch.

"Sammy will love it," Daisy said. "I'm pretty sure when Vi and Foster get a place of their own, they'll want to adopt a dog for him."

Serena went to her desk, shuffling some papers around as if she were distracted, as she asked Daisy, "Is that going to be happening soon? I know they're in the garage apartment at your place."

"Possibly sooner than I want it to be, but I know they

have to strike out on their own sometime. Still, I'm hoping they'll know when it's right so they don't step into hot water or high water, if you know what I mean."

Serena's expression was serious when she made direct eye contact with Daisy and said, "I do."

Suddenly, the front door opened, and Noah Langston came charging in. Noah was a few years older than Serena. His dark brown hair was the same color as hers. They had some of the same features with high cheekbones and pointed chins. Noah's hair was cropped short but looked good with his bushy brows and high forehead. He was tall and sinewy, and his chocolate-brown eyes were definitely his best feature. Daisy could imagine a number of women who might want to date him. But Noah's main focus seemed to be rescuing animals and taking care of them.

After greetings all around, Noah said to his sister, "If you want to leave, that's fine. I'm going to be here for a while checking over everybody."

Serena looked indecisive but then said, "I'm going to be here, too. I have paperwork I should take care of."

After goodbyes and a wave, Noah headed for the kennels. Daisy and Jonas wished Serena a good night and headed outside.

Daisy asked Jonas, "Did Serena seem herself to you?"

"Come to think of it, when I was around her today, I thought she seemed jumpy and nervous. Why?"

"I heard her take a phone call, and she seemed to be upset."

They'd reached Jonas's SUV by then. Instead of telling Daisy she shouldn't have listened or she shouldn't be worried about Serena, he put his dirty clothes inside the vehicle, then turned toward Daisy. Reaching out, he ran his hand through her hair and brought her close to him for a kiss.

She settled into him and let the kiss transport her to the future they were going to have together. There was no need to think about anything else.

This time of year was busy at the tea garden, not only with tourists, but with residents of other counties taking a drive for the day. Lancaster County's rolling hills, groves of trees with leaves turning in cooler weather, farms with fields being prepared for winter, and horses frolicking in corrals drew people simply for a look, for a drive, and for a taste of Pennsylvania Dutch food and fresh air.

Mid-morning the next day, the main room of the tea garden was full. Apparently, teas were just as popular as lattes. Daisy served scones, coffee cake, and cookies on flowered vintage plates. Her teapots varied from Polish porcelain to Royal Albert to James Sadler and even Pfaltzgraff. Her aunt had been collecting for years. Daisy had started as soon as she'd moved to Willow Creek and decided to open the tea garden with Iris.

Her latest find was a pretty vintage Sadler ceramic floral teapot. The Sadler teapots originated in England. This teapot was fashioned in swirled porcelain. A floral garland in pink, blue, yellow, and purple edged the top. A matching summer garland adorned the lid of the teapot. The handle, spout, and finial were trimmed in gold. She used it for a trio of women whom she knew appreciated the china as well as the ambiance of the tea garden. They had become regular morning customers at least once a week. They would visit for a little snack before they began their book club.

"No one brews tea like you do," said Tabitha Martin, the oldest member of the club, probably in her fifties. Her hair was brown with silver threads, and she wore it in a French knot.

Her two companions nodded. Clara, who was dressed in runner's garb and probably Daisy's age, said, "Especially with the Darjeeling. It's called the champagne of teas."

"I think it is," Daisy agreed. "My supplier mostly sells me first flush offerings."

"It's even pretty in the teacups," June, who was the youngest of the three, added. "That amber gold color looks like champagne. I love it with your wildflower honey."

The women had ordered cranberry scones this morning. They took bites of those while sipping their tea. Daisy could see they were content with their orders. She was about to return to the kitchen to help there when someone came in the door she didn't expect to see.

Gavin Cranshaw didn't even *begin* to look as if he wanted a tea service. He strode up to Daisy and asked, "Can we talk?"

Gavin, Foster's father, was a contractor and usually on the job this time of day. Lean and tall, Gavin had given his good-looking genes to his sons—Ben and Foster. However, his square jaw today looked more determined than friendly. His sandy brown hair had blonded in the summer. Now it looked as if he'd run his fingers through it several times.

Daisy suggested, "Take a seat in the spillover tearoom. I'll have someone cover for me. Would you like a glass of iced tea?"

"Sure," he said absentmindedly, already heading for the spillover tearoom.

In the kitchen, Daisy spoke to Iris who was taking a huge sheet pan of snickerdoodles from the oven. "Can you cover for me for a few minutes? Gavin's here."

Iris and Tessa asked at the same time, "This time of day?"

"That's what worries me," Daisy admitted, then left the kitchen with a glass of Darjeeling iced tea for Gavin.

After she placed it in front of him, he took several swallows and set it down. He almost accused her, "You think tea calms everyone."

She couldn't help but smile. "I hope it does. That's why I have a good business."

He leaned back in the chair and sighed. "Last night, Foster told me he and Vi want to move out of your apartment and find a place of their own."

"They told me that, too."

"Are you just going to let them do that?" he demanded.

Daisy could see Gavin was more worried than he was upset. "If they truly intend to move, there's not much I can do to stop them."

"But they can't afford it!"

"I think when they start looking, they're going to figure that out," Daisy reminded him.

Narrowing his eyes at her, Gavin seemed to relax a bit. "You believe they have enough common sense that it will stop them."

"I believe they won't look a gift horse in the mouth, whatever that saying means. I offered to let them stay there on a sliding scale until next spring when Foster graduates. They can look at their budget and figure out how much they can pay me. They really want to stand on their own, Gavin. I understand that. They need their independence."

"He didn't tell me about your offer," Gavin mused.

"That could mean they're considering it, or maybe not. I pointed out that once Foster graduates and has a job, other than working at the tea garden, they'll be able to estimate better what they can afford. You know I love having them and Sammy around, and I'm not eager to push them out."

"You're not ready for an empty nest?" Gavin gave her a weak smile. "Foster said Jazzi is sending out applications for college."

"She is. The change is going to be hard for all of us. But change is what life's about. I'm trying to roll with it."

"I know Foster can't afford a car if they decide to move out," Gavin ruminated as he once more picked up his glass. "Maybe that will keep them at your place for a while longer. I'm also concerned he's taking on way more than he can handle. I know he likes bringing more money in, but I don't want him to run himself ragged. On the other hand, I think we've helped them enough." Gavin took a few swallows of iced tea, as if to brace himself for the idea of setting the couple adrift on their own.

"Did you just figure out it's hard being a parent?" she teased. She and Gavin had always had a sense of honesty and humor between them when it came to their kids.

The tuba sound on Daisy's phone played.

Gavin took another sip of iced tea and stood. "I have to get going. I should be on the job. Thanks for the tea." He took his wallet from his pocket.

Daisy waved him off. "You know that's on the house."

With a grin, Gavin said goodbye and headed toward the door.

Daisy answered her phone and saw that Trevor was calling. *Her* instead of Tessa? She remembered when he'd called her before out of the blue. A shiver of foreboding made the hairs on the back of her neck prick up.

She answered, "Hey, Trevor. Does Tessa have her phone turned off?"

"No, I wanted to talk to you. She told me you went out to Wilhelm Rumple's place to buy a birthday present for Jonas."

"I did."

He went on, "And I know Jonas volunteers at Four Paws Animal Shelter."

"He does," she responded warily.

She heard Trevor let out a breath and braced herself for what was coming.

"There was a death at Four Paws. Wilhelm Rumple was found dead in a dog run."

Daisy swallowed hard. "Did he die from natural causes?"

This time, Trevor didn't hesitate. "I'm afraid not. Someone bashed him in the head."

CHAPTER FOUR

That evening found Daisy at her kitchen island, slicing sections of shoofly pie that her aunt had made. Earlier this afternoon, Iris had told her, "If you're going to talk about murder, you need something sweet."

Shoofly pie was the epitome of sweet with its gooey filling that included brown sugar and molasses. Daisy believed she'd need nerves of steel, too, but she didn't know where she was going to find those. Jonas, Jazzi, and Tessa sipped cups of Darjeeling tea as they waited for Trevor to begin his recitation of what he'd learned throughout the day.

The reporter didn't begin until Daisy had served him and everybody else. He used his fork to take a bite of pie topped with whipped cream and then a second. It was if he needed the sugar to rev him up for this conversation.

Finally, he revealed, "I went to the scene and discovered as much as I could there. Four Paws is shut down, at least until tomorrow. The detectives realized that the dogs' needs had to be taken care of, so they didn't seal it off completely. But there is crime scene tape around the perimeter. I think Bart Cosner is standing guard tonight until the crime scene techs decide that they're finished."

"We could have guessed all that," Jonas said. "Tell us what happened."

Jazzi piped up, "Isn't a reporter supposed to get to the facts first?"

Trevor shook his finger at her. "I'm not sure you should even be in on this discussion."

"You know I'll hear about it, one way or the other. And you'd rather I know the truth instead of gossip, right?"

Trevor shook his head after another glare at her.

Trevor dressed well. He was a good-looking man who could turn a woman's head. But he could also fade into the background when he wanted to. His brown hair straggled over his ears a bit, and it had a slight wave. Tonight, he was wearing a green-striped Oxford shirt with khakis, and he'd rolled up the sleeves on the shirt.

He took a sip of his tea then laid down his fork. "The bottom line is that the detectives believe Rumple was killed with something heavy that they haven't found yet. Someone hit his head with it. He fell and knocked his head a second time on the concrete floor. There'll be an autopsy, of course, but I think it's pretty clear what happened. Once he hit the concrete, he didn't have a chance."

"And you said this happened in the dog run?" Daisy asked, taking a seat at the island with the rest of them.

"It did."

Jonas said, "It sounds as if this was an impulse crime. I'm thinking about what would have been handy to use.

Often, there are buckets sitting in the dog runs. We use them to wash down the area."

"Can a bucket kill someone?" Jazzi asked, wide-eyed.

Jonas explained, "The buckets in the dog runs are metal, and they're heavy. They have to be substantial to last. I suppose if one hits a person in the head just the wrong way, it could crack a skull."

Glancing at Jazzi, Daisy swung her arm around her daughter's shoulders. "Are you sure you don't want to take Felix out to the backyard?"

"Felix is sleeping on my foot. I don't think he wants to go anywhere right now. It's okay, Mom. I'm old enough to know what goes on in the real world."

Daisy wasn't so sure about that.

"So I guess he couldn't have just slipped and fallen," Daisy mused.

"Not likely," Trevor said. "Rumple had volunteered last night. He was the one who belonged there. The time of death was ruled at about midnight. I don't know why he'd be in the dog run then."

Jonas asked Trevor, "Do they think someone called him out there?"

"Anything's possible," Trevor concluded.

For some reason, Serena's phone call entered Daisy's mind. She and Noah were going to stay late, but they'd probably left by the time Mr. Rumple had come on duty.

She could hardly believe the man she'd been talking to just over a week ago was now dead. He wasn't on this earth anymore. "What about Rumple's dog?" she asked.

"Dog?" Jonas looked at her with questioning eyes.

"Remember when we rode our bikes past his place and the police were there? Bart said he had a dog."

Trevor gave her a *good catch* look. "I went over to Rumple's property after I was at the crime scene," Trevor revealed. "He does have a dog, a Plott hound. The police rushed the paperwork through so they could search his house and grounds, too. They found the dog barking his head off."

"Who's taking care of him?" Jonas and Daisy asked at the same time.

"They had the dog in the yard for a while, but then I think a relative of Rumple's was coming over to pick him up. They'd had to get everything okayed, and you know that takes a while."

"When the three of us were bike riding the other night," Daisy said, "the police had been called to Mr. Rumple's. Do you know what that was all about?" She was curious whether or not that had any connection to the murder.

"I read the police report," Trevor said. "I managed to access that soon after the cops wrote it up. I'd heard on my scanner that they'd been called out there. But Rumple had insisted nothing had been stolen."

Maybe nothing had been stolen, Daisy thought to herself, but that didn't mean someone hadn't *tried* to steal something. One of those valuable statues? Certainly the break-in had to be connected. Didn't it? Was someone looking for a valuable statue? Or were they searching for something else?

Daisy made a phone call the following day that she'd been debating with herself about making. She called Detective Rappaport's cell phone number.

He picked up with a quick, "Yeah? Rappaport."

The way he answered didn't bode well for a good mood. "Detective, it's Daisy. Do you have a minute?"

"I probably have ten seconds of a minute. What can I do for you?"

"I have information for you, and I thought maybe we could meet somewhere other than the police station."

"Why don't you want to be seen at the police station?" he questioned her warily.

"Long story. I really want to tell it to you face-to-face, not over the phone. It could have something to do with Wilhelm Rumple."

At that, the detective went silent. "Just where do you want to meet?" he finally asked.

"Someplace we can both get to easily but isn't overrun by people. Someplace private."

"My mind is on a thousand other things right now. Do you have some place in mind?"

"What about in the park, near that dais they have set up for the concerts. It's not near the playground, so no one should be around there now."

"And you don't want me to tell anybody about this meeting?"

"Not if you don't have to. I'll explain why."

"I can't believe Rumple is the subject you want to talk about. I did get one of those Fitbit things, and I've been walking more. Can you meet me there in fifteen minutes?"

"I'll be there."

A few minutes later, Daisy told Tessa where she was going and why.

Tessa said, "It's the best thing to do. I know it is.

Hopefully, Jonas won't find out about your trip to Rumple's Statuary until after his birthday."

"That's what I'm hoping."

Daisy returned to her office, removed her apron, and plucked a violet-colored windbreaker from the clothes tree. She'd worn a pair of navy and pale blue plaid slacks today with navy clogs. Her pale blue crepe shirt had cold shoulders and a navy placket down the front. The jacket was necessary today. Some days, the sun was shining hot in Willow Creek as if it was still summer. But this morning, there had been a scent of damp leaves in the breeze that portended fall was on its way.

Daisy left through the kitchen's back door and turned left onto the asphalt that led past the door to Tessa's apartment. Circling around the Victorian, she headed out toward Market Street.

After checking for cars and horse-drawn buggies, she crossed Market to the other side of the street where Rachel's shop, Quilts and Notions, was located. She didn't want to pass by the main window outside of Woods on the same side of the street as the tea garden. This way, she could scurry along and not be noticed.

The colorful pots that some shopkeepers had positioned outside their doorways were filled with herbs, marigolds, and mums. The plants would last a few more weeks until the first frost. Willow Creek had decided to make the town a little prettier for the tourists by inviting shopkeepers to place potted flowers outside their doors. The town council had agreed to hanging pots on the lampposts, at least in the three blocks where the main stores were located. Beautiful waterfall begonias were still colorful and full-bodied.

Daisy veered left down a side street and was soon walking into the park. She cut across the grass instead of taking the path to the concert dais. She easily caught sight of Detective Rappaport standing near a grove of silver maples. The sun was shining bright, making any green leaves glisten. He had ducked into the shade and was taking a piece of chewing gum from his pocket as she approached him with a bag in her hand. Jonas had told her the detective was trying to lose weight. Walking and chewing gum was part of the regimen. She hoped she wasn't tempting him too much with the treat she'd brought him.

"Uh-oh," he said when she was close enough to hear him. "It looks as if you're going to bribe me, unless you brought yourself a snack."

"I was thinking about your new diet."

"Who told you about that?" he asked.

"Apparently, it's all over the station that the diet is making you suspiciously grouchy," she joked.

He narrowed his eyes at her. "So what's in the bag?"

She could smell the scent of cinnamon from the chewing gum he'd popped into his mouth. "Instead of whoopie pies, I brought you something a little more healthy. It's a carrot bran muffin."

He rolled his eyes. "Seriously, Daisy? If you think that's going to make up for not having chocolate whoopie pies, you're wrong."

"You didn't taste it yet. Don't pre-judge." She handed him the bag.

Opening it, he sniffed. "Are there nuts in the muffin?"

She nodded.

"Anything else that's good?"

"I take it you don't see bran as a treat?"

He snorted.

"The muffin has pineapple in it, too."

He made a face that told her that was a little better. "So what's this meeting about?"

"On Monday, I went to Wilhelm Rumple's to buy Jonas a birthday present."

"Now I see why you didn't want him to know. I *am* coming to your party, by the way, at least if an emergency doesn't come up."

"Good." Knowing his time was limited, she continued with what she wanted to tell him. "Foster went with me to Rumple's house. Wilhelm met us at the gate with his dog, and we went into the backyard."

"Crazy amount of statues back there."

"Did anybody tell you about the special safe in his office?"

"That was one secure safe," Rappaport said. "We had a locksmith open it for us. We had to take the whole mechanism apart. There were dog statues inside. Expensive ones, from what our tech discovered when researching them."

"Rumple told us he had a gold pug pin coming that would cost six thousand dollars."

Rappaport whistled. "Is that what you wanted to tell me?"

"No." She only hesitated a few seconds. "When Foster and I were there, someone came to the gate. It was Stanley King."

"Stanley King! The CEO Stanley King?"

"That's the one. His face has been all over the media with his new supplements, so I recognized him."

"So what? Maybe he wanted to buy a statue. He could buy everything that was in that safe."

She shook her head. "No, he wasn't interested in statues. Foster and I were looking around when he and Rumple argued."

Finally, she'd caught Detective Morris Rappaport's attention. "Argued about what?"

"I'm not sure exactly. It sounded like it was about money. King said he couldn't pay Rumple this month. He wanted to delay the payment. Rumple said that wasn't happening and that King should cut back the flower order for his son's wedding. In that case, he'd have enough money to pay. At least, that was the gist of it. King was really angry when he left. He slammed the gate, revved his car engine, and we heard his tires squeal. It all seemed out of proportion somehow."

"How did Rumple react?"

"He didn't seem too affected. He returned to us, and I bought the statue I wanted."

Rappaport chewed on his gum and then rubbed his jaw. "You said a piece of jewelry was coming to Rumple, a gold pug?"

"That's what he said it was."

"Maybe King bought something from him, like one of those statues or a piece of jewelry, and was paying it off month by month."

"I guess that's possible, but this is Stanley King we're talking about. It's possible Rumple could have been supplying him with something a lot more expensive than we're even thinking about."

"I'll follow up on this," Rappaport assured her.

"Do you have any other leads?"

Rappaport gave her a side-eye. "I'm not going to talk to you about an ongoing investigation. You are definitely *not* getting involved in this one. I'll take the tidbit you gave me and run with it. Don't worry about that."

"So if you won't tell me about the investigation, I guess you won't tell me about how someone tried to break into Mr. Rumple's house? Jonas, Jazzi, and I were riding by there on our bikes the night it happened. Bart told us that the property had quite the security system."

"Rumple did, but Bart shouldn't have said anything."

Daisy continued, as if Rappaport hadn't been so disapproving. "It makes sense he would, with all that inventory and what he had inside in that safe."

"Daisy, you're pushing."

In the same singsong voice, she said, "Not much."

The detective looked away from her and ran his hand along the bark of the tree. Turning back to her, he sighed. "I can tell you one thing and one thing only. Rumple's security system had quadrants, and one of them had been breached."

She jumped on that bit of news. "Had it really been breached? It wasn't just an animal or the wind?"

"Nope. Not either. A statue had been knocked over in the back. Nothing was taken, according to Rumple, and nothing else disturbed."

"Your theory?"

"In the light of what happened, I suppose somebody could have been trying to get to Rumple to kill him. On the other hand, somebody might have just been testing the waters. Or in this case, testing the security system."

Glorie Beck had invited Daisy and Jazzi over to her house for dessert and a chat that evening. Daisy had met Glorie when her granddaughter, Brielle Horn, had come to stay with Jazzi for a few weeks over spring break. That's when Daisy had become involved in Brielle's life.

Glorie lived a somewhat plain life in a rural area of Willow Creek. She liked to stand on her front porch when she knew visitors were coming so she could greet them. Her curly light brown hair, streaked with gray, floated like a cloud around her face. With her jeans, she usually wore an oversized T-shirt. Today the color was royal blue. Her arthritis bothered her daily, and Brielle now lived with her grandmother, partly to assist her and partly because it was just plain good for Brielle. Of course, that was the old story. The family was about to start a brand new one.

Daisy parked in the driveway of the white clapboard house. Its porch had a little roof and gray floorboards. Window trim around the house was painted the same gray. Glorie had lived here for more than seventy years, but now change was going to come.

Glorie looked happy as she stood outside waiting for Daisy and Jazzi, the folds of her T-shirt blowing in the September breeze. She was anchored by a pink flowered cane that Daisy knew Brielle had bought for her.

As Daisy and Jazzi walked up the porch steps, Glorie said, "Hot tea tonight with blond brownies?"

"Do they have peanut butter in them?" Jazzi asked with a smile, knowing that was how Glorie made them.

"They sure do. Come on in. Brielle's getting everything ready. Nola might come by later, but I thought it would be nice if *we* talked first."

Daisy wasn't sure what they were going to talk about, but she and Jazzi followed Glorie inside. Daisy always stopped to admire the eight-by-ten oval varicolored rag rug on the floor in the living room. Glorie had told her she'd used material in it from her daughter's dresses, her husband's shirts, and her own aprons. It softened the plank wooden flooring around the sofa, armchair, wood rocker, and coffee table. The green plaid curtains at the window—the material also used for slipcovers Glorie had sewn for the sofa—were a bit faded. However, the room gave off a shabby chic feel that was so popular nowadays. Glorie didn't care about shabby chic or décor. She simply knew what held memories and was comfortable. A flight of stairs led up to a loft that was Brielle's room now. Daisy noticed a patchwork quilt that hadn't been there before as it hung from the railing.

Brielle called from the kitchen, "Let's come in here. We have something to show you."

Even though Brielle's attitude had become sunnier over the past few months, her appearance was pure Brielle. She kept her hair short and spiked. Its natural black color made a contrast to her bright pink bangs. At first, Daisy had been taken aback by Brielle's nose ring, eyebrow piercing, and Goth tattoos on her forearms. But she'd soon grown affection for Brielle that rivaled the fondness she felt for her own daughters.

Following Brielle's voice, Daisy and Jazzi made their way to the kitchen and the square pedestal table and ladder-back chairs, where they often sat while they spoke with Brielle and her grammy. Brielle was standing at the counter that was gray-speckled Formica and had a few chips and stains. Glorie's refrigerator, with its rounded top and the white gas stove, were vintage.

After Jazzi and then Daisy hugged Brielle, they noticed that the table wasn't covered with teacups or a plate of cookies. Rather, there was a rolled tube sitting crosswise across the table.

Brielle informed them, "Tea is steeping. We want to show you something first and maybe ask your advice."

Both Brielle and Glorie looked excited about the cardboard tube on the table. Brielle pulled the roll from inside of the tube, spreading the papers over the table.

Daisy's gaze went to the corner of the architectural drawing and the name there. "You're using Wyatt Troyer?"

Jazzi came over to the table. "He's the one who designed the apartment on top of the garage where Vi and Foster live."

"Nola chose him because of his good reputation," Glorie said. "Now that we know he did work for you, that's a bonus."

Daisy leaned over the plans, studying them carefully. She knew what had been the instigator for them. Brielle's mother and father, who were both lawyers, were in the process of a divorce. Both Nola and Glorie wanted Brielle to go to college, but Brielle wouldn't do that as long as she felt her grandmother needed her. In the course of events, Glorie had realized that she shouldn't live alone any longer, and Nola had come to the realization that her high-powered career had interfered with her relationships with her mother and her daughter, let alone with her marriage. Now they were all trying to mend fences . . . at least, the women were.

Glorie owned a few acres of property and hated to sell the house where she'd been raised as a child and lived during her marriage. Because of her divorce, Nola was selling her house which was huge, and according to Brielle, a mausoleum. After much discussion, Nola had decided to build a house on her mother's property where the three of them could be happy. Glorie could keep and rent out her house. It seemed to be a good solution for all of them.

As Daisy drew her finger along the rooms pictured on

the plans, she noted to Glorie, "So you'll have your own room with a sitting area and a little kitchenette."

Glorie grinned and pointed to another area. "I will, but it's right off the living room, so I can go in there and spend time with Nola and Brielle when I want to."

Standing beside her grandmother, Brielle pointed to her room. "My room is right next to Grammy's, so if she needs anything, I'll hear her . . . or Mom will. Mom's having an intercom installed."

It was obvious that Nola's bedroom would be on the other side of Glorie's.

"And everything's on one floor," Brielle said. "Grammy can go wherever she wants. Mom's going to make sure Grammy even has one of those special tubs that you can just open the door and go in and sit. It has a hand-held shower and everything. She doesn't even have to stand up."

Glorie looked over at Daisy. "They're going to spoil me. I'm not used to it." She waved her hand around her home. "I mean, just look at this and what I'm used to."

"You *deserve* to be spoiled," Brielle asserted. "And if you rent this house to nice people, maybe you can come back over and look at it every once in a while."

Glorie pulled out a chair and sat on it. "There are two things we'd like to discuss with you, Daisy. Nola gave us the go-ahead. She's still sorting clients' files while she and Elliot make decisions on those."

"They're probably *fighting* over clients," Brielle said acerbically.

Glorie patted her granddaughter's hand. "Now, now. Your father's being fair otherwise. They were partners. Let's not forget that."

Brielle seemed unconvinced, her expression showing

it. She put her hand on her grandmother's shoulder. "Let's ask Daisy about Gavin."

Gavin. Daisy wondered why his name had come up, but then an idea came to mind.

"We know he's family now, sort of," Glorie said. "He's Vi's father-in-law. Nola met him and likes him. She looked into his work history and found he's worked with Wyatt on occasion."

Daisy nodded, guessing where this was going.

"What we want to know is," Glorie continued, "do you think he'd do a good job on our house?"

Daisy didn't hesitate to respond. "I'm sure he would. I know he's going to be busy with his contract for the homeless shelter. But he has more than one crew. In fact, he could probably have your house built before the homeless shelter is even started. The town still has to raise funds for that."

Glorie and Brielle exchanged a look and nodded. "That's exactly what we thought. Even if we could get started next month and be under roof by December, the finishing would take time, too. It would be February or March until we could move in. That brings us to our second point."

This time, Brielle took over. "Jazzi told me that Vi and Foster are thinking about moving out of their little apartment above the garage."

"They are, but I don't know if they can afford something else right now."

When Glorie smiled, it had a conspiratorial element to it. "I know you probably want to keep them near you. But when young folks make a decision, they make a decision. I intend to charge a reasonable rent for my house. How do you think Vi and Foster would feel about moving in here?"

Daisy felt her heart warming to the idea. Vi and Foster could be on their own but have somebody nearby to look over them. The idea gained traction in her mind.

Would Foster and Vi agree?

CHAPTER FIVE

Daisy was arranging a few tea cozies next to the teacups that were for sale on a shelf in the spillover tearoom. Rachel's daughters had made them, and Daisy was glad to showcase them in her shop. Since the shelf was high on the wall, Daisy had been using a stepstool to arrange the products. Tamlyn, one of her more recently hired servers, came into the room and looked up at her.

Tamlyn Pittenger was in her early twenties. She usually wore her long brown hair in a knot on the back of her head. Her cheeks were full and her lips wide. She'd recently had her bangs cut so they didn't cover her brows as they once had.

"Mrs. Wilson is in the tearoom," she said, looking troubled.

Unsure why Tamlyn was telling her this, Daisy asked, "Is she buying her usual weekly order?" Fiona liked to stock up on soup, salad, and goodies so that she could eat from them throughout the week.

"Yes, she is," Tamlyn assured Daisy. "But she seemed upset and a little baffled by what she wanted. So I suggested she sit and have a cup of tea before she placed her order. Is that all right?"

"Of course, it is," Daisy assured Tamlyn. "She's a regular customer, and we want to make certain she's fit to walk home."

Glancing over her shoulder at the main tearoom, Daisy spotted ten people being served. The tea garden wasn't overly busy this morning. "Why don't you bring me a cup of Darjeeling, and I'll sit with Fiona for a couple of minutes and see if I can find out if she's okay. We wouldn't want her walking home if she is shaky or confused. I've never seen either in her. Sometimes she can't make up her mind, but that's not unusual."

"I'll tell her that you're going to join her for a few minutes. Should I bring a plate of cookies?"

"Why don't you bring the cheese biscuits? It's near lunchtime, and she might enjoy those."

After a nod, Tamlyn hurried away.

Daisy folded up her stepstool and took it to their utility closet. Then she washed up and found Fiona in the main tearoom. The older woman was seated at a table for two near the side entrance.

Daisy pulled out the chair on the other side of the table from Fiona. "Hi, there. I hope you don't mind if I join you for a cup of tea."

"Oh, I don't mind at all," Fiona said with a smile. "I think I worried your server. I couldn't keep my mind on my order. I'm terribly distracted today."

At that moment, Tamlyn arrived with the tray with two

cups of tea in pretty Royal Doulton Arcadia-pattern teacups and saucers. She placed one in front of Daisy and one in front of Fiona. Then she finished emptying her tray. By the time she was done, she'd placed a nappy with slices of lemon, a shaker with crystal sugar, and a honey pot between their teacups. Then she set a plate of cheese biscuits arranged on a crystal dish on the table, too.

"Oh, my!" Fiona said. "I didn't expect the royal treatment."

Tamlyn, who was good with all the customers, grinned. "We like to give all of our guests the royal treatment. Daisy specifically said you might enjoy the cheese biscuits."

After Tamlyn left the table with the empty tray, Fiona sighed. "I suppose I haven't been eating as well as I should, either. That's why I stopped in today, so I could stock up."

Fiona was around seventy. Unlike her sister, Hetta, she was diminutive and slender. Daisy knew she bought her clothes at the thrift shop, A Penny Saved, but they were always colorful and trendy. Today she was wearing gray wool slacks, a pale pink pullover, and a gray and pink infinity scarf. She usually wore her chin-length curly hair with a gold clasp over her right temple. Today was no exception.

Daisy stirred honey into her tea and swirled it around, while Fiona took a slice of lemon and squeezed it into her teacup. "This is very nice . . . really. I'm grateful. I feel pampered."

"Everyone deserves to be pampered now and then, don't you think so?"

Fiona tilted her head and studied Daisy. "You know how to make a person feel comfortable."

"That's a nice compliment," Daisy said, meaning it. She decided to jump in while they were sitting here. "Is there a reason you haven't been eating properly?"

"I've been worried about my sister. Hetta told me you met her at Four Paws."

"I did. She and Jonas were cleaning out the kennels. Your sister says she has a Yorkshire terrier named Winkie."

Fiona chuckled. "Winkie is a character, the friendliest little pup I ever saw. She brings him over to visit, and I dog sit when she does her volunteer work. But for the past week, Hetta hasn't been herself."

This past week. Daisy didn't have to guess what that might be about. "Has this been since Mr. Rumple was found dead?" Daisy asked gently.

"It started a bit before that. His death had to have been a huge shock to everyone at Four Paws," Fiona mused.

"I know what it's like when the police come in and make the area a crime scene," Daisy empathized. "I heard the detectives realized that the dogs still needed care, so the shelter couldn't be completely closed off."

"I know Hetta was worried about the dogs, and she had to change her hours. Of course, that meant juggling hours at Bouquets To Go, too. And that affected her daughter. Her daughter Edith uses Hetta's kitchen to make the dog treats that she sells at Fur and Feathers and at the farmers market. So everything was topsy-turvy."

"A change in schedule can throw life off," Daisy agreed sympathetically. "And she's probably thinking about what happened to Mr. Rumple. Not knowing who did it is scary."

"Hetta's also afraid the adoption event will be affected. She's concerned that people won't come in to adopt because of what happened at the shelter."

"That might be true for a little while." Daisy stirred her tea, remembering how her business had been affected when a man had been killed in the tea garden's backyard. "But dog lovers who want to rescue a pet won't let what happened there keep them from adopting."

"Maybe you should talk to Hetta," Fiona suggested.

"She's lucky she has *you* to talk to."

Fiona eyed the cheese biscuits. "I might have to take her some of those. That might cheer her up."

"Try one first and see if you like it," Daisy advised her.

Fiona picked one up, and so did Daisy. The biscuits were warm, right out of the oven. Even to Daisy, who was used to the smells around the tea garden, the cheesy scent was wonderful and made her stomach rumble.

Fiona laughed. "I think you needed this break."

"I think I did, too."

Fiona already had more color in her cheeks and a smile on her face. That's what the tea garden could do for Daisy's customers. That's what her customers could do for her.

After work, Daisy strolled down Market Street, taking her time. A courting buggy hitched to a beautiful sorrel gelding clopped down the street with a young couple sitting about six inches apart on the seat. She was as used to the sound of buggies as she was to cars. Growing up in Willow Creek, she believed buggies were a natural part of the landscape . . . and a natural part of life. Some tourists complained about the buggies slowing down traffic, but to Daisy, the slowdowns were a good thing. They gave life a chance to ease.

She passed shops on her way to Woods—Vinegar and

Spice, Wisps and Wicks, a few business offices. The temperature had dropped some, and rain might even be in the air. She pulled her long sweater coat around her more tightly and buttoned the huge buttons. The coat was color-blocked with cat faces in each square. It made her and her girls smile, and they asked to borrow it now and then. She'd worn it today because she wanted to think of something other than Rumple's murder. She wanted to give herself lots of distractions.

At Woods, she studied the main window display. Jonas had been specializing in reclaimed wood. In the window, he'd set a bookcase made of reclaimed wood with a distressed blue paint finish. Books stood on the shelves along with a wooden train, something she wanted to buy Sammy for Christmas. She guessed Elijah Beiler had probably made the train. Jonas's friend ran his farm but sometimes worked in the shop. Someone had created a weaving that hung in a corner of the display. A glider rocker with a quilted cushion sat under the milk-glass globe of an antique lamp. An oval rag rug lay before the chair. It was the kind of display that pulled visitors into the shop.

After Daisy opened the door, she stepped into the warmth of the store. When she did, she glanced at the giant cubicle shelves that stood along one side of the store from floor to ceiling. Ladder-back chairs stood in each of the cubicles. They ranged in different finishes from distressed blue to teal to cherry wood and dark walnut. Customers could order whatever finish they wanted and as many chairs as they wanted.

Walking down the main aisle, she let her gaze play over the granite-topped islands built with reclaimed wood, a three-drawer accent chest done with a crackle finish, a mirrored cabinet that had a green base with foot pegs and a dark walnut top. Every piece of furniture was handcrafted by local craftsmen, including Jonas.

She easily spotted Jonas who was rubbing orange oil onto a small kitchen table. She liked the scent.

He always seemed to have a sixth sense with her, and he looked up before she was even three feet away. He dropped the rag onto the table and came to her, pulling her into his arms. The kiss was quick but sure, and she could have stood there for the next hour. But she didn't, and he didn't, either.

Looking down at the table, she said, "Don't you usually rub the oil back in the workroom?"

"I do, but this one had some happy little hands all over it this afternoon. A family came in looking for a table, and their two children sat at it for a little while. I'm just rubbing off the fingerprints."

Felix had been sitting under the table. Whereas cats didn't like citrus smells of any kind, Felix didn't seem to mind. He lifted his head, stood, and lumbered to her. She stooped, scratching behind his ears, rubbing down his flanks, and giving him a lot of love. He'd come to expect it from her.

"Felix wants to know if you'd like to pick up takeout or make something at your place," Jonas joked.

"That depends. Would he rather have a spring roll or a piece of a burger?"

Jonas laughed and finished polishing the table with a flourish. He said to Felix, "One bark is a spring roll. Two barks are a burger." He raised his hand in front of Felix's nose and lifted one finger.

Felix barked once.

Daisy had to laugh, too. "Did you teach him that?"

"Nope. Adele told me her son taught him. So I guess it's Chinese tonight."

"Unless Jazzi would like something different. She's angsting over her college essays. I don't think she's going to care what she eats. Chinese sounds good to me. There are some days I'd just rather somebody else cooked my dinner."

"I understand that. Did anything unusual happen today?"

"Fiona Wilson stopped in. She's worried about Hetta. Is there a reason for her to worry?"

After considering her question, Jonas responded, "I guess she and Fiona are close in spite of their age difference. I think Hetta is ten years younger than Fiona. Hetta has told me a few stories about their growing up. Fiona often took care of her while their parents worked. I don't know that anything's wrong with her, though. Everybody at the shelter is a little distracted."

"Are things back to normal there yet?"

"It depends on what you mean by *normal*. The crime scene tape is gone. The detectives are gone. But we never know if they'll stop in again and have more questions. No one seems to have any answers."

"Have you talked with Detective Rappaport or Zeke?"

"I have. They seem stumped. Whoever killed Rumple must have taken the murder weapon along with them. They grid-searched the property and beyond but couldn't find anything. There is no way to take fingerprints at the shelter with so many people going in and out of there. So unless the autopsy shows something for cause of death different from what they suspect, they're starting from scratch."

"They'll probably start with anybody who talked to Wilhelm or saw him the days before he died."

"I have a feeling they're going to be close-mouthed about this investigation. I know they've talked with Noah and Serena several times. The two of them are on edge about it. In fact, I wanted to make a suggestion."

"What?"

"I'd like to take Serena and Noah out to dinner. Maybe if the four of us just socialized for an evening, it would help them."

"Out to dinner is fine," Daisy mused. "On the other hand, if we invite them to my place, Felix can join us, and so can Bellamy. I get the feeling that Bellamy doesn't often leave Serena's side."

"I thought you said you'd like someone else to cook for you," he teased.

"That's tonight. By the weekend, I'll like the idea of cooking for someone else."

Jonas wrapped his arms around her and kissed her again.

Daisy usually patronized Guitars and Vinyl with her daughter Jazzi. But today, she wanted to talk to Ned Pachenko who worked there. It was a store that sold exactly what its title said—lots of guitars and plenty of vinyl. Daisy knew vinyl records were coming back in vogue. Her daughter had purchased a turntable and speakers and set them up in her bedroom.

The shop was divided into two sections. Guitars hung on the walls and on stands to the left. There was a selection of new guitars as well as old ones. To the right, vintage vinyl records stood in bins. Posters on the walls of

The Beatles, The Dave Clark Five, Heart, and the Bee Gees decorated that end of the shop.

Ned sat on a stool at the counter, looking through a catalogue. In his early twenties, he had a good-looking surfer vibe. His hair was blond and curly, and today he wore an *Abbey Road* T-shirt.

"Hi, Daisy," he said with a welcoming grin that was all Ned.

She knew Ned worked at the shop many mornings. He also took classes at Millersville University. "Foster told me you'd be here this morning, so I thought I'd stop in instead of calling. I just want to make sure we're still on schedule for the Storybook Tea."

Ned's grin grew even wider. "That is going to be such a blast. I'm having fun pairing songs with book titles. I even read some of the Newbery Medal winners to give me an idea of what kids are reading."

"That's wonderful. How about the old standards," she quipped.

He laughed. "You mean like *The Black Stallion*? I read that when I was a kid. I loved horse books."

"You're going to be well-prepared."

"I expect it will be a lot of fun," he enthused.

Daisy assured him, "Ticket sales are going well. If the weather holds, we can even serve on the patio that day. Not for the main event of you singing and playing, but for others who stop in without tickets. We're going to be filling both rooms for the event."

Suddenly, the double doors opened, and a pretty young woman with hair that looked like spun gold came in. She was slim, dressed in striped black, tan, and white slacks and a black cold-shoulder top. White sneakers were her shoes of choice.

Ned transferred his attention to the young woman. "Hi, Caroline. How are you today?"

"I'm good." She glanced at Daisy. "I don't want to interrupt."

"You're not interrupting," Ned assured her. "Caroline Miller, this is Daisy Swanson. Daisy runs Daisy's Tea Garden. I'm going to be doing a gig there soon. Daisy, Caroline works at her dad's bakery, Pastry Goods."

Daisy turned toward Caroline. "Congratulations on your wedding. My mom and dad run Gallagher's Garden Corner. I think they're going to be supplying your plants."

"They are. I believe everyone in town has heard about our wedding."

Caroline was positively beaming. She looked happy, and Daisy was glad to see that.

"Have you finalized everything?" Daisy asked.

"We have. There are so many details," Caroline added. "Andrew has been wonderful helping me with everything. He's the one who knows the vendors and where to go for tablecloths and glassware. And if he doesn't know, his mother does. They're used to that kind of thing. His family has been terrific. It's common knowledge Dad couldn't cover the reception cost, so the Kings are doing that and letting Dad handle the rehearsal get-together. I hope it won't be too simple for them, but Andrew insists I shouldn't worry about it." Caroline blushed a little. "My world was very limited before I met Andrew."

"Have you and Andrew planned a honeymoon?" Ned asked.

"We have, or rather *he* did. We're flying to Norway." She laughed. "I know that doesn't sound like the most romantic place in the world, but Andrew says there are lots of places there he wants to show me. He's traveled there several times."

"Any place can be romantic," Daisy said, meaning it. "If you're with the person you love, that's all that matters. And if you can see the Northern Lights as well, that's a plus."

"That's how we feel," Caroline agreed. "I've never been so happy in my life, except . . ."

Suddenly, Caroline Miller looked troubled, and Daisy wondered what that was about. She didn't know the woman well enough to ask, but apparently, Ned did.

"If you and Andrew are happy, what else can matter?"

"My father-in-law-to-be is very upset at the moment. Not with us. But he was called into the police station."

Ned looked shocked. "Why would he be called into the police station?"

Caroline looked down at her sneakers as if she shouldn't answer. But then, as if to get it off her chest, she did. "The detective questioned him about Mr. Rumple's murder."

A quiver of anxiety ran through Daisy. Had Detective Rappaport called in Stanley King because of what *she'd* told him? She'd told him because it was a lead, right? She'd done nothing wrong.

"I'm not sure exactly why," Caroline continued. "Mr. Rumple was an investor in Andrew's father's pet supplement company."

Hoping to allay Caroline's fears, Daisy explained, "The detectives often call in the people who were friends or acquaintances of the person who was murdered, especially if they'd had a conversation in the past couple of weeks. It's the way they gather their leads."

"You mean they question anyone who knew the victim?" Caroline looked a little brighter.

"Yes, especially if they're stumped, they try to look anywhere they can."

Looking relieved now, Caroline nodded. "That's good. I'm sure Mr. King will settle down after he realizes that's what they do."

Daisy had to wonder if Mr. Rumple being an investor in Mr. King's company was the only business they'd done together. However, that was a question for Detective Rappaport.

Ready for a dinner with Noah and Serena Saturday evening, Daisy gazed around her kitchen. She had prepared dinner with the care and love she always put into meals, especially when she was having company.

The beef roast had been in the slow cooker all day. Now she was making a sauce for hot German potato salad, while Jonas stood nearby, tearing lettuce and cutting carrots for the green salad.

"You said Jazzi had a date," he confirmed. "Was she going out with Mark again?"

This summer, Daisy had been surprised when she'd spotted Jazzi with a boy at the local carnival. She'd known her daughter had to start dating sometime, but Daisy didn't think she was ready for it. "Yes, she went out with Mark again."

"You said he was senior council president this year. And Jazzi told you he has good grades and has his eyes set on college."

"He does," Daisy agreed, trying to keep some distance from the subject.

She felt Jonas's gaze on her when he said, "You have to let go a little."

She sagged against the counter, facing him. "It feels like I'm letting go a lot. I didn't even ask her where they were going tonight."

"That's progress, I guess." There was amusement in Jonas's tone.

She gave his arm a gentle push and turned back to the sauce. "Aren't you worried at all?"

"I'm more concerned about the asparagus you're roasting in the oven. The timer's about ready to go off."

The doorbell chimed, and Daisy gave the potatoes and the sauce one last flourish before she switched off the burner. She pointed to the pan and the casserole beside it. "Can you pour the potatoes into the sauce and then put it all into the other slow cooker to keep it warm? We can have drinks and some of those little puff pastry quiches I made before we start dinner."

"I'll take the quiches out and bring them in with the drinks. You make Noah and Serena feel comfortable. I'll keep Felix in here until Bellamy has a chance to come in and get oriented. Are Pepper and Marjoram upstairs?"

"With the two dogs, I thought it would be better if they stayed in Jazzi's room, at least until we're finished dinner. They're napping on her bed. They won't mind."

Daisy often told Jonas what the cats thought. It seemed natural to her, and he accepted it.

She opened the front door and, after greetings, welcomed Serena, Noah, and Bellamy inside. Bellamy stayed right by Serena's side as she came deeper into the living room.

Serena glanced at the open space and then up at the wagon-wheel chandelier. "This is lovely. Jonas told me you renovated the barn and turned it into a home. Did you design the inside, too?"

"Along with a talented architect," Daisy confessed. "But I told him what I wanted to do with the space, and he executed it. Make yourselves comfortable in the living room. I'll hang up your jackets." She took their outerwear and hung it in the closet under the stairs. Bellamy didn't seem concerned with sniffing around but followed her mistress.

"Jonas is in the kitchen with Felix," Daisy explained. "We thought we'd give Bellamy a chance to get acclimated first."

"That's sweet," Serena, who'd worn gray slacks with a long-sleeved gray and winter-white sweater, said. "Bellamy doesn't usually go far from me, but when she does, she gets along with other dogs." Before she sank down on the sofa, she called in to Jonas who was in the kitchen. "Come in anytime you want. I know Felix is a gentleman. He and Bellamy will get along fine."

Noah had walked over to the deacon's bench and was studying the fireplace. "That's beautiful stonework."

"My contractor hired an excellent mason. He re-pointed the stones around the base of the barn, too, so we could keep them."

After waving at Jonas and greeting him, Noah spotted the reclaimed wood wall in the kitchen. "That's pretty spectacular, too."

"Actually, seeing that," Jonas said, "is what gave me the idea to make the pieces in my shop. And now it's sort of a specialty."

Felix entered the living room with Jonas and went over to Bellamy. They stood nose-to-nose, and communication seemed to pass between them. They both sank down, front paws to front paws, as if they were having a conversation . . . a silent one.

"Even though Felix wasn't at the shelter long, I think they remember each other," Serena said.

Noah picked up Jonas's conversation thread about reclaimed wood pieces. "The tourist trade will slow down now, but I imagine your shop will do okay with the holidays."

Jonas shrugged. "I'm trying to decide how far to extend my advertising. It all depends on how secure people feel about their lives and what they might spend for Christmas. We'll see. I'll craft pieces that I know are usually in demand in this area, like bookshelves, potato cupboards, and pie safes."

Conversation swirled around the coffee table as they ate hors d'oeuvres and enjoyed glasses of wine and each other's company. Then, however, the subject came up that they really couldn't avoid.

Noah inadvertently started it. "The shelter will be returning to full hours in the coming week."

Jonas exchanged a look with Daisy. "The police are finished there?"

"I certainly hope so," Serena muttered, looking tense. "The autopsy determined the murder weapon was a bucket. Something about the angle of Wilhelm's injury and residue left in the wound." Serena shivered. "They poked into every nook and cranny, trying to find that bucket. They examined every bucket they could find, upended our utility closet, and collected them all to test them. They upset all of the volunteers by either calling them to the shelter to question them or asking them to go down to the police station. The dogs are probably more intuitive than most people. They could feel all the tension. There was much more barking than usual, more accidents than usual, not as much playtime with all of us being distracted."

Noah glanced at his sister as if he were worried about her.

Daisy exchanged a look with Jonas. He'd been right about the bucket. Instincts that he'd developed in investigations were still at work. Daisy didn't want to add to Serena's upset, but she wanted to be sympathetic. "Did you know Mr. Rumple well?"

"Probably less than the volunteers," Serena answered. "That was because he was mostly there at night. I know he did dearly love the dogs. Their care was always on his mind."

"I probably saw him more than Serena," Noah admitted. "I was usually the one called in at night if there was a problem or when we had a new arrival. But I didn't know Wilhelm well. What I understand from other members of the staff is that he loved dogs, but humans not as much. They might have told their stories to the police."

"I heard that Mr. Rumple had a dog of his own," Daisy prompted, wanting to know what had happened to Hans.

"Yes, he did—a Plott hound. His nephew is adopting the dog. Dustan is Wilhelm's heir. He's going to sell Rumple's property and business. Dustan lives in York, so making arrangements shouldn't be too inconvenient for him. On the other hand, selling a business like that could be difficult."

Daisy wasn't sure about that because lawn ornaments were popular around Pennsylvania yards and farms.

"I just wish we could forget about the whole thing," Serena decided. "We've had multiple calls from news organizations. I don't want to talk to any of them. Neither does Noah. If they don't let us alone, we might have to hire a PR person, and we really can't afford to do that. We want all the donations for the shelter to go to the care of the animals, not to pay someone to ward off reporters."

Daisy could see how this whole situation was upsetting. Wilhelm Rumple's death seemed to have affected many people. The atmosphere in the room had changed considerably since they'd begun discussing the murder. Daisy decided it was time to change where they were sitting and what they were doing.

"Come on, everyone. Let's enjoy dinner and talk about happier subjects."

"I'm all for that," Noah said.

As they all stood to go into the dining room, Daisy noticed Noah and Serena exchange a look. She wondered just what that was all about.

CHAPTER SIX

Anxiety flooded through Daisy as she readied a table for tea service in the spillover tearoom Monday morning. She usually didn't set a service, but she had an appointment this morning. The idea of it was making her nervous, and she wasn't sure why. Dalton Ames had phoned her last evening and asked her if they could meet over tea. He wouldn't explain what the appointment was about, simply telling her they'd discuss it when he saw her.

Whatever could he want to discuss with *her*?

She'd soon find out.

At ten a.m., Dalton Ames walked in the door, right on time. She supposed it was good to know that he was prompt. As a fundraiser, he'd have to be organized and on schedule.

After she went to greet him, she motioned for him to

follow her into the spillover tearoom. She signaled to Cora Sue that they would be ready for tea. Cora Sue already knew what she was supposed to bring.

Today Dalton was wearing a pale gray sports jacket over a white V-neck T-shirt. Daisy wasn't fond of the slicked-back hair look or the beard stubble—at least not in the way Dalton presented it—but he was handsome in his way. He looked as if he belonged in the city, though, not in Willow Creek at her tea garden. Why she felt that way, she wasn't sure.

Again, her nervousness annoyed her. She had nothing to be nervous about.

Dalton waited for her to be seated, and then he sat, too, with a practiced smile . . . at least, it looked practiced to her. That was judgmental, and she shouldn't be thinking it.

They chatted about the attendance at the chamber of commerce meeting and Willow Creek ambiance for a few minutes until Cora Sue brought a pot of Darjeeling tea in a navy, flower-patterned china pot and two matching teacups. Daisy had already set up a bowl of sparkling sugar, a pot of honey, and slices of lemon.

Daisy asked Dalton, "Do you take cream in your tea?"

He waved his hand over the teacup. "No, this is fine. Thank you."

Next, Cora Sue presented a tiered tray of baked goods, from cheese biscuits to cinnamon scones to blueberry coffee-cake squares. For some reason, Daisy had wanted to go all out for this appointment. Was she trying to make a good impression on him about Willow Creek? No better impression than on any tourist who came in, she supposed.

After Cora Sue departed, he fixed his tea by squeezing

a slice of lemon into it. After he wiped his fingers on a napkin and set it on the table, he said, "I suppose you're wondering why I'm here."

"I am," Daisy conceded, fixing her own tea with a teaspoon full of honey.

He looked around the tea garden and then back at her. "This is a wonderful little business you have here."

She felt herself bristle at the *little* term. "My aunt and I have worked hard to make it a success."

"I suppose in tourist season, you're much busier," he noted.

Most of the tables in the main tearoom were filled, but she and Dalton were the only ones sitting in the spillover tearoom.

"Yes. It's quite challenging at full tourist season. This room is usually reserved for special teas."

"I understand you have one coming up called a Storybook Tea."

"We do," she asserted, still wondering where this conversation was going.

"I might have to buy a ticket." He sent her another practiced smile.

In other circumstances, she might offer him a ticket for free. Today, she wasn't feeling generous.

Choosing a blueberry coffee-cake square from the tray, he examined it and set it on his dessert dish, a Lamberton Ivory China Puritan plate with a Wedgwood blue pattern and a gold rim.

"We often have teas for children and their parents," Daisy explained, feeling the need to make conversation. "It's great socializing for the kids, and the parents enjoy it, too. They often become repeat customers."

"You're even having music," Dalton noted, as if he knew.

"We are. Ned has played for me before. We had a Fourth of July Garden Party."

"Yes, I heard about that. Your event teas are one of the reasons I'm here. Your day-to-day business is another."

She waited while he finished his coffee cake, brushed crumbs from his mouth, and then gazed at her with that same half-smile she was beginning to dislike even more.

"You have a lovely business, and from what I understand, you're well-liked in the community." His direct gaze was unsettling.

"I have family and good friends, no different from lots of other people in the community."

"You're being modest. From what I understand, you've even helped solve a few murders."

She kept quiet on that one. She didn't want to delve into anything with him that she didn't have to.

"I also understand that you support the homeless shelter," he went on. "Apparently, you helped a man who was homeless find his life again."

"Yes, I support the shelter. I think it would be good for the community to work together for something altruistic."

He nodded. "That's what I thought you would say. So I'd like to ask a few favors of you, representative of what we're trying to do to build this shelter."

She wasn't sure he was trying to build the shelter. He was trying to raise funds so that the town could build the shelter. And she didn't like the idea of doing him favors.

"What would you like me to do?"

He leaned over the table so his face was closer to hers.

"You're an influencer in this community, whether you'll admit it or not. Would you consider putting a fundraiser thermometer placard in your window and on your website? That would make your support public. You'd be showing you back this endeavor wholeheartedly."

After she thought about it for a moment, she nodded. "That's possible. I don't have a problem with that."

"Could you also talk it up on social media? I understand that your website is busy, that you have an employee here—your son-in-law—who's very good at the tech stuff."

She was uncomfortable with the fact that Dalton had apparently done research on her. "Foster does handle my social media. I'll be glad to do whatever I can to help with the fundraising effort and whatever else the homeless shelter needs."

He picked up his teacup and took a few sips of tea. "That's very good tea, and your pastries are delicious. I might call on you to cater a fundraising event or two. In fact, I've planned one at the King farm. It's the second Saturday in October. Maybe you could check your schedule and see if you can fit it in."

Daisy wouldn't turn down a gig that was good for tea garden promotion. "I'll check the date. I'm glad you like the pastries. Maybe you'll visit us again." She had to say that, didn't she? After all, she was running a business.

Dalton's gaze drifted over her as if he were thinking about asking her another question. He did. "Instead of simply tea, how would you like to have dinner with me sometime?"

She blinked. She hadn't expected that. Was he really hitting on her? Certainly, if he had done his research, he'd know that she was involved with Jonas. To squelch his request immediately, she responded, "I'm already in a relationship, and it's serious."

Dalton's eyes targeted her finger. She knew he was making an obvious point. She wasn't wearing a ring.

He didn't seem embarrassed as he shrugged. "These are uncertain times. Everything changes quickly. But keep in mind that my dinner invitation is open." He reached inside his sports jacket pocket and took out a business card. He slid it over to her on the table. "My personal cell phone is written on the back. Let me know about the King fundraiser."

If Daisy did accept the fundraiser party, she would keep her distance from Dalton Ames.

After work, Daisy walked to Woods, feeling not only the fall nip in the air but dampness, too. Clouds had moved in overhead, and dusk was falling earlier than usual. She didn't pay much attention to the few cars on Market Street or to the buckboard with benches that were empty now as the driver twitched his reins to drive the tourist buggy back to its home base and stable. On her mind was the tea she'd had with Dalton Ames. She wanted to discuss it with Jonas.

When she entered Woods, she saw immediately that Jonas was standing in the middle of the store speaking with one of his customers. Felix was sitting beside Jonas, looking up at the two of them while they talked. It was an animated discussion, and Daisy didn't know if she should join in.

Jonas saw her, however, and motioned to her to come

closer. The woman stopped what she was discussing with Jonas and turned to see Daisy. Jonas introduced them right away.

"Daisy, this is Berta Glassner. She and her husband often come into the store to buy furniture for themselves and their kids."

By Berta's dress Daisy suspected she was a Mennonite woman. The pattern of her dress was filled with pink flowers. Its length, her leggings, shoes, and *kapp* were sure signs that Daisy was correct.

"It's nice to meet you," Daisy said pleasantly, wondering why Jonas was including her in the conversation.

"Daisy is my girlfriend," Jonas explained to Berta. "She has much to do with the care of Felix. I'm sure she'll be interested in what you're saying."

Berta explained, "I came in to speak with Jonas this time, not about furniture, but about Felix."

That seemed curious to Daisy, though many people around town now knew that Felix was often at the store with Jonas, and they were a pair.

Berta continued, "I knew that Jonas adopted Felix from Four Paws. I wanted to know if Felix was sick at all after he was adopted."

Daisy's gaze met Jonas's as he answered, "No, Felix was perfectly fine. Daisy, did you see any signs that he was sick?"

"Absolutely not. He was full of energy and enjoyed his food. He'd learned many commands with his former owner, and we figured out what they were. He seemed, and *is*, perfectly healthy."

Berta said, "I was just telling Jonas that we adopted a dog from Four Paws. He's part schnauzer and part a hundred other varieties, we think. But he was sick. I won't go into details. We didn't take him back to the shelter, but to another vet. We thought it was best to get an independent opinion."

"I hope your dog's all right?"

"He is now, but he might not have been if we hadn't caught this in time. Noah Langston did tell us exactly what they were giving him in addition to food. They were giving him pet supplements."

Daisy's mind began spinning. Were those Stanley King's pet supplements? "What did the vet find out?"

"He found out that those supplements contained too much vitamin D, and that they could have killed him."

Daisy was so shocked that she didn't hear much of the rest of the conversation. As the woman and Jonas talked for a bit more, Daisy thought about everything that Serena and Noah had done to build up Four Paws Animal Shelter to be reputable. What was going on?

After goodbyes, Berta turned to leave.

"What was that about?" Daisy asked Jonas, baffled.

Jonas watched Berta leave his store and walk down the street. "I'm not sure. Have you heard any buzz around the tea garden about other dogs who were adopted being sick?"

Felix was bumping against Daisy's leg now and her sweater coat. Automatically, she stooped to him to rub behind his ears and along his back. "I haven't heard anything like that, and I'm sure we didn't see any signs in Felix that he wasn't feeling well."

"No, we didn't. But maybe when I adopted Felix, Four Paws wasn't using the same supplements. Maybe they weren't using any supplements at all."

"That's true," Daisy mused. "When Berta said *supplements*, I automatically drew the conclusion that they were

Stanley King's supplements. But that might not be the case."

"No, it might not. I did hear that Detective Rappaport had called King into the police station for questioning. I wonder how he knew Rumple."

"When I was at Guitars and Vinyl, Caroline Miller came in. I congratulated her on her wedding, and we talked a little. She said that Mr. Rumple was an investor in King's company."

"Ah, so that's the connection."

Maybe that *was* the connection. Maybe the detective had asked King to come in not because of what Daisy had said, but because Rumple was an investor. She wasn't going to go into that with Jonas, at least not until his birthday party was over . . . not until she surprised him with the celebration.

His birthday celebration was what she should keep her mind on, not her conversation with Dalton Ames, not Stanley King or Mr. Rumple or a murder that she was not going to get involved with.

Portia Harding Smith's visit was a surprise. Not that she wasn't welcome. Jazzi's birth mother was always welcome at Daisy's house. However, usually the visits were planned a couple of weeks in advance, over a weekend, to make sure they suited all concerned. But last night, Portia had texted Daisy and asked if she'd mind an overnight visit . . . tomorrow. Of course, Daisy didn't mind. She asked if Portia could be there for dinner. Portia assured Daisy that she could be. This would be a quick trip, and she'd return to Allentown the following morning.

Daisy suspected that there was something Portia wanted to discuss. It worried her a little. She'd accepted Portia willingly into Jazzi's life, but she was still a little fearful of sharing her daughter. Yet she knew she had to do it for Jazzi's sake. She knew if she didn't, Jazzi could pull away from her. Still, as she left the tea garden early to prepare dinner that evening, her thoughts were in a jumble.

She was preparing supper when Jonas opened the door to her house and came in. She was grateful to see him. Finally, he didn't think he had to ring the bell or announce his presence before entering. That made her happy.

She hurried to him, and he wrapped his arms around her. "You sounded anxious when you called me," he said after a long kiss. "Why are you worried about this visit from Portia?"

"I don't know. Maybe it was something in the urgency of it. I've been thinking all day about what it could possibly be."

"Stop thinking," he warned her.

With her arms still around his neck, she said, "Easy for you to say. You're a man."

He laughed. "You don't think I wake up in the middle of the night worried about anything?"

"I imagine you worry, but you seem to be able to compartmentalize better than I can."

"That's probably due to my police training rather than merely being a man."

She glared at him. "Why is it that you usually make sense?"

"That's my job with you, isn't it?"

"Only one of them," she teased. "How about peeling potatoes to go with the pork roast? It's in the slow cooker with peach salsa. This is an easy meal tonight. I brought home carrot-grape salad from the tea garden, and I have whoopie pies for dessert."

"What you consider *easy*, somebody else might consider *extravagant*. I'll be glad to peel potatoes. That keeps my wood-whittling skills honed."

Jonas could always lighten her mood when she was too serious, and she hoped she could do the same for him.

Jazzi arrived home soon after Jonas. She went upstairs to change out of her school clothes and into jeans and a T-shirt. She was happy about Portia coming, though she didn't understand the visit, either.

When she came downstairs with Pepper in her arms, she said, "Felix and Marjoram are having a discussion in my bedroom. Marjoram is meowing at him, and he's just sitting there, listening."

Jonas chuckled. "Felix knows the best way to a cat's heart is to keep quiet."

Jazzi giggled and set Pepper on the floor. The cat quickly jumped up onto the island chair and began washing herself. Her paw paused in midair when Daisy told her, "You'll have to go into the living room while we eat."

The look in Pepper's eyes said that she was terrifically offended, but then she continued washing.

"Do you have *any* idea why Portia's coming?" Jazzi asked.

"I'm sure she misses you. Your two weeks there in August probably gave her an idea of what it was like to have you around all the time."

Jazzi wasn't buying it. She narrowed her eyes at her mother. "You're worried about her visit."

"I'm not," Daisy protested. "There's no point worrying until I have something to worry about, right?"

"That's an old Amish proverb or something, isn't it?"
Jonas asked with a smile.

Just then, the doorbell rang, and Jazzi flew to the door
to answer it. Portia and Jazzi hugged, and Daisy's heart
did a little flip watching them together. They were definitely mother and daughter. Jazzi's black hair was sleek
and long. Although Portia's hair was black and in a short,
stylish cut, it had the same glossiness. They had the same
dark brown eyes, upturned nose, and wide smiles.

Daisy knew that Jazzi was soon going out into the big
old world. She'd be moving out of both of their orbits,
and there was nothing they could do to stop it. Did Portia
feel that urgency to be around her daughter, too?

Dinner went smoothly, and conversation flowed easily. After dinner, over second cups of tea, they played an
old-fashioned game of hearts. It was a card game that
Daisy had often played with her daughters when they
were growing up.

After three games, Jonas decided to leave.

Daisy stepped outside with him and Felix, breathing in
the near-autumn air, watching the leaves skitter across the
lawn. Still, for a few moments, she took in the sight of
Jonas on her porch.

He asked, "What?" before he put his arms around her.

"I like having you here."

"That's good because I like being here. I thought I'd
better leave so Portia can discuss whatever she wants
with you or with Jazzi or with both of you."

"I didn't get any sense about what it is from everything
we've talked about."

He kissed her forehead and gave her an extra tight hug.
"Go inside and find out why she's here."

Sitting beside Jonas on the stoop, Felix gave a little ruff, as if he agreed.

Daisy stooped and petted the dog. "You're a good boy. Thanks for treating Marjoram and Pepper like sisters."

He bumped his head against Daisy's leg.

After Daisy returned inside, she saw Jazzi and Portia talking at the island. From the dining room table, she asked, "Do you need a little privacy?"

Portia shook her head. "No, come join us."

Daisy did, still wondering what this visit was all about. She didn't find out until after Jazzi went to bed.

Usually when Portia visited, Daisy gave up her bedroom, and she slept on the couch. Vi's old bedroom upstairs had become a storage room of sorts. Daisy's couch was a pullout, and she was quite comfortable sleeping on it. However, after Jazzi had gone upstairs and they'd all gotten ready for bed, Portia came out to the living room where Daisy was undoing the sofa. Portia helped her with the mechanism and handed her the pillow that Daisy had deposited on the armchair.

Portia said, "I suppose you guessed that there is something I'd like to talk to you about."

"The truth is, I've been worrying about it," Daisy confessed, sitting on the corner of the open bed while Portia took the armchair.

"I'm sorry you worried," Portia said. "I didn't mean for that to happen. I wanted to talk to you alone about this, and I didn't think it was a conversation we should have over the phone."

"All right."

Portia sat forward on the chair. "Colton and I want to contribute to Jazzi's college education."

Not much could have surprised Daisy more. Portia and Colton had two daughters, and they'd have to fund an education for them in the future.

"I never expected that," Daisy said honestly.

"Colton was promoted, and with the promotion, there was an uptick in salary. We're doing well. I'm not saying we could pay for much, but we could subsidize the cost of Jazzi's books and maybe a monthly expense allowance."

So many thoughts were running through Daisy's mind. She decided to be frank with one. "Are you doing this out of guilt because you haven't been around Jazzi for most of her life? Because if that's the reason, it's not necessary."

Portia's eyes glowed with regret for all the years of Jazzi's life that she'd missed. "I have to admit, guilt is part of it. But I love Jazzi, and I want to take some responsibility for her. Don't you think it's about time?"

"And Colton is completely on board with this?" At first, Colton and Jazzi hadn't meshed well, but they'd gotten to know each other better.

"Colton understands how important this is to me, and he agrees."

"This isn't simply my decision to make," Daisy told her. "I think the best thing for you to do, is to talk to Jazzi."

CHAPTER SEVEN

On Saturday morning, as Daisy watched the Parade of Pets sponsored by Four Paws Animal Shelter trot by, she noticed the dogs available for adoption wore colorful collars and little signs that proclaimed LUV ME. However, not only shelter dogs were parading. The community had been invited to dress up their dogs and add them to the parade. There were even some cats—a Persian in a ruffled collar sitting in a baby stroller, and a calico with a harness and her cat mom walking beside her. The feline strolled proudly, head up, tail flying.

Jonas had met Daisy at the tea garden, and they'd walked down to Woods leisurely, enjoying the parade. Jonas had leashed Felix for the event. The canine was acting as if he were simply out for another walk. Every once in a while, he whined to make friends with one of the dogs in the parade, but then Jonas would give him a command and he would return to Jonas's side.

After they reached the front of Woods, Daisy noticed that Elijah had come outside and was shaking his head with a frown.

Jonas stopped beside him. "What's the matter?"

"I can't believe they dressed up those dogs like that. I shouldn't even be watching."

Elijah was New Order Amish but held on to most of the old ways. He used a cell phone for work and emergency purposes, a gas generator to run his washing machine and the like, but this display of frivolity was almost sinful to him.

"It's for a good cause," Daisy suggested. "Soon many of those dogs will find a home."

Elijah ran a hand over his beard, then shook his head again.

He was about to turn around and go back inside the store when he stopped. "Have you heard any more about Wilhelm Rumple's murder?" he asked the two of them. His gaze had targeted Serena and Noah, who were leading dogs past them. "I'm surprised the Langstons continued with this show."

"I suppose they're afraid the murder will affect adoptions," Daisy said. "They weren't sure they wanted to continue with the parade, but they had encouragement that the parade might help the community forget about what happened at Four Paws."

"Or remind them," Elijah muttered, "though I expect some Englischers accept crime as a matter of course."

"I don't think that's true," Daisy protested. "Everyone I know and talk to wants this crime to be solved and solved quickly. It's always scary when you don't know why something happened."

"I suppose that's so," Elijah conceded. "A cousin of mine who's a farrier is very upset about Rumple's murder. I *canna* see why. But as you say, not knowing the cause, not knowing what would make someone so angry that they would hurt another person, is very upsetting. I believe we have to look to *Gott* while the police settle this, ain't so?"

"We have to keep our faith, no matter what," Daisy agreed.

Daisy didn't know who Elijah's cousin was. Why would he be upset? She'd spoken with Serena this morning, and Serena still didn't seem to be herself. It seemed odd to Daisy that people who claimed not to know Rumple very well were affected by his death.

Vi and Foster suddenly appeared from the other end of the street, and Vi was holding Sammy. Daisy approached them, letting Jonas keep up his conversation with Elijah. She held her hands out for her grandson.

He went to her with a laugh and a hug.

"He kept us up a good bit again last night," Foster said. "It must be another tooth coming in. We took turns holding him and played tic-tac-toe until he settled down. One of his cold chew toys finally settled him. I guess it felt good to gnaw on it."

Daisy held her grandson away from her a bit. "He looks like a happy boy now."

"That's because we don't want him to fall asleep," Foster said, kidding.

Daisy assured them, "I'll be glad to hold him for a while and keep him entertained if you want to spend a little time by yourselves walking up and down. You could pick out a pup for him."

She hadn't yet discussed with her daughter and son-in-law Glorie's suggestion that they rent her house. She'd thought about talking to Gavin about it first. Still, if she did that, she wasn't treating them like the adults they were. Maybe they could get together soon and have a family meeting.

Vi leaned over and kissed her mom's cheek. "We'd love it if Foster and I could just walk around, get a croissant, and be a couple for a change without a kid."

"Understood," Daisy said with a smile. "I can take Sammy around to everybody, and they can greet him and play with him, and we'll have a good time."

"An hour?" Foster asked, the more practical one of the two.

"An hour sounds good," Daisy agreed.

Moments later, Vi and Foster walked away as the parade continued. A Saint Bernard guided a tall man, who must have been about six foot four, along with his leash. They looked like a good pair.

Suddenly, someone tapped Daisy's shoulder. She swung around to see Dalton Ames. She took in a little breath, because she wasn't particularly happy to see him.

Sammy stared and blew out a bubble.

Dalton was wearing skinny-legged black pants, an asymmetrical lapelled jacket, and a black scarf hanging down from that. The outfit was trendy, just as he was.

He smiled. "We meet again, Mrs. Swanson. Have you thought more about our offer for you to cater?"

"I have," Daisy responded, though she took a step back. "I can pencil in the fundraiser."

"Terrific. Your contact will be Andrew King. You can let him know what it will cost and what you need."

All at once, Jonas stepped forward beside Daisy, and Daisy introduced him to Dalton Ames. Ames said to Jonas, "You own this store, right?"

"I do."

"Your store carries weight with the Amish."

"I like to think my store carries weight with everyone."

"That's all the better," Dalton said. "Maybe you could do what I asked Daisy to do."

"What was that?" Jonas asked.

Daisy cut into the conversation. "Dalton asked me to put a thermometer in my window showing how well we have done with fundraising. He also wants me to post about the fundraising for the homeless shelter on my website."

"I see," Jonas said, though he seemed to be looking for something more than that from Dalton Ames.

Dalton transferred his attention back to Daisy. "So this is your grandson? I couldn't help but see Foster and your daughter hand him over."

"This is Sammy," Daisy affirmed, though she really didn't want to tell Dalton any more about her family than she had to. It was just a feeling.

"You don't look old enough to have a grandchild."

She'd heard that statement before from more than one person. Dalton saying it, nevertheless, made it *not* seem like a compliment. It seemed like it was fake flattery, as if he wanted an in with her.

"I have a birth certificate to prove how old I am," she joked. "Some days, I feel every one of those years."

Dalton rubbed his beard stubble. "You must have been young when you had your daughter."

"Not as young as some of the Amish women who start a family early."

He looked up and down the sidewalk at the mixture of people in Amish, Mennonite, and English dress. "Do you believe it's something that occurs more in this area?"

"Oh, I wouldn't say that." She didn't want to prolong this conversation.

Jonas took a step closer to her as if he sensed her discomfort, even though Dalton Ames didn't. "Daisy and I were going to take Sammy for a walk with Felix. So we need to be going. Right, Daisy?"

"Right," she said brightly, believing Jonas had read her correctly and was attempting to remove them from this conversation. Hiking Sammy up more securely into her arms, she said, "I'll see you around, Dalton. I'll phone Andrew King about the details." She headed down the street with Jonas, leaving Dalton Ames behind them.

They hadn't walked too far before Jonas asked, "What was *that* all about?"

"I don't know. He asked me to go to dinner."

Jonas was silent for a few moments. "What did you say?"

"I told him I was involved with *you*."

"Hmm." Jonas grunted. A few moments later, he said, "I think I'm going to take you to dinner somewhere special. What do you say?"

"I say, as long as I'm with you, I don't care where we go."

Jonas held out his arms to Sammy. "What if I carry you for a while?"

Sammy leaned toward Jonas and went easily into his arms. Daisy watched the two of them, her breath hitching a bit. Jonas loved kids as much as she did.

As Jonas and Daisy walked a little farther, she turned to him again. "Thank you."

Jonas just smiled in return.

The parade was almost at the end when Daisy spotted somebody she'd just met. Caroline Miller and a man who must have been her fiancé were playing with a dog that looked in large part like a King Charles spaniel. He was cute with those long ears, big brown eyes, and tan and white spots. He was looking adoringly up at Caroline.

"Uh-oh," Daisy said as she reached the couple. "I think you might have found a ring-bearer."

Caroline laughed and introduced Andrew to Daisy. Daisy introduced Jonas. After greetings all around, Jonas asked the couple, "Are you thinking about adopting her?"

"She *is* so cute," Caroline said, and sighed.

Andrew murmured, "We could keep her at the farm, at least until we find a place of our own."

"She won't get huge," Caroline said. "I know she won't. She's mostly a King Charles. They're supposed to be so lovable."

"For when I'm not around?" Andrew teased.

She flirted back, saying, "Of course, I'll need some comfort when you're not around."

Andrew eyed the dog again, almost forgetting he was in a discussion with three other people. "I might have to be away overnight now and then. It's not a bad idea."

Hetta Armbruster was the volunteer holding the dog on a leash. She said, "If you'd like to spend a little time with her, why don't you come back to the shelter?"

Caroline looked troubled. "I don't know if I want to go there. Just the thought of going in somewhere where someone was murdered makes my skin crawl."

Jonas offered, "They can come up to Woods with us. I

have Felix there all the time, and the shop is a place where they can sit and spend some time with the dog."

Hetta eyed him. "Are you sure you don't mind?"

"I don't mind at all."

"You *will* have to bring her back to the shelter," Hetta reminded them. "We'd have to do your paperwork with background information. You'll need to provide references, et cetera."

"Between us, we can do that," Andrew assured her. "Do you trust us to take the dog with us?"

She nodded to Jonas. "I know *him* pretty well. And you're a *King*. That name carries weight around here. Let me just give you this." She handed Andrew a paper with all the information for the dog on it. "Bring that with you. That will help move things along." She handed him the leash, then hurried to the front of the parade to catch up with Serena and Noah.

"That's kind of you to offer your store," Caroline said to Jonas. "We appreciate it. We'll just have to postpone our wedding preparations. We've been putting details together for over a year. Now and then, it's nice to take a break."

Suddenly, there was a shout from a man crossing the street.

Caroline looked his way. "That's my dad. I wonder what he wants."

Daisy studied Mr. Miller. He was around her dad's age. He had a clean-shaven face, with a high forehead that led to a bald spot across the top of his pate. Fine gray hair ringed his head. His furrowed brows and rings under his eyes made him appear older. The lines beside his nose down to his mouth cut deep into folds of skin, and the skin on his neck also showed his age. He was wearing a white long-sleeved shirt and black pants with a baker's apron over all of it. In red on the bib, it said PASTRY GOODS.

After he arrived at their group, Caroline introduced everyone.

Daisy was quick to say, "My older daughter loves your croissants. I don't make those."

"I'm glad to hear it. I know your baked goods are quite good. I hear about that all the time from your customers. I don't want to hold you up, but I have good news for Caroline."

"What is it, Dad?" She gave her full attention to her father.

"You know, originally we'd planned hors d'oeuvres for the rehearsal."

"I know," she said in a lowered voice. "You said a dinner would be too expensive."

"That's not true anymore." He gave her a slip of paper with the name of a Lancaster restaurant and a phone number. "I'm planning a dinner at this restaurant. Everyone should have a good time at the rehearsal dinner, and we'll all enjoy the food."

Caroline glanced at Andrew and then gave her dad a huge, meaningful hug.

As Daisy was riding her bike with Jazzi on Sunday after church, she thought about the month of September. It was a month of changes. Tree branches and their leaves rustled in the mild wind as they rode. Some of the leaves had changed colors. Others hadn't. When they passed pines, the scent seemed even stronger than in the summer.

As Daisy pedaled, she thought about the pet parade and everything she'd learned from the people she'd spoken to. A death caused families to be upset and acquaintances of the victim to mourn them. But it seemed that Rumple hadn't been a friend to many people. Why had his death been such an upset? Maybe because it was murder?

Her thoughts rambled, and she pictured Jonas working in his woodshop. He had lots of pieces he wanted to finish before the holidays, a good selling season for him. While she'd been petting the King Charles spaniel at Jonas's shop, Zeke Willet had come in. He and Jonas had their heads together for a while in intense conversation. However, when Daisy asked Jonas about it, he'd said they were just talking about guy stuff. Jonas and Zeke had had a good history, a bad history, and now a fresh new history. Their friendship had broken apart because of a romantic triangle that had turned tragic. They were mending their friendship now, and maybe their conversation had turned to deeper things. She and Jonas didn't have secrets from each other. After that thought, she knew she had to correct herself. She was keeping his birthday party a surprise.

Stones and gravel scattered on the rural road as Jazzi pedaled up beside her. With no traffic, they often rode side by side so they could talk.

Without preamble, her daughter said, "We haven't talked about Portia's offer."

Daisy looked over at Jazzi on her blue and purple bike with her fuchsia helmet. "No, we haven't. I was giving you time to think about it."

"I've been thinking about it. I've been thinking about how you would feel if they helped me."

"Oh, Jazzi, that shouldn't be part of your consideration."

"It's not. I want you to be honest with me. Would you mind?" Jazzi asked.

Being as honest as she could, Daisy tried to express her feelings. "Ever since you found Portia, I knew I had to open up my heart and let you bring her into it. Do you know what I mean?"

"I guess. You mean like there were barriers to you doing it yourself, so you kind of let her in through me."

"Exactly. I think we both know that Portia wants what's best for you, and now Colton does, too."

"I guess what bothers me some," Jazzi confessed, "is that I don't want to feel beholden to Portia and Colton. I don't want to feel like I owe them something."

"All you owe them will be gratitude. Your feelings are on you, Jazzi. And the truth is, I don't think they'll make you feel beholden. I'm fairly certain Portia won't."

"You mean because she feels guilty for abandoning me."

Jazzi's perception sometimes surprised Daisy. Yet it shouldn't. "If you want to put it that way. Is that the way you think about it? Because you could think about it in a different way. Portia wanted to give you a better life because she couldn't take care of you."

After pedaling a bit, Jazzi sighed. "That's what I tell myself. But that speck of doubt is always there. Let me ask you something, Mom. Would you have given me up? You were young when you had Vi. Would you have even thought about it?"

Immediately, Daisy wanted to dismiss that train of thought. "That's not fair, Jazzi. That's not fair to Portia. I had married your dad. We were in love, and we wanted to build a life and a family. You can't compare me to Portia."

"You didn't answer, but I understand if you don't want to. I think I *know* the answer. You *wouldn't* have."

"Jazzi, please don't weigh my life against Portia's. You have to think about Portia as she is now. She's a loving woman and a loving mother. She thinks you're the jelly on her peanut butter."

Jazzi laughed, and that's exactly what Daisy had intended.

"So you think I should accept what Colton and Portia are offering?"

Daisy sank back on her bike seat, glancing over at her daughter. "I think you should do what feels right to you. It would take a burden off of you. You wanted to get a job while you were at school, but if you accept Portia's help, you don't have to. On the other hand, if at any time you feel you don't want to accept Portia's and Colton's contribution, you can stop it. Life's made up of lots of little decisions."

"And I shouldn't turn it into a giant one?"

"Not if you don't have to."

They rode in silence a few minutes. "I'm still working on my essay to go along with my applications," Jazzi said. "Sometimes I find it hard to talk about being adopted. Maybe putting the words down on paper makes it not so matter-of-fact. Do you know what I mean?"

"I do know what you mean. Do you want any help?"

"No, I want to do it on my own. I'll let you read it, and maybe Jonas, too. You can tell me if I've said everything I've really wanted to say."

"I'm proud of you, you know."

Jazzi just smiled and pedaled up ahead of Daisy, her youthful energy apparent as she prepared for many new chapters in her life.

It wasn't long before they began approaching Wilhelm Rumple's property. Jazzi slowed her pedaling, and so did Daisy. To Daisy's surprise, there was a patrol car sitting there, though the crime scene tape had been removed. Daisy had read on the *Willow Creek Messenger*'s page that Rumple's funeral was tomorrow.

As she and Jazzi pedaled slowly past the property, Daisy could see Bart standing just inside the open gate. He was looking down at the ground. She wondered what he was looking for.

CHAPTER EIGHT

Daisy readied herself for bed that night, thinking about everything she and Jazzi had talked about. She looked around her room with its heavy pine furniture . . . its sunshine and shadow quilt on the bed. She loved the queen-sized sleigh bed. The furniture was all antiques. The bathroom upstairs had a double sink, but *her* en suite had only one. She looked at her shower which was nice enough. Two people could fit into it if they wanted to. But the bathroom was small. She'd designed it that way so she could have a small powder room near the utility room for anyone who came to visit. They wouldn't have to trek through her bedroom.

And the reason she was thinking about all this now?

Jonas. Would he be comfortable here? Could they make a life here together?

Daisy thought about that as she washed her face,

brushed her teeth, and donned her nightgown. She was ready to put lotion on her hands when her phone played its tuba sound. Picking it up, she saw Jonas's face on her screen, and she smiled.

"It's getting late," she said.

"I know, at least for us early risers it is," he agreed, a smile in his voice. "How was your bike ride with Jazzi?"

Daisy sank down onto her bed and plumped a pillow against her headboard. "It was good. I think she's going to take Portia's help."

"How do you feel about that?"

"I don't know. We'll see. This had to be Jazzi's decision. I'll be okay with it. I'll get used to it. Someone else is helping my daughter. That's a good thing, right?" Jonas's thoughts were important to her as they fit their lives together.

"It's a good thing, if you think about it that way."

Unsettled by the thought of Jazzi leaving for college next year, she wanted to change the course of the conversation. "We rode past Rumple's place."

"You did? Nothing going on there, I guess."

"Actually, there was. The crime scene tape was down, but there was a patrol car there. I saw Bart just inside the gate looking around."

"Maybe he was just going over the security system and where the motion detectors were."

"I suppose that's so. I really thought they'd be done with it."

"They might have gone back in for a second look . . . maybe an unofficial look."

Jonas's police experience often led him to see events in a different light.

Suddenly, Daisy's phone beeped that she had another

call. She said, "Jonas, I'm sorry. I'm getting another call. It's Serena."

"Maybe you'd better take it. I just wanted to say good night and tell you that you're on my mind."

"You were on my mind, too. I'll talk to you tomorrow."

Daisy quickly answered Serena's call. "Serena, hi. I was on another call."

"I hope I didn't interrupt."

"It's okay. I was talking to Jonas. It was just a good-night call."

Serena was quiet for a few moments. "I hope someday I'll have a relationship where a good-night call is important."

When Daisy didn't respond right away, Serena jumped in again. "Daisy, I have a favor to ask." Daisy's head spun with all the possible favors it could be. Maybe volunteering at Four Paws? She listened.

"Did you know Wilhelm Rumple's funeral is tomorrow?" Serena inquired.

"Yes, I know that. I saw it on the *Willow Creek Messenger*'s website."

"I need someone to go with me. Noah can't. He has surgeries tomorrow. But I don't want to go alone. I feel someone from the shelter should go, and no one else seems to want to."

This definitely wasn't a request that Daisy had expected. She asked, "It's at ten a.m., right?"

"Yes, and it's in York. So we wouldn't waste too much time traveling. I just feel that someone needs to represent the shelter. But I don't feel comfortable going on my own, and I know I can't take Bellamy."

That made Daisy smile. Would Serena really consider

taking her pet along? Maybe Bellamy was a therapy dog and not just a companion. Daisy hadn't thought about that before, but it made sense.

Serena sounded worried again when she asked, "Will you go with me?"

There was a tea service planned for tomorrow in the spillover tearoom. Customers had made reservations. There would be a lot of prep involved for all her staff. Her staff would have handled some of it today, but they always scurried around the morning before the tea, accomplishing everything to make it a rewarding experience. Still, she could call one of her other servers who liked to pick up more hours. She wasn't full-time, but she often told Daisy to give her a call if she needed someone else in a pinch.

Making a decision, Daisy assured Serena, "I can shift around my staff a little. I really should be back by two, though, as we have an afternoon tea service."

Serena sounded relieved when she said, "Since the funeral's at ten, we should easily be home by one."

"All right, Serena. I'll go with you. Do you want to meet me at the tea garden?"

"That sounds good. Thank you, Daisy. I really appreciate this."

After Daisy said good night to Serena and ended the call, she texted Jonas and told him what she'd be doing tomorrow.

The church in West York was old and stark. Inside the double black doors, Daisy sat next to Serena in a pew near the back of the church. Tan walls surrounded them, along with small windows without stained glass. There was a dark wood altar with a cross hanging high above it. Light poured in from a round window at the point of the roof over the cross.

Daisy shivered as she watched anyone who'd come to pay their respects to Wilhelm Rumple cross in front of the pews where the closed wood casket stood. They spoke a few words to the man who was seated on a folding chair to the right of the casket.

Serena leaned closer to Daisy, her light floral perfume a nice contrast to the dank atmosphere of the church. "The graveyard is around back," she said. "I don't think anyone's going to eulogize Wilhelm in here."

"I haven't seen anyone else from Willow Creek, have you?" Daisy asked.

She'd been on the lookout, maybe even for one of the detectives. They were good at fading into the crowd just to keep an eye on anything that happened. From Daisy's experience in other murder investigations, she knew they believed the murderer sometimes couldn't stay away. The detectives had been right before. But today, this sparse crowd simply seemed eager to have the service over with.

Serena whispered again, "The nephew's name is Dustan. I can't imagine that his father, Wilhelm Rumple's brother, wouldn't be here. But he'd be seated up there with Dustan if he was, don't you think?"

"Probably. But there's no knowing what goes on in families."

Daisy was hoping she could find out, though, merely by talking to other people who were here. Serena had told her that after the graveside service, there would be a gathering in the social hall. Wilhelm's nephew must have some regard for him if he was willing to put all this together.

After the allotted time for everyone to pay their respects, a minister came to the podium. He said that the pallbearers would take the casket out to the cemetery, and everyone else should leave their pews in orderly fashion and follow. He stopped to talk to Dustan, and after a few nods, they separated.

Watching him, Daisy saw Dustan leave the church through the side door. There was a small house near the church where the minister lived. Daisy wondered if he was going there, maybe to compose himself before heading for the graveside service.

Daisy had dressed in a slim black suit with a substantial fitted jacket. She hadn't wanted to bring a coat. She'd worn black flats, not knowing what kind of ground they would be covering in the cemetery. Serena had dressed similarly in a navy dress with a jacket. She'd even worn a small navy pillbox hat. Daisy wished she could wear such a hat with that kind of aplomb.

At the tail end of the line of mourners, they exited the church by a side entrance and walked along the cement pavement to the cemetery behind the church. Cast-iron fence surrounded it. A green canopy had been set up over the particular plot of land that was designated for Rumple's grave.

Daisy suddenly heard a dog bark behind her. When she turned, she spotted Hans, Rumple's Plott hound! Dustan was leading him on a leash. Hans, maybe remembering Daisy, guided Dustan toward her. Before Dustan could guess what he was going to do, Hans sidled up to Daisy and rubbed his head against her leg.

Dustan hurried to apologize. "I'm so sorry. I don't know what he's up to."

While Serena kept her distance, Daisy turned to Dustan and extended her hand. "Hello. I'm Daisy Swanson."

Dustan raised questioning eyes to hers. "Do you know Hans?"

"I met him at your uncle's. He liked sniffing my jeans because I think he smelled my cats and my boyfriend's dog. It's a little unusual to see a dog at a graveside service."

Dustan looked embarrassed. He was about five-nine, fortyish, with a bookish look. His dark brown hair wasn't particularly styled, and he wore tortoiseshell glasses. He was wearing a suit, but his brown tie was crooked, and the collar on his off-white shirt a bit mussed. "It *is* unusual, I suppose," he admitted. "Hans is usually pretty mellow. He's been having separation anxiety. He and my uncle always went everywhere together if they could. He hasn't wanted to leave my side since I brought him home."

"Were you and your uncle close?"

Dustan didn't hesitate to shake his head. "Not particularly. The only thing we had in common was our love for dogs. I have two others, a lab and a mixed breed. Hans is making friends with them, but he still wants to stick with me. I'm hoping he'll become more secure the longer he's with me."

"Is he a good guard dog?" Daisy asked nonchalantly.

"From what I can tell, he does perimeter checks. But he's not at all aggressive."

"I know someone tried to break into your uncle's house while . . . while he was living there. Do you have any idea why someone would want to break in?"

Dustan looked away as if he were hiding something.

Then he met Daisy's gaze. "I do know my uncle kept expensive statues in a safe inside. I suppose it's possible an intruder wouldn't think all of them would be in the safe. But I don't know."

If Dustan knew about those statues, did he know about anything else?

Daisy noticed that Serena had pretended not to be listening. On the other hand, however, she must have overheard some of the conversation. Was she truly not interested?

The church social hall was a separate building, more modern than the church in some ways, but not in others. It was cement block with high windows, cafeteria-style tables, and a cafeteria line. It was a square box, really, with an institutional flavor. Daisy felt awkward and, from Serena's body language, she imagined Serena felt the same. After all, they didn't know anyone, and they were in strange territory. Dustan hadn't come inside with Hans, and she wondered if the nephew would make an appearance later without the dog. Certainly, he knew the people who had joined together to celebrate or mourn his uncle's passing.

Daisy and Serena passed through the food line, choosing from ham and cheese or chicken salad sandwiches, potato chips, and cups of punch. Afterward, they found a table with three other people sitting there. One was a woman who looked to be in her fifties with gray hair, wearing a black dress with blue flowers. The two men were wearing brown suits and looked like brothers. They could have been in their late fifties or maybe a little older. Daisy wasn't sure.

Daisy and Serena introduced themselves.

One of the men who was wearing a tan-and-white-striped tie introduced himself as Rex Clauson. He pointed to the man next to him and said, "This is my brother, Corbin. We're twins, if you hadn't guessed."

Daisy, not one to be shy in situations like this, though she did try to be tactful, asked, "Did you know Mr. Rumple well?"

The twins exchanged glances. "Let's just say we knew him years ago," Rex said. "We took some master's degree courses together in business administration. How did *you* know him?" he asked the women.

Serena explained that she managed Four Paws Animal Shelter and that Wilhelm was a volunteer there.

"Yep, he liked dogs back then, too. I think he had a rottweiler. Small apartment and big dog. He cared more about that dog than anybody else," Rex concluded.

"My boyfriend works at Four Paws," Daisy explained, "and I got to know Mr. Rumple through his business."

"Oh, yeah, that concrete statue business he started. That was a surprise."

"Why do you say that?" Daisy asked.

"I don't think of Wilhelm as a particularly good salesperson. Though he did have a head for numbers."

The woman, who might've been in her late fifties, joined the conversation. She put down the sandwich she was holding. "I'm Doris Jackson. I taught Mr. Rumple in high school."

Daisy's eyes widened, and the woman laughed. "Yes, we don't think of adults as ever going to school. Wilhelm was smart. Too smart for his own good sometimes. He was bitter, even as a teenager."

"Did you ever find out why?" Daisy asked, fingering a potato chip.

"His brother Herman was a year ahead of him, and a very different type of boy," Doris revealed. "Sometimes I thought Wilhelm was just jealous of his brother. He didn't particularly attract the girls. His brother did. More than once I heard Wilhelm mumble that he never thought he'd marry. So I presumed he never thought he'd have a family. He definitely lacked confidence." Thinking about the past, the retired teacher went on, "He did like dogs, though. He volunteered at an animal shelter even back then to get in his service hours. But they became more than service hours. Wilhelm made connections with those dogs. Somehow, he and the canines communicated on the level that Wilhelm couldn't reach with humans. At least that's the impression I got. Believe me, I'd never be talking like this if he was still alive. He was a student, and we keep their confidences."

"So you think he was lonely?" Daisy asked the teacher.

"I do think he was lonely, and lacking in a good sense of self. From his records, I remember that Wilhelm's father died when the boys were in grade school. I think the mother stoked the rivalry between the brothers. She died a few years ago."

Rex added, "Wilhelm and his brother stopped talking altogether. I don't know why. I assume that's why his brother isn't here today. When I talked with Dustan, he said his father wasn't coming."

Serena looked pensive as Daisy asked the others, "Was there a particular argument that made Wilhelm separate from his brother?"

"That's a question I don't have the answer to," Rex responded. "You'd probably have to ask Wilhelm's brother."

"Do you know what work he does?" Daisy asked as a way of searching out personal information without being overly obvious.

Rex's twin answered that question. "Herman has a car lot—Colonial Motors on the Industrial Highway. Why are you so interested?"

Daisy decided to be blunt. "Mr. Rumple didn't just work at Four Paws Animal Shelter, he was murdered there. I'd like to figure out the reason why."

CHAPTER NINE

Jonas dropped off Daisy at Rachel Fisher's house the following morning. Before he watched her go inside, he'd kissed her soundly. She was still smiling as she knocked on the door of the Fishers' mudroom, then turned and waved to him. He waited until Mary had opened the door, and then he drove up the lane to the rural road."

Guder mariye," Mary said with a smile as Daisy stepped into the mudroom.

Daisy returned the Pennsylvania Dutch *good morning* greeting as she hung her jacket on a peg in the mudroom. She'd learned quite a bit of Pennsylvania Dutch when she was a child and playing on the Esh farm with Rachel and her brother. They'd often wished they could go to school together, but Amish school and English school were very different. Most Amish children stopped their education at eighth grade. Some kept reading and learning, but unless they left the faith, they rarely went on to higher education.

Daisy had understood then and now that Amish day-to-day life was very different from hers. Rachel and her siblings were up at four o'clock in the morning, caring for livestock, feeding them, gathering eggs, mucking out stalls. Their lives were about their farms and the care of them, about their families and the basics they needed daily. They grew produce in the summer and canned it for winter. Girls learned early on how to do that. Without electricity, families turned in early and used battery-powered and gas lanterns in their homes. They were not wasteful.

Rachel and Levi hadn't opened the store until their girls had finished their schooling and could help. Their son Luke's life included learning everything about the farm, since he would inherit and run it someday.

"You didn't drive today?" Mary asked.

"No, my car's being inspected, and Aunt Iris needed the work van for a catering job. So Jonas dropped me off. He'll pick me up again when I give him a call. How is Rachel feeling?"

"She'll tell you all about that." Mary lowered her voice. "She's going to ask you a favor. If you don't feel good with it, just say *nee*."

"Of course I'll do Rachel a favor."

"Maybe not this one," Mary muttered.

Curious now, Daisy was particularly interested in the favor. What type of ask would be so out of her realm?

Rachel, who had been putting food in a basket in the kitchen, turned to greet Daisy. "You look wonderful bright as a berry this morning."

Daisy laughed. She'd worn jeans and a raspberry-colored sweater.

"I told *Ma'am* you wouldn't have your car today, but she must have forgotten." Rachel's arm cast was cumbersome, and she was having trouble loading food into the basket one-handed.

"Do you need help with that?" Daisy asked.

"I want to say *no*, but I've learned I can't be prideful about this injury. This basket is for Luke to take to the men who are helping with the feed corn. Gathering it takes many hands."

Daisy helped Rachel load the basket with sandwiches, cookies, and two thermoses of coffee. "How are you feeling, besides being frustrated by what you can't do?"

Still hobbling on her hurt ankle, Rachel used the counter to lever herself as she walked. "The arm doesn't hurt so much, but the ankle still does. When I stand on it too much, I just have to sit and pray for a while. I have so much to do, Daisy . . . for the wedding."

"You have to give your foot time to heal."

"I know, and I use the walking stick if I go outside. But even that doesn't always do *gut*."

"Why don't you sit while I load the rest of the cookies into the basket," Daisy offered. "Did you make these?"

The huge molasses cookies were a specialty of Rachel's. "*Ma'am* had to help. Too much standing and stooping. I praise *Gott* that I wasn't more hurt in the fall. I have learned I need to work harder on my patience."

Daisy smiled softly. "You have plenty with *kinner*, just not with yourself."

"For certain sure," Rachel confirmed.

"Mary said you had a favor to ask me. What is it?"

"I need to go to my sister's to use her sewing machine."

Daisy knew Rachel's sister had a treadle sewing machine. "I don't have my car," Daisy reminded her friend. "Would you like me to call Jonas to drive us?"

"*Nee.* I have another idea."

Rachel looked askance at Daisy, and Daisy wondered what this idea could be. She already knew Luke and Levi would be busy in the fields. "Do you want me to call a driver for us?"

"*Nee*, I could do that." She gave Daisy a sideways glance. "I was wondering. Do you remember how to drive a buggy?"

Half an hour later, Daisy couldn't believe she'd agreed to do what she was doing. Before she'd left for college, she'd often driven one of Rachel's or her family's buggies. Not only a cabin buggy, but a courting buggy and a pony cart. Those had been adventurous days and loads of fun.

Rachel and Levi's buggy was gray-topped, made of fiberglass. Its windows could be opened. Daisy and Rachel had them open now so that the fall air could blow through.

Battery-powered operator lights and turn signals helped keep Amish drivers safe on the roads. The orange triangle at the rear of the buggy indicated that it was a slow-moving vehicle. Amish buggies in Lancaster County taught everyone in the community an important lesson—slow down and enjoy the scenery. Daisy could enjoy the scenery better if she wasn't worried about controlling the horse. Earlier, Rachel had rung the porch bell. Luke had answered the summons and hitched up the buggy. Daisy was sure she wouldn't have remembered how to do *that*. The horse, whose name was Rusty, was a beautiful Tennessee walker with a burnished coat and white forelock.

"You are doing wonderful *gut*," Rachel told Daisy as the horse clomped along at a steady pace.

"We're not even a quarter mile up the road yet," Daisy joked.

Maybe driving a buggy was similar to riding a bicycle. Once you did it, you never forgot how. The reins felt comfortable in her hands, and she was glad she could do this for Rachel. They wouldn't have to drive onto any busy roads, simply take back ones to a neighboring farm. That's the only reason Daisy had agreed to do this.

"You're trusting me with your life," Daisy teased.

"I *do* trust you with my life," Rachel said, so seriously that Daisy glanced at her.

"To tell you true, I do," Rachel assured her. "You know that."

"I'm honored."

The gray ribbon of road, with its yellow line down the middle, seemed to lead to forever. To Daisy's left was a field of corn ready to be harvested. Harvesting corn with horses, one row at a time, was serious work. That's what Levi, Luke, and other men were doing today. Daisy knew the ear corn was put in a crib, then later taken to a sheller to pick the kernels off the cob. It would feed livestock over the winter.

As Rusty's clomping set a mesmerizing rhythm, Rachel asked, "Have you heard anything more about Mr. Rumple's murder?"

"Serena asked me to go to the funeral with her, and I did. I learned some interesting things about him. He had a degree in business administration, but he also had a falling out with his family. He and his brother hadn't spoken for years."

Rachel tilted her head in question. "Did anyone know why?"

"Not that I know of. The gentlemen we sat with went to school with him. An older woman there was one of his teachers. She said there was always a bitterness about him that bothered her." Daisy rethought her comment. "Maybe not *bothered* her, but worried her."

"Bitterness about what?"

Fingering the reins, Daisy recalled what the teacher had said. "Bitterness that his brother had more luck with the ladies. Bitterness that he couldn't seem to make friends. But one overriding fact stood out no matter who I talked to. Mr. Rumple loved dogs, and he was better with dogs than with people."

"Puzzling, ain't so?"

"It is." Daisy considered something else. "Elijah Beiler is in your district, isn't he?"

"Jonas's friend from the store? Certain sure, he is. Why?"

"I was speaking with Elijah when the pet parade was marching down Market Street. He couldn't believe dogs were dressed up in costumes."

"I won't comment on that." Rachel suppressed a smile.

"Anyway," Daisy went on, smiling back, "he has a cousin, Zebediah Beiler."

Shifting toward Daisy on the buggy seat, Rachel said, "We haven't had many dealings with Zebediah, but we know who he is. He's a farrier, ain't so?"

"Yes, he is. Elijah said that Zebediah seemed upset about Mr. Rumple's death."

"Did Mr. Rumple have horses?"

"Not that I know of," Daisy responded.

"Then I guess he wouldn't need a farrier," Rachel said practically.

"I suppose not."

The two women exchanged a glance, and Daisy knew what her friend was thinking. Then why had Mr. Rumple and Zebediah, an Englischer and an Amish farrier, had any association?

When Jonas picked up Daisy from Rachel's in the early evening, he asked, "You drove a buggy?" His grin was wide, and he glanced at her perplexed as they drove to her house with Felix in the back seat.

"You sound surprised. I'm a woman of many talents."

"Indeed, you are," he agreed after another chuckle. "That's one I wasn't prepared for. If our vehicles need repair, we could always borrow a horse and buggy."

She sent him a mock glare. "Someday, you'll be grateful for my many skills."

"I'm sure I will be." He gave her another look that was warm but with some sizzle in it, too.

Changing the subject, she informed Jonas, "In my conversations with Rachel, Mr. Rumple's murder came up."

"Why would that be?"

"Do you know Elijah's cousin Zebediah Beiler?"

"He was at the sale that Elijah and I organized. He's been to the store now and then. Why?"

"Rachel knows Zebediah is a farrier. Like me, she doesn't understand why Zebediah would have any dealings with Mr. Rumple."

"I might know a reason," Jonas offered. "Zebediah has

made metal sculptures, especially from horseshoes. Do you remember seeing those at the sale?"

"Now that you mention the sculptures, I do remember one. It was pretty large. I didn't know Zebediah made it."

"It sold for about three hundred dollars. That could be quite lucrative. The problem is he doesn't have many places he can sell them. The farmers market isn't exactly the right venue. I wonder if Rumple might have sold some for him on his property. They could be put outside or inside. I could see those sitting around with the concrete statues . . . or in someone's garden for a custom piece."

Thinking about the backyard on the property, Daisy couldn't remember seeing anything like that at Rumple's Statuary. She could have missed them because she had been mostly interested in dog statues, and that's where her focus had been. She'd have to ask Foster if he'd noticed anything like the metal sculpture.

Jonas switched on his turn signal, and they headed toward Daisy's road. "There was interesting scuttlebutt buzzing around Four Paws today," he commented.

"About Rumple's murder?"

"No, it wasn't. Apparently, Noah and Serena are going to stop using the pet vitamins that Stanley King developed. Rumor has it that other shelters have stopped using them, too."

"Why?" Daisy asked.

"I don't know if it has to do with the vitamin D problem. They didn't want to discuss it."

"Do you think it has anything to do with Rumple's murder?"

Jonas shrugged. "I talked to Morris this morning. He

stopped into Woods looking for a TV stand. Apparently, he's buying a flat-screen for his bedroom."

Detective Morris Rappaport had moved to Willow Creek from Pittsburgh. He'd never seemed to really settle in. However, over the past few months in particular, he seemed to be enjoying Pennsylvania Dutch food more.

"Did he say why he's doing this now?"

"He's moving into new digs. He's renting a two-story row house. I think it's on the same street as Marshall's office."

"How interesting. Maybe Morris is going to make Willow Creek his permanent home. Did he give you any news about the investigation?"

"Nope. Zeke and Morris are being particularly close-mouthed this time. No leaks that I've heard of."

Daisy couldn't help but say the obvious. "Maybe there aren't any *leaks* because there aren't any *leads*."

The following morning, Daisy worked on coffee-cake batter, while Tessa baked trays of chocolate chip cookies. Checking the time on her watch, Daisy asked, "Do you think I should call Iris? She's late, and she's never late."

"I was thinking the same thing," Tessa agreed. "Maybe after you make that batter, you can give her a buzz."

Daisy worried about her aunt just as she worried about her mother and everyone else in her life. They both put in long hours working and had pastimes, too. She couldn't remember her aunt saying that anything unusual had come up.

Suddenly, the back door opened, and Iris bustled in. She was apologizing before she took off her green all-weather jacket. "I'm so sorry I'm late. I forgot to set my alarm."

Her aunt, who usually had a smile and pink cheeks and a glossy lipstick across her lips, looked . . . rundown and a little bit haggard.

"Were you up late?" Daisy asked.

"I don't want to talk about it now," Iris said as she went to the office to hang up her coat.

In a low voice, Tessa asked, "Do you want to go after her and find out what's wrong? I'll make sure everything's okay here."

"Thanks, I probably should."

"The Darjeeling's ready if you want to take two cups along."

"That might be a good idea, too. Iris looks as if she needs something to brace her."

Instead of using china teacups, Daisy poured tea into two mugs. Many of her customers preferred mugs and would tell her so. Jonas was one of them. She hurried into her office and saw Iris staring out the window. Daisy pulled the chair in front of her desk over to the side of the room and went around her desk to the wheeled chair and brought it around to the front.

She motioned to the mugs of tea. "Sit and catch your breath," she suggested to her aunt.

Iris looked as if she was going to refuse and then suddenly deflated. She sank down into the ladder-back chair, picked up the mug of tea and held it between her palms. "Thank you. Maybe this will give me energy to start work."

"Do you need the day to yourself?" Daisy asked gently. "I'm sure we can cover for you."

Iris brought the mug of tea to her lips, took a small sip, and then set it on the desk. "I didn't sleep very well last night. In fact, I tossed and turned most of the night. I didn't hear the alarm when it went off." Iris picked up the mug of tea again. It seemed she had to have something in her hand or else something to do. She didn't want to look Daisy in the eye.

"Did something happen last evening?" Her aunt had seemed fine at work yesterday.

"I had a date with Russ."

Her aunt had been dating Russ Windom, a retired teacher, for over a year. Daisy had suspected they were becoming serious.

"What happened?" Had Russ told her he was sick, or . . .

"I thought we were close. I thought we might spend more of our lives together," Iris said morosely.

"And you're not going to do that?" Daisy prompted.

"Russ is going to move to Ohio where he has family. His brother lives there, and he lost his wife last year. Russ has nieces and nephews there, too."

"I see." Daisy could see how hurt her aunt was about Russ's move.

"He feels if he doesn't do this now, he won't. I never even considered that he might move somewhere else. He never told me he wanted to be close to the rest of his family. Sometimes"—her aunt sighed—"I suppose a single life is my vocation."

Daisy didn't want to merely give her aunt platitudes, but she didn't know how to make her feel better, either. "How can I help?"

Now her aunt met her gaze. "You help by listening.

You help by being here. I have to remember my family is here."

"Would you have gone with Russ if he had asked?"

"I sincerely don't know. But he didn't ask. He didn't even make it sound like it was a possibility."

"I'm so sorry." Suspecting sympathy alone wouldn't help Iris, Daisy decided to offer more than emotional understanding. "I think you need to come to dinner at my house tonight. I have all the supplies to make fall wreaths for our houses and for the tea garden. You can help me."

Iris didn't immediately turn down her offer. "Don't you have plans with Jonas?"

"He'll come to dinner, and Jazzi will be there, too. If they don't want to help with the wreaths, they can take Felix out for a run or a walk. And that's something else I wanted to talk to you about."

"What would that be?"

"As I told you, Adele Gunnarson, Felix's original mom, had to give him up when she went into an assisted living complex. She likes company, and Jonas and I take Felix over to visit her. Maybe you and I could visit her sometime."

Her aunt's eyes grew misty. "I'd like that, Daisy. I like being included. That's what I need right now."

"You're included, Aunt Iris. You always have been."

Iris took Daisy's hand and squeezed it. "If I had had a daughter, she'd be just like you."

Daisy and her aunt both took sips of tea and smiled.

CHAPTER TEN

Daisy sat in her office the next morning, going over the supply order for October. She'd be ordering pumpkin spice tea from her supplier, as well as other fall flavors like caramel peach tea and cinnamon chai. She should increase her order for cinnamon, cloves, and nutmeg with her baking supplies, too. Molasses cookies, apple gingerbread coffee cake, and chocolate macaroons were fall-to-Thanksgiving treats.

She considered the wreaths that she and her aunt had put together last night while Jonas, Felix, and the cats had enjoyed a movie and popcorn. At the dining room table, Daisy had laid out orange, rust, and checkered black and white ribbon, burnished copper foil ribbon, as well as yellow, orange, and green velvet strips of material to wind around the burlap wreath forms. She and Iris had attached pine cones, silk leaves, and an assortment of artificial berries. They'd talked in low tones while they'd worked, and their conversation hadn't seemed to bother the movie watchers.

Venting and remembering, Iris had spoken of Russ and more about the whole situation. She'd been trying to process it and decide how she felt about Russ leaving. It would take some time.

In the meanwhile, to shift her thoughts from Russ, Iris had asked, "What are you going to do next about the Rumple investigation?"

"I shouldn't do anything."

"That isn't what I said or asked," Iris had advised her. "I know you. Your mind is sifting through what you know, what you don't know, and what you want to do. What have you come up with?"

Daisy's aunt had always been a confidante, and Daisy had confided in her last night. "The idea of Four Paws dropping King's vitamin supplements bothers me greatly. In addition, I know that Rumple invested in those supplements. Caroline told me he did. What if that had something to do with his murder?"

"Don't you think the detectives are looking into it? Especially after you met with and told Detective Rappaport?"

"He said he wouldn't let Mr. King slide by him, but I don't know if he's actively pursuing it. He and Zeke have their own suspect list and people to interview. They might not connect the vitamins to Four Paws."

"Back to my original question then," Iris said. "What are you going to do next?"

After a thought-filled pause, Daisy had decided, "I'd like to talk to another shelter that stopped using the vitamins . . . just to get another take on the situation."

Her aunt had given her an understanding look and had kept winding ribbon around the wreaths.

After Iris had gone home last evening, and Jazzi had gone to bed, Daisy had spoken with Jonas about the idea. He'd told her to sleep on it. If she wanted to visit shelters, he'd go with her.

Today, she made her decision. By half an hour later, she'd accumulated a list of shelters in the Susquehanna Valley. When Daisy phoned them, though, she was disappointed with the results. The shelters were closemouthed, even after going up the chain of command. She couldn't coax very much information from three of them. They simply wouldn't tell her what she wanted to know about the vitamins. They wouldn't admit to using them or not. She wondered if that had anything to do with legal repercussions. Finally, on her fourth try, she spoke to a woman named Alice, who worked at Waggin' Tails Animal Shelter near Marietta.

Daisy simply asked, "Do you use Stanley King's vitamin supplements at your shelter?"

Alice didn't hesitate long. "I can't speak with you about that, but our manager could. She's not here now, but she'll be in this evening."

"Could I make an appointment to see her? A friend and I would like to talk with her."

"I'm sure she'd talk to you," Alice said assuredly. "She'll be here around six."

"What if we're there around seven?"

"That should be fine," Alice confirmed.

"Can you tell me her name?" Daisy asked.

"Sure. Her name is Juanita Cortez."

That evening, Jonas picked up Daisy at the tea garden, and they drove about an hour away to Marietta. It was easy to find the shelter. Daisy could see it was about the same size as Four Paws. She wondered what it would be like inside.

She soon found out. The lobby held several blue vinyl chairs in an area about as small as Daisy's office. Behind the desk sat a woman who looked to be in her forties. She had beautiful auburn curls.

At the desk, Daisy said, "We're here to see Juanita."

The woman stood and studied Daisy and Jonas. "I'm Juanita Cortez. How can I help you?"

Jonas explained, "We're from Willow Creek, and I volunteer at the Four Paws Animal Shelter."

Juanita's eyes widened when he said Willow Creek.

"That's where—" she stammered. "That's where that incident happened."

Jonas nodded. "Mr. Rumple was killed in one of our dog runs, but I'm not here about anything to do with that. Neither is Daisy. I adopted a dog from the shelter before I started volunteering there."

Juanita looked puzzled. She said, "I see," but Daisy could see that she didn't.

Daisy jumped in. "Alice told me that you used Stanley King's vitamin supplements."

Now Juanita's eyes showed understanding. "We don't use them anymore."

"We heard that they were making dogs sick," Jonas said.

Juanita didn't hesitate long. She sighed. "That seemed to be the problem with the new line of vitamins. We stopped using those as well as the first supplement line he developed for general dog owner use."

"I didn't know there was more than one line of vitamins," Daisy said.

"Mr. King created a more economical line of vitamins specifically for animal shelters so we could keep our costs down. Sure, we were worried about cost, but I'm much more concerned about keeping our dogs healthy."

"Do you have any details about the vitamins and why they were making the dogs sick?" Jonas asked.

Juanita shook her head. "There are rumors about vitamin D in high doses being the problem. They're being tested, but I don't have any more information than that."

Jonas pulled a business card from his jacket pocket. "I'm the owner of a store called Woods in Willow Creek, but I'm involved with the animal shelter. I'd appreciate it if you learn anything else that you give me a call."

"I can do that," Juanita said with a smile. "We need to band together to keep the dogs healthy."

Daisy wondered if Stanley King had made shortcuts in the economical vitamins. If he did, those shortcuts could mean disaster for his brand.

Detective Rappaport had asked for a seat at a table on the outside patio at the tea garden on Friday. The yellow-striped umbrella above him flopped in the breeze. Daisy realized the seasonal weather would soon prevent her staff from serving out there.

As soon as Daisy had spotted the detective, she'd known he was there to see *her*, no other reason. Of course, whoopie pies used to be the reason. Knowing he was watching his diet, she'd taken a carrot muffin out of the case, fixed a glass of iced Darjeeling tea with no sugar, and carried them outside. The sun was bright and hot, and the temperature had risen to about seventy degrees.

The detective seemed comfortable in his tan light-weight sports coat and chocolate-colored slacks. His white shirt was open at the collar, and he wasn't wearing a tie. He did have black circles under his eyes, though, and Daisy felt sorry for him. Yes, this was his job. But it wasn't the job Morris Rappaport had signed up for when he'd taken on the post of detective at Willow Creek Police Department. He'd expected traffic stops and jaywalking and a domestic dispute now and then, not murder.

As soon as she sat down with him and pushed the drink and food over to him, he didn't hesitate to say, "Tell me what you've found out."

"How do you know I found out anything? Did you get a report on the funeral?" Daisy asked.

"Oh, I had a report, but I'm sure it's not as good as whatever you learned. Tell me." He picked up the muffin and took a bite, maybe trying to put her at ease.

Sometimes Daisy felt as if she were a sponge, soaking up conversations around her. "I didn't really learn much— basically, a few personality traits about Wilhelm Rumple."

"What kind of traits?" Rappaport asked around a bite of muffin.

Since the information might help the detective, Daisy related what she'd heard. "A former teacher said he seemed bitter at a young age, maybe because of his looks, maybe because his older brother was handsome and better in school. He had an argument with his brother at one point, and they didn't talk for years. His nephew brought Rumple's dog to the graveside service. Have you spent time with the nephew or his dad?"

The detective licked a finger that had caught crumble from the muffin. "We've interviewed them. But I can't say we got much out of them. Same story as you said . . .

the two brothers stopped speaking a few years ago. But the brother wouldn't say why. He told me he wouldn't attend the funeral, so their split must have been serious. Why did the nephew bring the dog?"

"Apparently, Hans was very attached to Wilhelm Rumple. The nephew says he gets anxiety attacks when he leaves him for too long."

"The nephew or the dog?" Detective Rappaport asked.

"The dog," Daisy said seriously.

The detective's expression was one for the books.

"I'm not pulling your leg," she assured him. "Dogs can have separation anxiety. If he was really attached to Wilhelm, suddenly being without him is a trauma. The nephew's handling it the best way he can."

"Then the nephew must like dogs, too. What did you learn at the dog shelter in Marietta last night?"

At that, Daisy leaned back in her chair and stared at him. "And just how did you find out I went there?"

"Daisy, word gets around. Bart has been going into the shelter to see one particular dog. He heard about it. Something to do with vitamins, I hear."

"Apparently, some shelters have stopped using Stanley King's vitamins because the dogs were getting sick. At the shelter Jonas and I visited, we found out that King developed a special line of economical vitamins that he was selling to the shelters. They must have been inferior. That's really all I learned. I know that Rumple had an investment in King's company, but I don't know what one has to do with the other. Do you?"

The detective finished the muffin and wiped his fingers on his napkin. "No, I don't. And that's the problem. We have plenty of leads, but we're stuck until one of them pays off."

"Pays off how?"

"We haven't found a suspect who has a *motive* for murder."

With harvest season over, Daisy stood in her garden that evening, attempting to clean it up for winter. Jonas was helping, while Felix snuffled here and there and chased a ball that Daisy or Jonas tossed every once in a while. There was a nip in the air, so Daisy wore jeans and a teal flannel jacket. Her gardening gloves were worn, but she could actually feel what she was doing with this pair because they fit tightly. She'd banded her hair in a messy topknot to keep it out of her face if the wind blew or she stooped over to weed.

She'd pulled her third tomato plant when she stopped to study Jonas. He was working on the spaghetti squash vines.

He said, "You might get another squash or two here."

As he straightened, Daisy admired his broad shoulders in a navy sweatshirt, his slim hips in his black jeans. She knew he worked out in the privacy of his townhouse every morning. He'd been shot in the shoulder, and he had to work it to keep it loose. He'd also been shot in his leg, and he stretched every morning for that injury. He didn't let either of the injuries limit him. Come to think of it, he didn't let anything limit him.

The wind had tossed his black hair over his brow. Every once in a while, he brushed it back. She liked looking at him. She liked being with him. She liked thinking about their future. They hadn't discussed details yet, and she imagined that was soon coming. It gave her a nervous exhilaration when she thought about it. They'd moved very slowly, making sure they were right for each other. They hadn't taken their physical relationship to the most serious step. Because they were afraid they wouldn't last? Because their lives had been in too much of an upheaval? Because Daisy's life had changed so drastically, first with Vi's pregnancy, and now with Jazzi soon moving out?

Jonas held an oval white spaghetti squash in his hands after he'd dipped to the vines and stood up straight. "Supper tomorrow night?" he asked with a grin. But then he realized she'd been watching him. "Do you have more on your mind than supper?" he asked with a twinkle in his eyes.

"I might," she said coyly, not exactly sure of what she wanted to say. "I was just thinking about how sexy you look standing in the breeze in jeans and a sweatshirt."

Her honesty surprised him. She could see it in his expression. He walked across the garden to her. "If we're talking about sexy . . ." He flipped one finger through her hair. "What about this hair of yours that's floating all over the place, and the pink in your cheeks, and the sparkle in your blue eyes?"

Her mouth went dry until she found a few words. "My mind is not on that spaghetti squash tomorrow night for supper, even with parmesan cheese and olive oil."

He laughed and pulled her into a fierce hug. They were about to kiss when her phone dinged.

Jonas leaned away, his brows arched. "You'd better get it."

She checked the screen and saw it was Gavin. There was a text. "Gavin's out front," she said. "I'm going to text him to come around back."

"I wonder if he was at Vi and Foster's and something happened," Jonas surmised.

"Or maybe he just wants to discuss them moving out of the apartment."

"It's their choice now." She had discussed the idea Glorie Beck had presented about the couple renting her house. They were thinking about it.

"Are we done here for tonight?" Jonas asked. "I'll start putting the plants in that basket. We can spread the straw another night."

"Yes, we're done. I can go in and make a pot of tea. Maybe Gavin will stay."

As they cleaned up the plants and collected the garden tools, Daisy spotted Gavin walking around the house. He met them at the patio.

"Hey, Gavin," Daisy said. "What brings you over? Were you at Vi and Foster's?"

Gavin shook his head. "I had to vent to someone, and I knew you and Jonas would understand."

"Let's go inside." Daisy suggested, "I can make tea or coffee. I might even have a chocolate espresso cookie or two lying around."

"Don't let her fool you," Jonas said. "She has a whole can of them."

Even their joking didn't make Gavin smile, and Daisy considered how serious this meeting might be.

After they went inside, jackets thrown over the back of dining room chairs, they stood around the island until Daisy brewed a pot of tea. While it was steeping, she took out the can of cookies and opened the lid.

She motioned to the chairs at the island. "Come on, let's sit. Tell us what's going on."

While she poured tea out of a favorite teapot that Jonas had given her with cats decorating the sides, Gavin said, "I had a meeting with Dalton Ames."

"Uh-oh," Jonas muttered. "Professional fundraising can get sticky."

"It's not only sticky. I'm beginning to think it's no different from politics," Gavin grumbled.

After Daisy poured the tea, she sat at the island with the men. "What did he say?"

"First of all, I never planned to get involved in the fundraising. I'm the contractor. I work with the architect. That's all I really want to think about. That and my crew."

"I can understand that," Jonas said. "A community project is very different from a private one."

"I'm finding that out," Gavin admitted with a scowl. "And I'm not at all happy about it. Dalton is used to big city projects. He thinks what we're raising is a mere pittance. At least, that's the impression he gave me. But to this community, we'll have our hearts in the project as well as money. I don't like Dalton's strategy."

"What *is* his strategy?" Jonas asked,

"His aim is to reel in wealthy investors. I told him we don't have that many wealthy folks in Willow Creek. He wants to go outside of the community to find them. He wants to convince them it's a good cause. He wants them to feel as if they're doing important charity work. That's hogwash to me. I think the whole community should be involved in donations. If normal folks are invested in this homeless shelter, they'll care about it . . . they'll care about what happens there . . . they'll care about whoever stays there. Am I wrong to think that?"

"Not wrong," Daisy agreed. "Maybe Dalton thinks we

can't raise the money by just keeping it to the community. If it's a matter of the shelter getting built or not, I can see his point. I'm catering a fundraising event at the King farm on Sunday."

Gavin ran his hand through his sandy hair and shook his head. "It's not my job to convince Dalton one way or another. It's the town council's. They're the ones who are going to have to decide what strategy they use for this fundraising. I simply wish we could start building."

"When do you think you *will* be able to start?" Jonas asked.

"Dalton has set out a timeline to raise the money by January. If that's possible, we can start as soon as we have a break in the weather. In March at the latest." Gavin swiveled on his chair to face Daisy. "By the way, I think I have you to thank for a new project."

Daisy exchanged a look with Jonas. "Glorie Beck and Nola Horn's house?"

"Yes. We signed the contracts today, and they told me what they suggested to you about Vi and Foster renting Glorie's house."

"What do you think about Vi and Foster moving in to Glorie's old house?"

"I think it might be the answer they're looking for."

Daisy quickly turned to Jonas so he wouldn't be left out of the discussion. He didn't look uncomfortable at all, but rather appeared to be listening intently. "Jonas and I have been discussing it for the past week, whether we should promote it or not."

"Maybe we should all be quiet," Gavin decided, "and let them come to a decision on their own."

Jonas covered Daisy's hand with his.

She smiled. "I'm glad we're all in agreement . . . that we'll take a step back. Then we can convince each other it's the best thing to do."

Gavin's expression finally relaxed. "On that note, I think we should eat the chocolate espresso cookies. Parents definitely need chocolate to keep them in the right frame of mind."

They all picked up their teacups and touched them to each other in a toast of agreement.

CHAPTER ELEVEN

Before Daisy accepted a catering job, she weighed the benefits. At the top of the list was whether she and her catering staff would enjoy the event. Of course, one of the other points at the top of her list was the monetary benefit for the tea garden as well as the publicity it would garner.

When Dalton Ames had suggested this event at the King farm, she'd asked the usual questions—how many guests would be invited . . . what kind of dishes would they enjoy . . . would it be a sit-down service . . . would she be supplying everything from table linens to dishes to silverware to teacups? All of those questions had been answered to her satisfaction by Andrew King, so she'd accepted this gig, knowing fundraising for the homeless shelter was on the line.

Last evening, she'd said to Jonas, "I can possibly get an invitation for you, if you'd like to come."

He'd narrowed his gaze and given her a perceptive smile. "You're going to be busy. Besides, you can handle Dalton Ames on your own, can't you? I'm sure you don't need my support."

"Your vote of confidence in me warms my heart," she'd quipped, placing her hand over her heart. She'd sighed. "Sometimes I feel like decking him, and I don't know why."

At that, Jonas had laughed. "I don't think you have to worry about that. You're much too restrained to let loose, especially at a public venue."

"I think this event might be classier than I bargained for."

"Classy how?" Jonas had asked.

"Dalton supplied me with the guest list. I think it was to impress me."

"Did it?"

"No, but it did make me consider what I'm going to serve. Two of the couples have positions on the board for Philadelphia Museums. There are Willow Creek bank presidents as well as Daniel Copeland on the list, a hedge fund manager from Harrisburg and his wife, and several doctors from municipalities around us."

They'd been sitting on the sofa, and Jonas had leaned away from her and eyed her. "And just where did you get all of this information? Certainly not from Dalton's list."

"You're not the only one who can do background checks," she'd reminded coyly.

"You Googled *everyone*?" There'd been laughter in his eyes.

"I wanted to know what I was getting into . . . what my servers were getting into."

"And what did you tell your servers about this bunch?"

"I told them to be professional but to be themselves."

Jonas had put his arm around her and pulled her close.

She tried to remember that hug now at the King residence as she faced the open concept living room, dining room, and great room combination in the rambling house. From the outside, the white-sided house looked as if it had been an old farmhouse with more than one addition. There were two barns on the property. She supposed one was for equipment and the other for horses, though she knew that one was probably called a stable in this family.

She hadn't known what to expect when she'd walked into the kitchen with her staff. She'd been directed to come in that way with their boxes, bins, and refrigerated items. But she should have expected the completely modernized kitchen with its granite countertops and La Cornue Grand Palais range. The giant island held a drawer for the microwave and storage as well as an eat-in section. She imagined what had once been the old farmhouse had been completely gutted to create the open concept atmosphere, at least on the first floor. All the furniture had been removed from the space to make room for the tables and chairs for the event. The white wood looked pristine with the white tablecloths and napkins.

Daisy had planned the tea service menu carefully. This wasn't a dinner, but it was a food experience for refined palates. Cora Sue, Iris, Foster, and Tamlyn were helping her today. They each knew their jobs, the number of their table, and what courses they were serving. Foster had offered to clear tables between courses, which helped Daisy a lot. She was offering Darjeeling tea—hot as well as iced, both sweet and unsweetened. She'd let fall be reflected in the foods she'd chosen for today, beginning with creamy butternut squash soup with a sprinkle of ground cloves on the top. She herself was serving the table that included Caroline, Andrew, Dalton, and three other guests. From their *ooh*s and *aah*s, they seemed to enjoy the creamy soup, perfect for an autumn day.

As she refilled teacups, Dalton asked her, "Do you come up with recipes, or do you hire someone for that?"

She had vowed to herself to be pleasant to him. "I create some of the recipes, and my kitchen manager creates others. It's a joint effort."

"And the soup?" he asked with one of those half-smiles.

"That was my creation."

He gave her a wink, as if he particularly had enjoyed it. She turned away before she said something she shouldn't.

When she served the second course, a ribbon salad with poached pears and pecans, Caroline said to her, "Andrew and I decided to adopt that cute little puppy. But we didn't want her to have to be inside today with all these people around."

Andrew added, "My stable hand is keeping her in the barn until we're finished here."

"She was so adorable," Daisy said, meaning it.

"Do you ride?" Andrew asked.

"I haven't ridden for a while, though I did drive a horse and buggy recently."

After a startled expression, he laughed. "Maybe after this is all finished, I can take you on a tour of the barn, and you can see the pup again as well as the horses."

Daisy felt honored that he would give her a tour. It was

obvious he didn't want her to feel like a servant while she was here. She appreciated that.

She responded, "We'll see how cleanup goes, and if everything's in hand, I'd love to tour the stables with you."

After Foster cleared the salad course and brushed crumbs from the tables, Daisy brought out the savory course—a tiered tray with spinach quiche pastries, avocado with prosciutto rounds, cheddar biscuits, and smoked salmon and beet bites.

Caroline chose one of the salmon and beet bites. Then she picked up the conversation where she and Daisy had left off during the last course. "Andrew taught me how to ride."

"Do you feel secure in the saddle?" Daisy asked.

"I like the English saddle better than the Western one. He let me try both, and he always lets me ride Goldenrod, who's a Tennessee walker. When I ride her, it almost feels like sitting in a rocking chair."

When Andrew and Caroline beamed at each other, Daisy could tell simply from looking at them how much in love they were.

She heard Dalton mutter, "Young love," under his breath.

If that was supposed to be funny, Daisy didn't find it so. She appreciated young love.

She made conversation with other guests at the table, too, as they seemed chatty. One of the women from Philadelphia, wearing a fascinator in orange that accompanied her black suit with its orange and yellow blouse, asked Daisy, "Do you actually know many Amish families? The Kings don't. I imagine the Amish keep to themselves."

"That depends," Daisy answered truthfully. "There's an Old Order Amish district to the east that does isolate. They try to keep their community self-sufficient. Many families living around town on nearby farms are New Order Amish. I have a friend who runs Quilts and Notions. Her family has a farm, and I grew up knowing her when we were kids. We're still friends."

"And the difference between Old Order Amish and New Order Amish?" the woman asked.

"Old Order Amish, taking cues from their bishop, stay off the grid entirely. They do have plumbing but not many modern conveniences. They cook on wood stoves. They will not ride in vehicles except horses and buggies. My friend's New Order Amish district allows propane gas for cooking rather than wood stoves, gas-run refrigerators, and battery-powered lanterns for their buggies and barns. It can get complicated, but each district knows what they're allowed to do. It's called the *Ordnung*, which is German for *order*."

"From what I understand," Andrew said, joining in the conversation, "it's a book of rules."

"It gets even more complicated," Caroline added, "when you talk about *Rumspringa*. Those are the teenage running-around years for Amish youth before they decide to commit to their faith. The young people drive cars, have cell phones, and do anything an Englischer would do."

"Do many leave after that?" the woman asked.

"Surprisingly not," Daisy answered. "The Amish community is important in ways the general public no longer understands. They depend on each other for everything. If a barn burns down, the community comes together to build a new one. If there's a medical emergency, there's a community fund that pays for it since they don't buy insurance. Families live together, old and young. Amish families are often large, so there are no childcare worries if you have a sister or a brother's wife who can take care of children whenever needed. Their lives are much more intertwined than ours."

The woman said, "Thank you so much for answering my questions. It gives me some idea of why the homeless shelter is so important to the Willow Creek community. Maybe you're trying to emulate what the Amish do."

"Maybe we are," Daisy agreed.

When she crossed to the kitchen for the final sweet course, Eva was fixing the tiered trays, and Cora Sue was just arranging hers.

"The people at my table are very snobby," Cora Sue said under her breath. "But maybe that's because I have four men who are doing nothing but talking finances. I'm not sure they're even interested in what they're eating."

"It's the presentation that counts, Cora Sue," Daisy reminded her. "They might be putting the food away quickly, but after the fact, they might remember how it was presented and how good it tasted."

"Mr. King is at my table," Cora Sue said. "His feathers are a little ruffled at what some of the men were saying."

Daisy was dying to ask what that was, but now wasn't the time or the place. "Maybe the sweets tray will improve his mood. The triple chocolate torte, or the peanut butter cup pastry, or the pumpkin spice mini-cookies could be all he needs."

Cora Sue gave Daisy a look that said she doubted it, but then picked up the tray and went on her way.

After everyone had been served all of their courses, Daisy made the circuit of tables, checking for anything that might need to be changed or enhanced for future events of this nature. She also liked to hear the comments the guests were saying to each other. Two men in gray business suits had gotten up from their table and gone to stand by French doors that looked out over a patio.

Daisy stopped near a serving center nearby to pick up a teapot. She heard one man saying to the other, "A donation to the homeless shelter is one thing, Todd. I think it's worthwhile, and of course, it will be a write-off. But putting any more money into King's company is something else. I heard it's in trouble. For all we know, that trouble could have something to do with Rumple's murder."

The other gentleman responded, "The list of investors in King's vitamins is long. What happened to this Rumple person might not have anything to do with King. He insists the vitamins are going to be cleaned up, and everything will be good as new."

"I don't think they'll be cleaned up that easily if someone has made a complaint to the FDA."

Daisy couldn't stay there any longer without looking obvious, so she picked up the teapot and took it into the kitchen.

An hour and a half later, the tea service had wrapped up, and most of the guests had left. Daisy's staff was packing up her van. The rental company would be coming later to pick up the tables and chairs.

Daisy was standing outside, making sure everything was in its proper place, when Andrew approached her. "Would you like to take a tour of the stables now?"

Iris had overheard, and she gave Daisy a thumbs-up sign that all was secure and she wasn't needed.

Seeing Dalton coming toward her, she said to Andrew, "I'd love to see the stables."

Andrew grinned at her and asked in a conspiratorial tone, "Are you trying to elude Dalton Ames?"

"I plead the Fifth," she responded.

Andrew motioned her toward a path that led to the stables. "He can be a bug, I'll say that," Andrew concluded. "But I suppose that's how he raises all the money he does. I'm not sure how he'll do from today, but everyone seemed happy to be here. They were certainly pleased with your tea service."

"I'm glad," Daisy assured him.

"Your staff knows what they're doing. I know from experience that it's hard for my parents to keep good staff."

"I try to put them in positions where they can use their talents to their best advantage. It all depends on how much employees are willing to learn, too."

"I suppose that's true. Of course, we have to worry about something you don't."

"What's that?"

"We don't want our business broadcast to the world. Confidentiality is important to us. Anyone who's in the house overhears things."

"I suppose that's true. Do you do NDAs?"

She'd heard non-disclosure agreements were the norm in many households that employed maids, housekeepers, butlers, and chauffeurs.

"We do."

"My tea garden staff has to be discreet. I've never had a problem with what they overhear and them disseminating it. For my regular customers, sometimes I feel like a bartender—listening to confidences or family issues. When customers come in regularly, they think they know me, or they think I know them. And in a small town, it's often true."

"Like when your older daughter got pregnant?" Andrew asked, not looking at all embarrassed about bringing it up.

Daisy shrugged. "Exactly. Because my customers know me, they think they need to know my business."

"You're notorious in your own right."

"Excuse me?" she asked with a smile.

He motioned to the side door of the stable and opened it. The door swung open easily on its big black hinges. They stepped inside onto concrete that was so unlike many Amish barns. This was a modern stable with well-spaced stalls and a wide walkway down the middle. Daisy had been in many Amish barns, and she liked the ambience of them—the dirt floor, the hay, the old wood smell, the dust motes floating past the small high windows. This stable reminded her more of a business than a home for horses. But she could be all wrong.

"I understand you should be on the police payroll," Andrew continued.

"I don't know where you've heard that. Jonas is friends with Zeke Willet, and Detective Rappaport comes into the tea garden now and then."

"Now, Daisy," Andrew admonished. "You're being too modest. You've helped solve murders. I've read the stories in the *Willow Creek Messenger*. Trevor Lundquist has written several about you."

"Perhaps Trevor exaggerates the part I play."

This time, Andrew shrugged. "One clue or a different lead can make all the difference. Are you helping them with the Rumple murder?"

When she thought about her trip to the animal shelter, she wondered if that was considered *helping*. "Now and then, I've become involved because of friends in trouble. Since Jonas works at Four Paws, he was affected by what happened there, at least when it was roped off as a crime scene. But I'm really not involved."

They had only taken about ten steps down the walkway when the pup who seemed to be mostly a King Charles spaniel came running to Andrew with a happy *yip-yip*.

Without hesitating, Andrew stooped to pick up the pup. "Did you escape from Billy?"

The pup began licking Andrew's face, and he laughed. Looking up, he waved to someone down the aisle and called, "I've got her. I'll take her to the house with me."

"So she's found her forever home?" Daisy asked seriously.

"She has. Caroline loves her, and I do, too. Just another reason why we need a house with a yard. We've named her Duchess."

Daisy petted the pup. "A fitting name if ever I heard one."

Andrew tucked the pup into the crook of his arm, and Duchess seemed to like it there. As he showed Daisy around the well-equipped tack room, she admired the saddles that were pristinely kept on their pegs. The scent of leather cleaner wafted around them.

A stable hand, dressed in jeans and a sweatshirt, stopped in the doorway. He looked to be in his late teens. His black hair was pushed back behind his ears. He smiled at Duchess. "I exercised Goldenrod and groomed her, since Miss Miller won't be riding her today."

"Thank you, Billy," Andrew said. "We're going down that way to take a look at her now. Will you exercise Thunderbolt today, too?"

"I already did, sir. I'm going for supper now, and then I'll take a last look around the barn before I leave tonight."

Andrew nodded that that was acceptable.

After Billy left the room, Daisy asked, "I take it you help run the estate?"

"I do, but I don't know how much longer I will. I have a suite in the house now, and Caroline and I spend a lot of our private time there. But soon, we'll have to start looking for a house for after we're married. My parents want us to live here, but I think as a newlywed couple, we need our privacy."

He took a step sideways and studied Daisy. "What do you think about that?"

"I think you have to know your family and what kind of life you want to start with your wife."

"You mean how much I want them involved in my business?" His expression was wry.

Daisy chuckled. "Something like that. I would think most newlyweds need their privacy, as you've indicated. How does Caroline feel about it?"

"She's just happy we're getting married."

"She thinks of you as Prince Charming?" Daisy teased.

Andrew blushed. "Possibly. I *have* told her that's a mistake."

"We all have dreams, no matter what our age," Daisy confided.

"True, but I think those dreams have to be rooted in reality."

Andrew seemed to be a practical man as well as a nice one. After exiting the tack room, he settled Duchess on the walkway and tapped the side of his leg. Duchess ambled beside him as he walked along with Daisy.

Each of the stalls was labeled with a plaque and a horse's name. Daisy spotted Goldenrod's head before she saw the plaque on the stall. The Tennessee walker was a beautiful golden brown with an almost blond mane.

"Is she friendly?" Daisy asked.

"Caroline says she's the most loving horse she's ever met. But I'm not sure Caroline has met that many horses."

Daisy held her hand out to the horse, and Goldenrod nuzzled her fingers with her soft-as-silk nose. Daisy stroked the horse's forelock, noticing the four white boots on the animal.

But she also noticed something else . . . a bucket sitting in the corner of the stall. It was a heavy, galvanized bucket, very much like the ones used at Four Paws Animal Shelter.

Daisy remembered that the bucket—the murder weapon—was missing. It would be so easy to hide a bucket in a stable.

Daisy and her Aunt Iris had finished fashioning the autumn wreaths. They'd attached them to the front and back doors of the tea garden that morning, to the front door of Daisy's home, and now, this evening, they'd brought a few over to Iris's house.

Iris said to Daisy, "I think these are gorgeous, if I must say so myself." She fingered the orange and rust tulle surrounding the burlap wreath that she was going to hang on her back door. Pine cones were intertwined with the tulle, and a pineapple decoration, a welcome symbol, stood in the middle.

"I *could* put this one on the front door," she said, as if the choice were a difficult one.

They'd laid the wreaths on Iris's front porch and were looking from one to the other. The second wreath was also a burlap one, wound with orange and yellow ribbon. Copper-colored mesh wrapped it, as well. Tiny sunflowers gave pops of extra color. Iris had attached a wooden welcome sign in script letters across the center.

The evening was chilly, and Daisy wrapped her cat sweater more tightly around herself. She buttoned it as Iris made her decision. Her aunt seemed to be accepting the fact that Russ was leaving. Or else, Iris was just focusing attention on everything else except that.

"The tea went exceptionally well, don't you think?" Daisy asked her aunt.

"We didn't spill anything," Iris returned with a smile. "Mrs. King seemed pleased. Did you notice the bonus she included in her check?"

Daisy had opened the check after she'd received it and been pleasantly surprised. "I think the Kings are just generally thrilled about this wedding between Andrew and Caroline. The couple certainly seems to be happy. I talked with Andrew while he showed me the stables. His family might have money, but he and Caroline are just like any other young couple starting out. As far as what they want and what they hope for, anyway—a happy marriage, and eventually, a family."

"I wonder if Caroline will keep working at the bakery," Iris mused.

"I don't know. The way Andrew sounded, I think he's thinking of separating from his dad's business."

"Really? I think his future is made for him there," Iris decided.

Daisy considered all the conversations she'd had with Andrew. "I get the feeling that Andrew wants to be his own man. He told me he has a degree in economics and public affairs. I think he'd like to work for a local or state government, helping to work out the finances and the running of the town or the state. I think he might be interested in public service."

Daisy thought again about the buckets that she'd seen in the stalls, how they looked exactly like the ones Four Paws used. She imagined lots of places used buckets like that. Still . . . should she say anything to Detective Rappaport about them?

"I made a decision," Iris said. "I'll put the one with the welcome sign on the front door. Can you attach that one while I do the back door?"

"No problem," Daisy answered.

She would be removing the summer wreath that was hanging on Iris's door and attaching the new one. Picking up the roll of twine that she had laid on the porch, she got started.

She'd just finished hanging the wreath when she noticed Iris's neighbor come out of his house. He was cleaning out a birdbath that was nestled between two golden mop bushes under his bay window. As she took another look at the birdbath, she noticed that it could have come from Rumple's Statuary. She'd often exchanged greetings with Mr. Timbow, Iris's long-time neighbor. He and his wife were friendly and had mentioned that if Iris needed anything, she should call them. Mr. Timbow was tall and thin, with a bald pate and wire-rimmed glasses. He had a long face that his nose fit into nicely.

After Daisy finished with the wreath, she crossed the property line to his yard. "Hi, Mr. Timbow. How are you?"

"I'm just fine. I'm cleaning up my yard for the new season. This birdbath will be good until the first freeze; then I'll have to take it in so it doesn't crack."

"That's a lovely and sturdy birdbath. Can I ask if you bought it at Mr. Rumple's business?"

"I did. It's the last thing I bought from there." He motioned to his front porch, where a duck sculpture sat. "That's from Rumple's, too, and I have a squirrel ornament out back. His business will probably be sold now, I imagine. It's such a shame what happened."

"Yes, it is. I had purchased something from Mr. Rumple, too. My boyfriend works at Four Paws Animal Shelter, where Mr. Rumple had contacts with much of the staff."

"He wasn't a particularly friendly sort. He was all about business and that dog of his. He and that dog had quite a bond."

Daisy nodded. "I met Hans. He seemed like a mellow sort of hound."

"I think he was. He was friendly enough with me, and he always let me pet him. Rumple was an odd little man, though, wasn't he?"

"How do you mean?"

"I remember the first time I bought something there. Rumple went inside for change because I had paid cash. He didn't return for a while. I began to be concerned. I went inside and didn't see him anywhere inside the house. So I went back outside, talked to Hans, and was getting ready to leave, thinking he could just keep my change for a tip."

"Is that what happened?"

"Oh, no. That was the weird part. Rumple suddenly appeared from the house again as if from nowhere. It was very odd."

Odd things and Wilhelm Rumple seemed to go together. She wondered if it was something odd that had gotten Wilhelm Rumple killed.

CHAPTER TWELVE

The tea garden was full . . . absolutely full.

As Daisy looked around, she could only see one spare chair. Two tour buses had arrived at around the same time. They must have all put the tea garden on their schedule for ten a.m. Someone from each bus had come into the tea garden, looked around, and decided she could seat all of them. She could.

Between the two rooms, the tea garden could seat sixty customers. She and her staff had scurried into fast gear, brewing tea, taking dough from the walk-in and scooping it into cookies that would be baking in the oven for fifteen minutes. She'd made a double batch of cheesy cauliflower soup, intending to take some of it home. Now they might be using that for customers who believed the soup would be a good substitute for baked goods for breakfast.

Daisy loved a full house. She was simply hoping all of

her customers would be well-satisfied. The carrot-grape salad and peach salsa were going fast, and they might run out of those. But otherwise . . . she could prepare more soup for the lunch crowd, and the same with the salad.

She'd been covering two tables in the spillover tea-room and was on her way to the kitchen for another pot of Darjeeling tea when the front door opened and a male voice called her name.

She'd swung around to face him when the man practically yelled, "Daisy Swanson, I want to talk to you."

With two four-cup teapots in her hands, she froze when she saw Stanley King.

Before she could even think of saying "good morning," he began his diatribe. "How *dare* you give information to the police about me? How *dare* you insert your nose into my affairs? My business is none of yours. If you don't stay on your own property and stay away from mine, there will be consequences, and you won't like them. I'm a powerful man, and I can *ruin* you."

His diatribe overflowed with vitriol. Everyone in the tea garden was gaping at her and Stanley King.

Foster rushed up beside her and put his hand on her shoulder. Also standing close to Daisy, Tessa, phone in hand, looked as if she wanted to pummel Stanley King with both fists.

However, the man had said his piece, and he wasn't staying. He swiftly turned, his expensive black suit jacket flaring out in back of him as he opened the door and left the tea garden.

Daisy was still staring at the door when chatter erupted all around her.

"Who was that man?" people were asking.

"What did he want here?"

"What did Mrs. Swanson do?"

Daisy could hear commotion around her as her staff soothed gossipy patrons, refilled teacups, and replenished breakfast plates.

Daisy was rooted to the spot.

Foster leaned close to her. "Daisy, come into your office for a few minutes."

She heard him, but she still felt icy fingers run up and down her spine.

Iris took the two teapots from Daisy's hands. "I'll take care of these," she said. "You go with Foster."

Daisy had turned and headed toward her office when the front door opened again. Glancing over her shoulder, she turned, afraid Stanley King had come back. To her relief, she saw Jonas.

He came up beside her and hung his arm around her shoulders. "Tessa called me. Come on. Let's talk in your office."

Tessa was on her phone again, and Daisy didn't know whom she was calling. Trevor? No, couldn't be. He wouldn't be interested in what had just happened, would he?

Jonas led Daisy into the tea garden's office. Seconds later, Iris bustled in with a cup of black tea. She set it on the desk, while Daisy took the chair behind the desk.

"I put sugar in it," Iris admitted. "Drink it."

While Daisy didn't make a comment, Jonas picked up the ladder-back chair in front of her desk and carried it around to the back.

Jonas advised her, "Take a few sips and then talk to me."

After a quick glance at him, she took a few sips and made a face. "I like honey in my tea."

"Iris must think the sugar will do you more good,"

Jonas suggested, and then swiveled her office chair around to face him. "Tessa phoned me to tell me what was happening. Why did King go after you like that?"

With dismay falling over her, she realized Jonas's birthday surprise wasn't going to be a surprise any longer. While he wouldn't know the gift would be a dog statue, and he wouldn't know about the dinner, she was going to have to tell him about her visit to Rumple's Statuary.

"I went to Rumple's Statuary for a birthday surprise for you. Foster went with me."

Jonas's eyes softened as he realized why she hadn't told him before now.

"That's how I knew about his Plott hound. I met Hans when I went over there."

"Hans?" Jonas asked, with a quirk of a smile on his lips.

"That's his name. He's a beautiful dog." She knew she was distracting herself from the rest of the telling, and maybe trying to distract him, too.

"What does your visit to Rumple's have to do with Stanley King?"

Clasping one hand with the other, she explained, "Foster and I were in Wilhelm's backyard with him. We'd been inside the house for something Mr. Rumple had wanted to show us, and that's how I knew about the safe, too."

"I see."

It was easy for Daisy to imagine that Jonas was bubbling with questions, but he wasn't going to ask them, because they might be part of her surprise.

"We were outside and were talking with him after we'd been in the house when Stanley King came to the gate."

"The backyard gate?" Jonas asked.

She envisioned what had happened. "Yes. Wilhelm had left it open. Wilhelm went over there to talk to King. We were at the far side of the yard, so we couldn't hear everything, but they were arguing. I recognized Stanley from the *Willow Creek Messenger* and the local news. Foster recognized him, too. We heard him say, *My son's wedding is costing me a mint. You're going to just have to wait for this month's payment.*"

Jonas's brows arched, and she could see from the tightening of his lips that he had a million questions.

She rushed on. "Wilhelm responded that he wouldn't wait. He told Stanley, *You'll just have to scale down your flower order for the wedding.* It was weird. The dog stood there as if it was protecting Wilhelm Rumple, but he didn't growl. The thing is . . . it sounded as if Mr. King growled. Foster and I couldn't hear what he said. When he left the yard, he slammed the gate."

"Did Rumple act rattled?" Jonas asked in his detective tone.

"No. After Wilhelm came back to us, we heard a car start up outside the gate. It revved a few times, and then the tires squealed. I assumed Stanley was pulling away. Mr. Rumple didn't look as if that bothered him."

Daisy picked up the teacup, took another sip, and made a face again because of the sugar. She continued with, "When Detective Rappaport talked to me, or rather I talked to him—I asked him to meet me in the park, so you wouldn't know about my visit to him if I went to the station and ask me what it was about . . ."

Jonas just shook his head and covered her hand with his. "You told him about your visit to Rumple's?"

"I did. I thought I should, and that King and Rumple

didn't seem to have a friendly relationship. But then I learned that Rumple had invested in King's vitamin supplement company, so I was hoping that King thought the police asked him in for questioning because of that."

"But someone must have let it slip that you mentioned his name," Jonas murmured.

"I guess." She started to rise. "I'd better get back out there. We're so busy. Anybody who was thinking about coming back for a return visit might not do it now because of what Mr. King said."

"My guess is, what he said reflects badly on *him*, not on *you*. Sometimes, you have to take what customers dish out."

"He startled me so badly I couldn't even respond. I think Tessa would have decked him if she could have."

Jonas offered his hand to her and pulled her up out of the chair. Then he hugged her and gave her a fiery kiss. It almost made thoughts of the last fifteen minutes flee.

Leaning a few inches away from her, he asked, "Did that make you forget about what happened?"

"Almost," she joked.

"Then I'll just have to do it again." And he did.

Jonas had left, and Daisy had returned to serving the busloads of customers. Many of them were finishing up, paying, and leaving, but at least half of her customers were still seated at their tables, chatting, and enjoying cheese biscuits, whoopie pies, or slices of shoofly pie.

Daisy had just set down a folder with her Daisy logo, which contained customer receipts for each member of a four-party group, when the front door opened and Zeke Willet strolled in. He was wearing jeans and a gray flannel sports jacket over a round-necked navy T-shirt. He seemed to dress more casually when he was always on the go for a murder investigation. Zeke was classically handsome with his squarish jaw. His usually short blond hair had grown out a bit with the fall season.

His dark brown eyes were apologetic as he approached her. "Can I talk to you for a few minutes?"

"I don't know if I should," Daisy said. "Everything I say to you might get around."

Zeke looked embarrassed. "We deserve that."

She nodded to her office. "Come on. Tea and a cookie?"

"You can't be too mad at me if you want to serve me that."

She gave him a glare that said that wasn't true at all.

On their way to the office, she met Foster. "Chocolate espresso cookies if we have any left, and mugs of Darjeeling."

They didn't speak until Foster had brought in the cookies and mugs of tea. Then Zeke was the one who closed Daisy's office door.

He stood with his hands in his pockets, looking sheepish. "You know, don't you, that neither Detective Rappaport nor I would put you in danger."

"I didn't think you would. I thought my conversation with Detective Rappaport was private."

Zeke came over to the desk and sat on a corner. "It was private as far as that goes. But you know we have to write up our notes and a report, especially for a murder investigation."

"I know that. Don't you have a murder book that you hand around or something like that?"

Zeke picked up the mug of tea and took a few swallows. "We do. Morris had a bunch of notes. And when he gave them to an assistant to type up, your short talk with him was in there. He would have come today himself, but he's out of town following up a lead. I came as soon as I heard what happened."

She picked up one of the chocolate espresso cookies and nibbled it. She needed more than chocolate and tea, but this would have to do. "It doesn't take long for gossip to travel in Willow Creek, does it?"

He set down his mug. "It's the beauty of small towns and a community like this. But you've got to admit, that was as public as an altercation can get. Of course, it's going to race through town like a thoroughbred rather than a buggy horse when a well-known figure like King is involved, let alone the police department."

She chose to concentrate on the lesser of all evils. "Some of the buggy horses I've known are pretty fast."

He leaned down and looked her straight in the eye. "Whether the notes are in the murder book or not, most of us know not to say anything at all. But this was a new patrol officer—Carl Crouse—who got a glimpse. King was in more than one time for an interview, and when he asked Carl who spilled his business to us, Carl mentioned your name was in the notes. I'm truly sorry, Daisy. You don't deserve to be made a public spectacle."

"I get it, Zeke. I'm not angry with you or Detective Rappaport. It's just one of those things that happened. Good citizens sometimes get shafted."

"You've been around Jonas too long," Zeke muttered, and picked up a cookie. "I suppose he's going to want to wring my neck, too."

"Not yours, but probably the patrol officer's."

After Zeke took a couple of bites and swallowed, he

said, "I'll tell you a secret. Tessa's the one who called me to tell me what happened. By the time I left the station, I was hearing it from all sides."

"Tessa's a good friend."

"I've seen that," Zeke said. "It's a shame she's going out with Lundquist."

It wasn't the first time Zeke had made a comment about Tessa. However, for now, Tessa seemed to be enjoying her relationship with Trevor.

Zeke finished his cookie, took another couple swallows of tea, and then said, "I'm out of here. I have a murder to solve."

As he stood ready to leave, Daisy stopped him. "Thank you, Zeke. Your apology means a lot. Tell Detective Rappaport I understand."

Zeke gave her a smile, said "Will do," and then he was gone. Daisy hoped one of them cracked this case soon. She wondered how she could give them more help.

Daisy's trips to the farmers market were among her most enjoyable errands. Iris had insisted she leave the tea garden early this afternoon to recover from what had happened with King. To relax, Daisy had headed for the old building where the farmers market was located. It had housed stands with produce, baked goods, and other paraphernalia for at least the past fifty years. The building had been fashioned of wood, almost like a barn, until about ten years ago, when the town had decided it needed to be preserved. The outside had been re-sided. The blue stood out on the road where other shops, including antiques and used items, were located.

If Daisy remembered the story correctly, that blue siding had been donated because a roofer couldn't sell it. The roof had been re-shingled, too, in green shingles that didn't exactly complement the blue. But none of that seemed to matter to the patrons.

The farmers market was open three days a week—Tuesday, Friday, and Saturday. Tuesdays weren't as busy as the weekend days.

Daisy's footsteps clicked from her clogs on the concrete floor as she walked down an aisle and passed a produce stand with fresh broccoli, cauliflower, celery, potatoes, sweet potatoes, and onions. She took in a breath with the combined aromas from around the market, inhaling the scent of cinnamon rolls from the baked goods stand, potato chips from one of the many snack companies in the area, grilling burgers and French fries from a lunch counter. She next passed a long, refrigerated meat counter. The farmer sold beef products like steak, roasts, and fajita meat. They also had a section for pork and sausage. The deli case next to it showcased everything from pimento cheese to prosciutto to various salads. Daisy always felt like a kid in a candy shop when she came here. Today, however, she was limiting her focus to Ruth Zook's stand.

Ruth was Mennonite. She was wearing a pale green dress printed with tiny darker green flowers. She carried a few produce items at her stand—various varieties of apples, and sweet potatoes, including the white ones that Daisy liked best. They had a more delicate taste and weren't as fibrous as the orange variety. She would buy a bag full of those, as well as Stayman apples, when she was finished asking Ruth about jams for the Storybook Tea.

Daisy used Ruth's jams regularly at the tea garden when she planned her full tea services. They ranged from raspberry to strawberry to peach. Daisy also wanted to talk to Ruth about her two daughters—Priscilla and Louise—who were good workers. In the past, they'd helped Daisy serve at her special teas. She wanted to see if they would help with the Storybook Tea she'd planned.

Ruth focused on Daisy, her blue eyes bright and sparkling when she spotted her. "What brings you to me today? Did you run out of strawberry jam?"

Daisy laughed. "Not quite, but I *am* going to need more varieties for the special tea I'm planning. I want to make sure you save me about ten jars of each."

Ruth's face took on a considering expression, her smile adding animation to her pretty round face. "You're fortunate you stopped in today. My raspberry jam is getting low, but I think I'll have ten jars for you. Peach and strawberry are no problem. What kind of scones will you be baking to use with them?"

"Tessa developed a lemon-blueberry scone recipe, and we'll serve cinnamon scones, too."

As Daisy stood at Ruth's stand speaking with her, she realized the wonderful cinnamon scent was coming from the Miller's bakery two stands down.

Ruth saw Daisy looking that way. "Those buns smell wonderful *gut*, don't they?" Ruth asked.

"Yes, they do. You'd think I'd get enough of baked goods from baking them at the tea garden, but those cinnamon rolls are special, and Vi especially likes their croissants."

Mr. Miller was laughing and speaking with a customer as he handed the man a waxy bag of cinnamon rolls.

Ruth watched him and mused, "Mr. Miller and his daughter seem much happier lately."

"Do you think Caroline's wedding is the reason for that?" Daisy asked.

"I'm not sure," Ruth responded. "A wedding certainly does make a family smile though, don't you think?"

Daisy remembered Violet's wedding. "It can. It can also bring some stresses."

"I imagine so," Ruth agreed. She leaned across the stand closer to Daisy. "Not long ago, many rumors ran around the market."

"About Mr. Miller?" Daisy asked.

"Oh, yes. His business was doing poorly. Many sellers thought he might go out of business, and there would be a stand available for someone else."

"What happened?"

"Suddenly, the rumors stopped, and things seemed to turn around for him. He started carrying more baked goods again, and refurbished his stand with that Plexiglas in front of it. All seemed well in his world, and he wasn't grouchy so much anymore."

Daisy wondered if the wedding of Caroline and Andrew had more benefits than a happily-ever-after. Had Stanley King given Miller an influx of cash or perhaps a loan? The Miller–King wedding could possibly mean happiness for both families.

After Daisy finished at Ruth Zook's stand, making arrangements for her daughters to help at the Storybook Tea in two and a half weeks, she looked around to see if she wanted to stop at any other stands before she headed out. On the other side of the aisle, about halfway down, she spotted Hetta Armbruster with a younger woman.

Maybe that was her daughter? They were selling dog treats. She'd have to stop there and buy some for Felix, but first . . .

Maybe she'd bring home a few sticky buns or cinnamon rolls for something different. They were ooey-gooey, and Jazzi particularly liked them. She was sure Jonas would, too.

As she stopped at Pastry Goods, Mr. Miller was busy on the other side of the table with a customer. Caroline, however, was free, and smiled when Daisy stepped up to the stand.

"It's good to see you again," Caroline said. "Your tea was fabulous, and I don't just mean the beverage. I mean the whole thing. Everybody was talking about it. In fact, you might be getting a couple of calls soon for holiday parties and that kind of thing."

"That would be wonderful," Daisy enthused. "The holidays can be so iffy on tourist traffic, but special events can carry the day."

"I told Andrew that, but he's been distracted lately. You don't want to hear about that, though," Caroline said, her smile shy as she looked embarrassed.

"I'd be glad to listen if you need to talk," Daisy said. "Why don't I give you my order, and you can think about it if you want to tell me."

Daisy decided on six sticky buns and six cinnamon rolls. Whatever they didn't eat tonight, she could freeze or take over to Vi and Foster. Foster had a sweet tooth as much as Jonas did.

Mr. Miller had moved on to another customer on the far side of the stand, as Caroline bagged Daisy's purchases and handed the waxy bags to her.

"Maybe it would help to tell someone," Caroline decided. "My dad doesn't want to hear about the King family."

"Because he feels . . . different from them?" Daisy hadn't been sure how to ask that question.

"That's one way of putting it. Mr. King acts like a powerful man, and my dad's a lot more humble. Anyway, Andrew's been worrying about his father. Mr. King's blood pressure is skyrocketing." She leaned closer to Daisy. "I heard what Mr. King said to you this morning. Everyone here has been talking about it. One of your customers stopped in here, gossiped about it, and it spread. That had to be awful for you. Andrew and I feel so sorry you had to go through it."

"He shocked me when he blew up like that," Daisy said honestly.

"He's definitely not himself," Caroline revealed. "But he's hired a Philadelphia lawyer, and he doesn't intend to tell the police another thing."

"Having the detective question you is stressful," Daisy acknowledged. "Especially if they do it more than once."

Caroline went on, "I don't know if they found out that pet shelters were suing him and that problems with his products were reported to the FDA. It sounds serious. I'm not sure what that would have to do with Mr. Rumple, though. If Mr. King was in some kind of partnership with Mr. Rumple, Andrew's father's whole business would be affected, and the investors would be, too." She stopped for a breath. "The thing is—"

Glancing toward her dad and lowering her voice again, Caroline almost whispered, "My father had business dealings with Mr. Rumple, too. I saw an email from Mr. Rumple to my dad that his payments would be increasing."

"Do you know what payments those were?" Daisy asked, keeping her voice just as low.

"When I asked my dad about it, he said I shouldn't worry. Now that Rumple was dead, there wouldn't be any more payments."

"But you still didn't find out what they were for?"

"Not exactly. But Dad said they were for insurance that he didn't need any longer."

Insurance. That was a new one. Had Wilhelm Rumple been an insurance broker?

After a few more minutes of more normal conversation about Duchess and her settling into her surroundings, Daisy turned from the Millers' stand. She headed for Hetta Armbruster's table, and she was delightfully surprised by the array of dog treats there.

Hetta greeted her. "Are you shopping for Felix?"

"I am. Look at all these treats I can choose from."

The other woman at the stand came over to stand beside Hetta. She grinned at Daisy. "I've heard all about Felix."

Hetta put her hand on the younger woman's shoulder. "This is my daughter Edith. She can tell you all about these wonderful treats that she makes herself."

Hetta's daughter was a pretty young woman around Daisy's age. Her medium brown hair was full and wavy and lay across her shoulders. She had a big, wide smile, dimples, a high forehead, and chocolate-brown eyes. She was wearing a red pashmina and a red scarf of the same material that wrapped around her neck. She greeted Daisy as if she knew her, or maybe had just heard about Felix.

"Your boyfriend adopted a cream golden retriever,

right?" Edith inquired. "They are the sweetest dogs . . . calm and friendly."

"Felix certainly is," Daisy agreed with a soft laugh. "He's a great companion and watchdog, too."

"I hear he goes along to work with your guy," Edith said, brushing her hair back over her shoulder.

"He does, and I think the customers are beginning to like him a lot. Do you have a dog?" Daisy asked Edith.

The woman's bright expression wavered. "Not now," she said. After a brief hesitation, she added, "I lost Poncho last year. He was the cutest little mutt." Her eyes glistened. "But cancer took him. One of these days, during my volunteer sessions at Four Paws, I'll find another soulmate pup. But I'm just not ready for that yet. So instead, I make dog treats to sell. Besides the farmers market, I've been doing quite well at the pet store, Fur and Feathers."

"They're beautiful treats." Daisy looked down at the dog cookies. "Good enough to eat."

"Humans could eat them," Hetta said. "They're made with the best ingredients."

Daisy looked over the selection and stopped at one that looked like a donut. "What's this one?"

"Those are peanut butter dog donuts topped with Greek yogurt and bacon bits," Edith answered.

"I'll take three of those," Daisy decided.

Next, Edith pointed to cookies in the shape of pumpkins. "These are pumpkin ginger biscuits. They're good for a dog's digestion. They contain whole-wheat flour, pumpkin, coconut oil, and are easy to make."

"And what are these?" Daisy pointed to more decorative treats. "They look like cupcakes."

"They have carrots and peanut butter in them. The dog biscuits over there have wheat flour, wheat germ, and peanut butter. I use organic peanut butter in the treats. You don't have to worry about preservatives."

Daisy pointed to another treat she was interested in. "Those look like pretzels."

"They are. They're made with egg, oat flour, rolled oats, and applesauce."

"I'll take three of the pretzels, too. I think Felix is going to be a happy camper tonight."

Hetta rearranged some of the treats on the table, while Edith packaged Daisy's purchases. There was pride in Hetta's voice when she said, "Edith makes these for Winkie. She made all of her own food as well as treats for Poncho."

Nodding, Edith explained, "There's no telling what's in pet food anymore. Have you heard about the vitamin D problem?"

"I did hear something about that," Daisy said, without saying where she heard it or why.

"You can easily make your own pet food," Hetta said.

Edith jumped in. "I'd be glad to give you some recipes if you'd like them."

"I would," Daisy responded. "Why don't you stop in at the tea garden sometime? I'll offer you human treats."

Edith laughed. "I'll have to stop in at Woods, too, and meet Felix. I hear he had good training."

"He did. His previous owner loved him to bits, and her son trained him."

"Dogs need pre-school and kindergarten just like kids," Edith advised with another laugh.

As Daisy walked away from the stand, she remembered what Fiona had said about her sister. Hetta had seemed down, disturbed, and out of sorts. But today, she seemed fine. Maybe Mr. Rumple's murder hadn't affected her as much as Fiona had thought. A death in Willow Creek affected many people besides friends and family. But a murder in Willow Creek affected the whole town. Folks would be grieving and worrying until the murder was solved. Daisy hoped that would be soon.

CHAPTER THIRTEEN

The following day, Daisy was standing at the sales counter when Detective Rappaport came in. He looked around the main room of the tea garden, then shifted into the spillover room and canvassed it. Next, he approached the sales counter, his gaze speeding by Daisy before it came to rest on her."

Good morning, Detective. Tea or conversation?" She wouldn't mind picking his brain. Of course, he would try to pick hers at the same time. That seemed to be the way they operated.

"Zeke told me he apologized to you for our leak. Crouse was reprimanded. I'm sorry, Daisy."

"Thank you. I believe you. Things happen."

The detective shuffled his feet for a second, which wasn't like him at all. Today he was dressed in a dark brown sports jacket that wasn't wrinkled, a white shirt, and a tan tie. She wondered if he was going to a business meeting. She didn't think he'd dress so dapper to interview a suspect.

"On your way to a conference somewhere?" she asked, hoping to elicit a smile.

Instead, he turned red. "No, not a conference. I wouldn't mind a glass of iced tea and a carrot muffin, if your aunt is free."

If her aunt was free? "Aunt Iris?"

"I don't think you've changed aunts in the last month, have you?"

Her confusion dropped away, and she suspected why he was here. Interesting. "No, I haven't changed aunts. I thought you were here for another purpose. Aunt Iris is in the kitchen. I'll fetch her along with your tea and muffin." She motioned to the spillover tearoom. "If you need a more private table, just choose one."

If it was possible, he turned even redder. He shook his finger at Daisy. "This isn't a teasing matter."

"I suspect not," Daisy returned seriously. "I'll get my aunt."

Fifteen minutes later, her aunt was seated with the detective, who was talking animatedly while taking a bite of his muffin.

After another glance their way, Daisy noticed Hetta Armbruster and Edith enter the tea garden. Leaving the sales counter, Daisy showed them to a table in the main tearoom.

After they were seated, Edith asked Daisy, "Can you sit with us for a few minutes? I brought recipes along, and I want to explain them."

Since Iris was tied up for the moment, Daisy considered the fact that there were three other tables for four.

Cora Sue, Jada, and Tamlyn seemed to be serving them with no problem. She knew Tessa and Eva were holding down the kitchen.

Cora Sue saw Daisy estimating how busy the staff was and came over to her. "Can I get you something?"

"Do you think service will be adequate if I take a few minutes? I don't usually take a break now, but I'll split it today."

Cora Sue gave her a *you've-got-to-be-kidding* look. "You're the boss, Daisy. Sometimes I don't think you realize that. You can take a break whenever you want."

"Not if it overloads my staff." Cora Sue had always been blunt, and Daisy appreciated that about her.

"We're good," Cora Sue assured her. "Would you like me to bring you anything?"

"I'll take Hetta and Edith's orders and get myself a cup of tea. I'm good. I think you're all going to deserve bonuses for Christmas."

"That's something to look forward to," Cora Sue agreed with a bright smile. "You're fair, Daisy. That's why we all like working for you."

Daisy patted Cora Sue on the shoulder with a *thank you* and turned to take Edith's and Hetta's orders.

She motioned to the board above the sales counter. "Whatever you like. It's on the house."

Hetta was the first to speak up. "Fiona said your peach Darjeeling is delicious. Could I have a cup of hot tea? She also likes your cheddar biscuits that are the special this month. I told her I'd pick up a dozen for her, and she can freeze some of them."

"Cheddar biscuits and Darjeeling tea it is. How about you, Edith?"

Edith was studying the sales board, squinting a little as if that helped her see better. "Is it okay if I have a cherry tart?"

"Absolutely."

"And like my mom, there's something I'd like to take along. Fiona said your peach salsa was so good. She put it over a pork loin when she baked it."

"Wait until before you leave, then go to the sales counter and ask for the extra purchases. That way, they'll be as fresh as they can be. Would you like tea, Edith?"

"I see up there that you have a Daisy's Fall Supreme Tea. Can you tell me what that is?"

"We're going to use that for our Storybook Tea. It's decaffeinated green tea mixed with some raspberry and vanilla notes. The kids and adults should like it. Would you like to try that?"

"Can I have that iced?"

"You certainly can. I'll be back in about five minutes. Make yourselves comfortable. Look around, chat, see if there's anybody here you know. I've had mostly local customers this morning rather than tourists."

"I heard Stanley King made quite a scene," Edith said.

Hetta shook her head and patted her daughter's hand, as if she shouldn't have brought it up. Had they known about the altercation yesterday when she'd been at the market? Maybe. Maybe not. Had they come in today to find out about it? No. Edith had said she'd brought recipes.

Daisy made her expression as bland as she could. "Don't worry. You won't offend me by talking about it. He did make a scene. I was shocked, shocked so badly I froze."

"I heard you told the police that Mr. King and Mr. Rumple had a fight," Edith went on, as if she wanted to know details about the encounter.

Daisy didn't mind discussing what had happened at the tea garden because that had been public. But the rest . . . "I'm not sure why the detective questioned Mr. King. I overheard them exchange a few words."

"We all get angry sometimes," Hetta said, surmising those words hadn't been friendly. "It's what we do about the feeling that matters." She lowered her voice. "Stanley King has a sense of entitlement about him. He always has. He thinks he's better than everyone else."

Daisy had to lean closer to hear Hetta as she went on, "I guess money does that. But I don't see why. Just because you can buy nice things and have a big house doesn't mean you have a good heart. It doesn't mean you have people around you who love you." She reached over and held her daughter's hand. "Right, Edith?"

"Right, Mom."

To Daisy, Edith's voice sounded a little thick, and her eyes looked moist. Mother and daughter had a strong bond . . . that seemed obvious.

After Daisy went to the kitchen and returned with their orders, Edith handed Daisy recipe cards for the dog food she and Jonas could make. Then they settled into drinking and eating.

Edith said, "This place really is amazing. Did you take business courses at school?"

"I took courses that had to do with what I was learning about nutrition—how to counsel people, what to eat, the healthiest way to cook food. I did take a bookkeeping course. Thank goodness my computer program handles the bookwork. I concentrate on trying to use wholesome ingredients in the food we make here . . . no preservatives. I like to think our soups and salads are particularly healthy. The baked goods are comfort food."

"Just running our stand at the farmer's market can be a bookkeeping headache," Edith supplied.

"Now that I have a new program for my computer, it should be easier," Hetta protested. "I'll teach you how to use it. Or better yet, we'll learn together."

Changing the subject, Edith asked Daisy, "How is Felix doing?"

"He's great. He's with Jonas at Woods today."

Edith nudged her mother. "We'll have to stop in and meet him. I missed him when he was at the shelter. I hope this week at Four Paws everything will be back to normal. The police popped in so many times."

"Officer Cosner was back on my last shift," Hetta supplied. "All of the volunteers said they were questioned again. I guess that was better than us going down to the station."

"Bart's a good guy. I'm sure he handled it well." Daisy hoped that that was so.

"He was very respectful when I spoke with him," Edith said. "He asked the same questions over and over—like how did Mr. Rumple seem when he was at the shelter? Most of us couldn't answer that one because our shifts weren't at the same time his were. He asked if we ever saw Mr. Rumple talking to someone who wasn't a volunteer there. But between you and me, I think Officer Cosner also came to the shelter so often to visit with one particular pup."

As if that wasn't of consequence right now, Hetta said,

"I don't know how many times Officer Cosner asked if Mr. Rumple was really good with the dogs, if that's the reason he was there. I'm sure all of us said that he was."

'   "So do you believe Officer Cosner is going to adopt a dog?" Daisy asked, returning to that idea.

"We can only hope." Hetta winked. "We can only hope."

Daisy's heart beat fast as she and Jonas walked the path to the big red barn on Friday evening. Would he be surprised?

"There are quite a few cars here tonight," Jonas said, glancing around at the parking lot. "I guess The Farm Barn's name is getting around."

The door to The Farm Barn was trimmed in white, as were the windows. Jonas opened the door for her.

As soon as they both stepped inside, a shout of *Surprise!* erupted from the two long tables that had been set up in the middle of the space. There were also shouts of "Happy birthday" and "Do you feel another year older?" from everyone Daisy had invited. Her parents were grinning at Jonas, along with Vi and Foster, Sammy and Jazzi, and Gavin and his children Emily and Ben. Trevor and Tessa, along with Rachel, Levi, and their children, lined up with others around the table. Zeke and Detective Rappaport, as well as Serena and Noah, also joined in the happy gathering.

Jonas turned to Daisy. "What did you do?"

"Do you see those balloons rising from the center-pieces on the tables? They say HAPPY BIRTHDAY. I wanted to give you a celebration you'll remember. I wanted to show you how much you're loved."

Jonas was dressed in black jeans, a white shirt, and a silver bolo tie with black strings. For a moment, Daisy didn't know what he thought about the surprise, whether he liked it or not. He was quite still, quite immobilized, and she thought maybe this focus on him might be uncomfortable to him.

Then she watched his green eyes go shiny as he swallowed hard. The set of his jaw went a little slacker. He took her into his arms and hugged her close, his cheek against hers. "No one has ever done anything like this before for me. Thank you, Daisy."

She let out a relieved breath and hugged him back . . . hard. "Come on. Let's greet everyone. My guess is Lydia will bring out the food soon. She's the manager and oversees everything."

As Daisy and Jonas approached the tables, Jazzi came over and gave him a big hug. Daisy heard Jazzi whisper in his ear, "Gram made your birthday cake. She said she wanted to be the one to show you that you mean something special to this family."

Daisy did see that Jonas was trying to absorb all the care that had gone into this day.

Zeke crossed to them and thumped Jonas on the back. "Another year older and another year wiser, right?"

"How long have you known about this?" Jonas asked him.

"About a month. Daisy doesn't leave anything to the last minute."

Jonas looked down at her with so much feeling that she felt her own throat closing.

Glorie Beck, with Brielle on her other side, used her cane to point to the servers starting to file in from the kitchen. "Lydia Aldenkamp has planned quite a feast for today, in collusion with Daisy, of course. There's a beef barley soup appetizer, and then we'll all be scooping out salads, from chow chow to three-bean to pickled beets."

"And the main courses are supposed to be your favorite," Brielle added. "Pork and sauerkraut, ham and scalloped potatoes, and fried chicken. We're all going to be ten pounds heavier when we leave."

Jonas lightly laid his hand on Daisy's waist. "You've planned a feast."

"The Farm Barn makes family dinners a specialty of theirs. I wanted you to experience the full effect. After all, it's a long way to go until the holidays."

"About six weeks until Thanksgiving," he reminded her, looking around again at the table filled with presents, at the side bar with cold drinks and ice, at the coffee and hot water urns.

The inside walls of the barn were rustic, the high beams sturdy and long. The floor itself, however, wasn't barnlike. It was luxury vinyl that could withstand the wear and tear and cleanup that it needed. However, it had wood-tone colors and added to the barn effect. Bunches of dried flowers and herbs tied with plaid ribbons hung along the barn posts. Daisy imagined that Lydia changed them according to the celebration going on . . . maybe tulle and satin for weddings instead of burlap and gingham for family dinners.

As if thinking about her made her appear, Lydia came through the door from the kitchen. She was wearing a high-necked gingham dress with long sleeves. Spotting Daisy and Jonas, she came over to them and introduced herself to Jonas. Her hair was burnished brown, and she wore it in a bun at her nape. Her brown eyes were alight with the pleasure of serving people dinners like this.

She said to Jonas, "If there's anything you need, just let one of the servers know. We'll stay out of your way as much as possible so you can talk with your guests. We truly hope you enjoy your celebration. That's what we're here for."

"Everything looks wonderful," Jonas assured her. "Daisy told me the food here is top-notch. I can't wait to taste it."

After Lydia wished them another good evening and went to see to everything she had to manage, Daisy touched Jonas's elbow. "We should take our seats. You're over here at the head of this table."

"You want me to stick out like a sore thumb." Jonas's voice was teasing.

"You're the guest of honor. We all want to be able to see you."

Shaking his head, Jonas followed Daisy to his chair. Before the meal started, everyone bowed their heads for a couple of minutes for silent grace. Daisy watched Levi, who was sitting in her row, for the signal that he was finished. She wanted Levi and Rachel to enjoy this evening. The Amish celebrated with meals with their family and friends, but they didn't do over-the-top decorations or anything that would be considered pomp and circumstance. Daisy respected that. It was one of the reasons she hadn't included liquor in the evening. She had surmised that Jonas wouldn't mind.

After the main courses were passed around, Rachel nudged Daisy's arm. "This is really a homey place to have a celebration, ain't so?"

"It is. That's one of the reasons why I chose it. I'm glad you feel comfortable here."

Rachel nodded to a quilt hanging on the wall. "That

star quilt is beautiful." The quilt had been fashioned with blue, red, yellow, and gold diamonds. Daisy had been told that the circle in the middle represented the earth. She knew that in Native American traditions it had been named after the morning star.

Rachel's daughters and son were sitting nearby with Foster and Vi. The girls were talking to Vi animatedly during the meal. Luke, her youngest, was speaking with Hannah's betrothed Daniel in between bites of a fried chicken leg. Everyone at the table looked as if they were enjoying themselves as well as the food.

About half an hour later, Jonas's hand covered Daisy's as they waited for the cake to be cut. Jonas said, "I'm going to thank your mother for that gorgeous cake. She must have spent a lot of time on it."

"She did, and I'm sure she'll like it if you tell her."

Jonas rose from his seat as a server went around the table pouring coffee or tea into cups for anyone who wanted it.

Trevor suddenly pulled out Jonas's empty chair and sat beside Daisy.

Surprised, she asked jokingly, "Are you taking over the seat of honor?"

"No, this is Jonas's night, and he looks as if he's liking it. I've never seen the man look so relaxed. You're good for him, Daisy."

"I hope I am. Did you want to talk to me about something?"

"I do. I didn't know if we'd get another chance." Trevor lowered his voice. "I found out something today that's interesting."

"About the murder?" She kept her voice as low as his.

"The police want to look into Rumple's finances, but they can't find his computer."

"What about checkbooks and that kind of thing?"

Trevor was already shaking his head. "They've managed to access his credit card statements and utility bills, but nothing about his business finances. It's weird. He had one ledger with weird notations, but the detectives can't decipher them."

"Weird notations?"

"Just letters with numbers after them, nothing that leads in a specific direction."

"And they have no idea where it leads?"

"No."

"Can they find out if any local banks do business with him?"

"My guess is that will take time and subpoenas. His lawyer claims he can't divulge anything until the will is probated."

"And Rumple's nephew?"

"Apparently, he has no knowledge of his uncle's personal business. He's stated unequivocally that he has no knowledge of checkbooks or ledgers or even the computer. It's very odd, don't you think?"

"It *is* odd. It's definitely something to think about."

Jonas came back to his seat, and Trevor stood. Trevor shook Jonas's hand. "Glad you made it another year."

Jonas laughed as Trevor went back to his seat.

Daisy glanced at her mother, and she was absolutely beaming. "Apparently, you said the right thing to my mom."

"I think she and I are starting to get along." There was amusement in his voice, but Daisy knew it was true.

At the beginning of her dating Jonas, her mother hadn't liked the idea of her dating a former cop . . . not at all. And with Jonas operating Woods, her mother had thought he lacked ambition and that he was settling. But since then, she'd learned differently. She'd learned Jonas had a talent for woodworking. She'd learned he was a man of integrity, and the man Daisy loved.

"I'm going to give you your present," Daisy said, "before we get caught up in everybody else's congratulations and opening gifts. Be right back."

Foster had been watching her. He nodded to her and then followed her to a storage closet, where he helped her pick up the golden retriever statue. Daisy had tied a big blue and silver bow around the dog's neck. Together, they carried it to Jonas's place and sat it on the floor beside him.

"Since Felix couldn't be here, you thought you'd bring me a substitute?" Jonas joked.

Foster saluted Daisy, and then he went back to his seat.

Daisy explained, "I thought you might like this for your porch."

A shadow passed over Jonas's face, but it was gone in an instant. She thought maybe she'd imagined it. He ran his hand over the dog's head. "It's a beautiful replica. This is what you bought at Rumple's Statuary?"

"It is. I feel like that visit started life spinning out of control."

"Maybe. It definitely pulled you into the most recent murder investigation. I do love it. I'm sure Felix will, too."

Daisy leaned over, her arms around Jonas, and gave him a quick kiss. More than anything, she wanted him to move in with her. Maybe soon they could have that discussion.

CHAPTER FOURTEEN

On Sunday afternoon, Daisy brought Felix, along with her Aunt Iris and Glorie Beck, to visit Adele Gunnarson. Adele seemed happy at Whispering Willows Assisted Living facility, which was about two miles outside of Willow Creek. The willow trees surrounding the property gave the campus a peaceful air. Suite 23 welcomed them with a wreath of sunflowers hanging on the door. As usual, Felix rushed inside before the women could.

Adele reached for him like a long-lost friend.

Adele had been Felix's pet mom. Daisy always thought she looked a little like Betty White, with her snowy white hair and curly bangs brushed over to the side. A bobby pin held her hair back over her left ear. Huge dimples appeared on either side of her mouth when she smiled. Using her wire-rimmed glasses for distance clarification, she wore them on a turquoise beaded chain around her neck. Adele liked flowers, and today she was wearing a blue, rose-flowered blouse that hung out over her pleated slacks with tan tennis shoes.

After greetings all around and an introduction to her Aunt Iris, Daisy placed the goody basket she'd brought on the small, white round table. She glanced over the living room area where a gray and black tweed rug lay under the coffee table on the vinyl tile floor. After she'd crossed to the living room area again, she chose to sit on the sofa that was upholstered in a sunflower fabric. The easy chair Adele chose was covered in pale green, the same color as the cabinets in her kitchen. They coordinated with the dark sage laminate on the counters.

Preparing for company and tea, Adele had set a white tea table next to the chair she occupied.

An hour later, they were all enjoying cups of peach Darjeeling tea in the teacups and saucers Adele had provided. Daisy asked Adele, "What would you like to try for teatime?" She uncovered the goodies and let Adele choose first.

"Tell me what they are," Adele said.

"There are cucumber canapés, apple scones, smoked salmon triangles, and lemon drizzle cupcakes."

"Is it all right if I have one of each?" There was a girlish gleam in Adele's eyes.

"Of course, it is. I brought plenty, so there will be leftovers to snack on later if you want them."

"You spoil me," Adele pronounced, "with tea garden goodies *and* visits from Felix. My son says he's glad I found new friends."

"That's why I brought Iris and Glorie today. We can all use more friends."

After Daisy, Iris, and Glorie chose their treats, as well, Daisy said, "I gave Felix an extra little meal before we came so that he wouldn't want to chomp on all our goodies. But he's really well behaved about that, even at mealtime. Your son trained him so well."

"He'd always been such a good dog, even when he first came to live with us. He and Horace bonded right away. After Horace died, I just didn't know what I was going to do. Thank goodness, your Jonas connected with him at Four Paws."

Iris said, "I always thought about adopting a pup, but working all day just didn't seem fair to the canine. Jonas has the perfect situation . . . he can take Felix to work with him."

Glorie asked Adele, "You didn't mind giving up your home to move in here?"

"Oh, at first I thought I couldn't do it," Adele responded. "But my son lives an hour away, and he couldn't take care of my outside work. Sure, I could have hired a cleaning lady, I suppose, or gotten help another way. But this just seemed to be the best idea for me."

"I'm going to be moving in with my daughter and granddaughter after we build a house together," Glorie revealed to Adele. "I'm a little afraid about how it's all going to work out."

"I'm sure it will be an adjustment at first," Adele offered. "But won't you enjoy having family nearby?"

"I fell in the spring," Glorie confessed. "That scared me. My granddaughter's been living with me since then, and I enjoy her company. But she needs to have a life of her own. Moving in with her and her mom will give us all a shared responsibility, I suppose."

"It's so important to have people we care about

nearby," Adele reminded them all. "Some older folks aren't so fortunate."

Daisy watched Felix change position on the floor and rest his head on Adele's foot.

"I haven't had a tea party in years," Adele confirmed. "This is so wonderful. It's nice to have something good to think about. I've read what happened to that Mr. Rumple at Four Paws Animal Shelter." Adele focused on Daisy. "Did Jonas have anything to do with that? I mean, was he there when it happened?"

"No, he wasn't," Daisy answered. "Whatever occurred, occurred at night, when no one else was around."

"I knew the Rumple boys," Adele revealed. "At least I knew *of* them. My son was at school when they were."

"They were friends?" Iris asked, looking curious.

"No, but you can guess how it is when boys especially are around the same age at school. Parents hear things."

Glorie finished an apple scone and then took a sip of tea. After she'd set the teacup on the saucer, she focused on Adele. "What did you hear?"

"I heard that the older brother tried to protect Wilhelm, but Wilhelm didn't appreciate his protection. I had the feeling Wilhelm was bullied a bit as a boy."

"After the funeral service, I spoke with a teacher who knew him. She said something similar," Daisy confided.

"The thing is," Adele pointed out, "Wilhelm just preferred to isolate himself. That was self-protection, I guess. He didn't want his older brother standing up for him, yet he couldn't make friends on his own. Still . . . there was also something about Wilhelm that seemed . . . calculating."

Iris took another cucumber canapé and put it on her plate. "How do you mean?"

"Wilhelm was bullied, but from what I understood, there were also boys who were afraid of him."

"That doesn't seem consistent," Iris noted.

"No, it doesn't," Adele agreed. "It was almost like Wilhelm played whack-a-mole to take care of one bully somehow, and another would pop up."

"Physical confrontation?" Daisy asked, though that was hard to believe of Wilhelm Rumple.

"No, I don't think so. That was the odd thing," Adele said. "No one knew exactly what Wilhelm did or how he did it."

"Not even his brother?" Glorie asked.

Adele shrugged. "No one ever knew."

There seemed to be a lot about Wilhelm Rumple and the people he interacted with that no one knew about.

When Jonas called Daisy late afternoon on Monday, she was closing out the register at the tea garden. As soon as she saw his face on the screen, she thought he was calling about dinner.

She answered, "Hi, handsome. What are you hungry for?"

"Daisy, right now, I don't want to think about dinner."

There was a tone in his voice that alerted her that something was going on.

"What do you want to think about?" she asked warily.

"Noah Langston is here at Woods. He and I were talking, and I think it would be good if you sat in on the conversation."

Daisy guessed that Noah might be close by Jonas, listening to what he was saying. She motioned to her aunt and the cash register.

Iris nodded and called, "I'll take care of the deposit, too. Don't worry about it."

Within five minutes, Daisy had pulled her sweater coat from the clothes tree in her office, her purse from her desk drawer, and headed out the back door of the tea garden. A few minutes later, she was at the back door of Jonas's shop.

He must have been watching for her because he opened the door before she could knock.

After she stepped inside, he gave her a hug. She sent him a questioning glance, but he gave her a shrug and motioned to where Noah was sitting on a deacon's bench where she and Jonas often had conversations.

"Hi, Noah. How are you?"

"I'm not sure," he answered, while Jonas pulled up a ladder-back chair near the deacon's bench.

Daisy sat beside Noah. "Jonas called and said you might like to speak to me?" She sent questioning looks to both men, wondering where this was going.

Noah flushed when he said, "I know this is an imposition."

Daisy still didn't understand how he was imposing. She unbuttoned her sweater. "How can I help?"

"Serena isn't herself. I think she's having panic attacks again."

Daisy didn't understand what those had to do with *her*. "You said *again*. Has she had them before?"

"We went to different colleges. After she graduated, I noticed her anxiety symptoms. However, after about a year, they faded. Now they're back."

"This is a stressful time," Jonas reminded him.

"Yes, it is, especially with the police in and out of the shelter. I can understand why she's upset. But it's more than being upset about the murder . . . at least, I think it is. She jumps at the slightest noise. She startles when someone walks in the room. She can't seem to concentrate."

"How did she get through it before?" Daisy asked.

"Truthfully, I'm not sure. She wouldn't talk to me about it then, either. I think she saw a therapist at some point. All I know is that she was good. I hadn't seen symptoms for years. Now I don't know what to do for her."

"What do you think *we* can do?" Daisy inquired gently.

"When she asked you to go along to Rumple's funeral, I was surprised. Serena doesn't seem to make friends easily. I know that sounds odd because with shelter clients and business, she can talk to anyone. She can be friendly, and everybody likes her. But as far as real friends, I always thought she's been too busy to make them."

"I like Serena," Daisy said. "She was quiet at the funeral and at the reception afterwards. But funerals are a serious business. I didn't see anything out of the ordinary."

"She manages to hide her symptoms well," Noah admitted. "But now I think they're so serious that she can't. I think she asked you to go along with her to the funeral because she trusts you, Daisy."

"I don't know, Noah. I haven't known her very long."

"No, you haven't. But sometimes there's an instant connection. I think she made that with you, maybe because she knew Jonas, maybe because she knows you like dogs and animals in general. For whatever reason, I think maybe she'd talk to you."

"What would you like me to do?" Just walking up to Serena and asking what's going on wasn't going to work.

"I thought you could invite her to lunch or tea or something and have a chat. Once she gets started, perhaps she'll tell you what's bothering her. And if not that, it's possible she'd relax a little just being with you." Noah gave Daisy a winning smile. "You have that effect on people."

Jonas chuckled. "Yes, she does. Her customers sometimes reveal things to her they wouldn't reveal to anybody else. So your idea might be a good one. What do you think, Daisy?"

"I think I can make time for the two of us. If she comes over to the house and brings Bellamy, I can have Felix there, too. Animals are a great buffer. Do you think that would work, Noah?"

"Right now, I think it would be a godsend," he responded. "She's like a teapot that's ready to blow. Maybe you can just open the spout a little."

Daisy had to smile. Noah was trying to use imagery she'd understand. Still, her smile soon faded, even though she was going to do what Noah asked. If Mr. Rumple's murder had something to do with Serena's sudden anxiety attacks, could that mean his sister was directly involved somehow?

"Serena hasn't returned my call yet," Daisy said to Jonas as they sat in the York restaurant, candlelight glimmering on their table. It was unusual for them to make reservations during the week at this type of restaurant, but Jonas had insisted.

They had sampled appetizers and were waiting for their main courses to arrive. This was a restaurant that Daisy knew many people used for special occasions because it was pricey. She wasn't sure if Jonas had made the reservation for them here because she'd put together his birthday celebration . . . or because he just wanted romantic time for the two of them.

Tonight, she'd dressed in a leopard-print jacket with a black collar and wide black cuffs. Underneath, she'd worn a soft off-white sweater. Her black slacks were leg-hugging. Jonas's eyes had gone a deeper green as he'd studied her outfit. After all, he was used to seeing her in her tea garden apron and her work clothes or jeans. Her breath had caught when she'd opened her door to him. The sight of him always made her heart skitter, but in a charcoal suit, white shirt, and pale gray tie, he looked strong, accomplished, and so sexy.

"What do you think I should do if Serena doesn't call back?" Daisy asked, corralling her thoughts back to their conversation.

"Maybe give it one more try? Who knows, sometimes voice mails go the way of spam calls. I know if I don't recognize the number, sometimes I don't answer. My phone doesn't either if I have it set to ignore those calls."

"I could call again. I could also stop in at the shelter. It might be harder for her to say no face-to-face."

"It might also be embarrassing if she really doesn't want to do it," Jonas pointed out.

"I don't know why Noah thinks I can coax Serena to confide in me, when he's known her all his life and *he* can't. I've gotten the impression that the two of them are close."

"The two of them *are* close," Jonas agreed. "But talking to a woman might be different from talking to a man. Some women think that some men are just clueless." Amusement tinged his words.

She replied by patting his hand. "I would never think that of you."

He gave her an askance look. "My guess is it depends on the subject, ain't so?" He used the popular Pennsylvania Dutch tag question that many Amish used.

"It is so, I suppose." She said more seriously, "I'll wait to see if Serena calls me tomorrow. I don't think she's the type who doesn't return phone calls."

Jonas took a sip of wine from a crystal glass, and so did Daisy. He looked undecided for a few moments, but then his expression changed, and he launched into another subject. "I saw Trevor briefly today. Since Detective Rappaport isn't giving us any information, I thought Trevor might get it first. I asked if he'd heard anything more about Rumple's computer."

"What did he say?"

Jonas fingered his wine glass and then turned it in a circle. "It's very odd, don't you think, that the detectives can't find any financial records?"

"So Trevor didn't hear anything else?"

"No. He and I were tossing ideas around."

"Toss some my way," Daisy suggested lightly.

"Trevor still thinks it's possible that either the nephew or the brother might have Rumple's financial records."

"But they've told the police they don't?"

"They said they don't, but who knows. Maybe the split between brothers wasn't as serious as everyone thinks."

"But his brother didn't even attend the funeral."

"That might be for show. After all, his brother is dead. What does it matter?"

"You mean Herman Rumple doesn't know the people that resided in his brother's circle of contacts, so his attending the funeral didn't matter?"

"Something like that. Or maybe keeping his brother's secrets is merely more important."

"Any other ideas?" Daisy asked.

As if he could conjure up a few, Jonas gazed into his water goblet. "I wonder if Rumple has a safety deposit box somewhere that nobody knows about. Maybe he hid the key, and the detectives haven't found it."

Daisy always appreciated this give-and-take with Jonas as they batted around suppositions. "Where would *you* put a safety deposit box key?"

"Somewhere where I could find it. For security sake, I would probably tell one other person."

"And you believe it has to be the brother or the nephew."

"Exactly. Unless Rumple had friends we don't know about. From his reputation, that seems unlikely."

"Still," Daisy mused, "nobody knows everything about somebody."

"True. Usually a person's life is in pieces," Jonas surmised. "A brother knows one part of a person, while a sister knows another, parents know another, and a husband or wife knows another. What the detectives do is put all that information together. It makes up the picture of the person who was murdered. Usually it's consistent. If there's an inconsistency, that's where the detectives look."

"That makes sense."

Jonas smiled. "That's how I solved a lot of cases, and I know Zeke does it that way, too. The problem is—the usual method doesn't add up with Rumple."

"Explain," Daisy encouraged him.

"Everything about Rumple's life is inconsistent. No one seemed to know him well. My guess is his teachers had the best handle on his personality. That means every person who knew Rumple is a lead, in a way. The only information that really rings true is that Rumple didn't like people very much, and he liked dogs a whole lot."

"His house was neat and tidy," Daisy pointed out. "That trait might have had a presence in the rest of his life."

"Really? I don't think anybody mentioned that."

"Unless Rumple straightened up expecting Foster and me to go inside, the house seemed pristine. That kitchen was state-of-the-art but didn't look used. Everything seemed to have its place, even in his office. The items in his safe were lined up perfectly. I saw a grid on his desk. It looked like he'd numbered every statue outside, and the grid duplicated the order. The rooms that Foster and I walked through were neat."

"What do you surmise from all that?" Jonas asked her.

His question prompted her to analyze her descriptions. "Rumple didn't seem like a man who left anything to chance. So either somebody knows a whole lot more than they're saying, or there's something we haven't figured out about him yet."

The waitress arrived with their main courses, setting them before them on steaming hot dishes. Jonas had ordered duck breast with an orange-mango glaze and a side of green beans with bits of ham, accompanied by garlic and sour cream mashed potatoes. Daisy had ordered baked crab cakes with lemon aioli, grits with cheddar cheese, and sweet corn succotash. With those dishes, the waitress provided spicy bread-and-butter pickles for them to share, as well as a basket of buttermilk biscuits.

While they enjoyed their meals, they gazed into each

other's eyes often and talked of anything and everything from Sammy's latest growth spurt to Jazzi's college applications to Portia and Colton's offer to help Jazzi when she went to college. Nothing was off limits, and they didn't tiptoe around any subject.

Daisy felt so free with Jonas now, and she hoped he felt the same way. They decided to split a chocolate caramel tart for dessert. They had just finished when Jonas picked up his napkin and reached across the table to swipe a bit of chocolate off the bottom of Daisy's lip. She stared at him, mesmerized by his green eyes and the expression in them.

He cleared his throat and then set down the napkin. He looked uncertain and then cleared his throat again. He started, "I've been wanting to—"

Daisy's phone played its tuba sound, and she quickly silenced it. She saw that Jazzi was calling.

"It's Jazzi. She's with Mark. I'd better take this."

The expression on Jonas's face changed to one of concern, and he motioned to her phone. "Go ahead."

Jazzi's voice was shaky as she said, "Mom, we were in an accident."

Daisy felt the color drain from her face.

Jonas reached across the table and took her hand that wasn't holding the phone.

"We're all right," Jazzi was quick to say. "Really, we are. The police are here."

Daisy found her voice. "Where's *here*?"

Jazzi named a road near Lancaster that they'd taken to come home. Then, her voice quavering, Jazzi added, "Mom, Mark was driving."

"My car?" Daisy asked.

Jazzi said simply, "Yes."

"We'll be there as soon as we can. Text me your exact location."

"Mom, I'm sorry."

"We'll talk about it when I get there." After Daisy ended the call, she turned to Jonas. "Jazzi was in an accident. She's okay, but Mark was driving the car."

"Let's go," Jonas said, motioning to the waitress. "Try not to think about it until we get there and find out what happened."

That might be good advice, Daisy thought, but she wouldn't be able to take it.

CHAPTER FIFTEEN

When Daisy saw her car, she started shaking all over. Her PT Cruiser was turned on its side in a ditch.

Seconds later, however, she spotted Jazzi, and the shaking stopped. Her daughter was talking to Tommy Kruger, a patrol officer, and she looked to be in one piece.

Daisy pushed open her door.

Jonas's hand rested on her arm. "Easy," he advised. "You don't know the story yet."

She glanced over her shoulder at Jonas. "I know my daughter wasn't driving, and it's *my* car."

"I know. I'm just suggesting you don't scare Jazzi more than she is. From the looks of the accident, she could have been hurt."

"She still might be. That's why I have to get to her."

Suddenly, the medic unit drove up, its lights flashing. Now the whole area was lit up with the patrol car's strobe bar and the mobile unit's glaring beams. A sedan had driven up on the other side of Daisy's car, and it looked like a couple had gotten out. They went to another patrol officer who was speaking with Mark.

Daisy didn't want to talk about what had happened. She wanted to get to her daughter. She ran to Jazzi and put her hands on her daughter's shoulders.

Jazzi winced when Daisy gripped her right arm.

"Are you hurt?" Daisy asked.

"That's what the medic will find out, Daisy."

Daisy turned around to see Bart Cosner. "Oh, Bart. It's you. Tell me exactly what happened."

"It was a deer, Mom," Jazzi said with pleading in her eyes and in her voice. "Mark didn't want to hit it. We swerved, and that's where we landed."

Daisy's mind was already spinning. "So you were on the passenger side?"

"Yes."

"How did you get out?" The passenger side was the one in the ditch.

"Mark helped me climb out the other side, Mom. It wasn't hard."

Jazzi had white powder on her nose and cheeks. That would have come from the airbag. Daisy had heard of noses being broken by airbags opening, but Jazzi's nose looked okay.

"What hurts?" Daisy asked her daughter.

"I'm fine, Mom, really."

"What hurts, Jazzi?" she demanded in that mother's voice her daughter knew she couldn't evade.

"My arm. I think I have a brush burn on my face from the airbag. Crawling out, I banged up my knee on the steering wheel."

The paramedic came up to Jazzi. "You were in the accident?"

She nodded.

"Come over to the vehicle, and we'll look you over. Can you walk on your own?"

Jazzi nodded again.

Jonas had been standing back and observing. "I think Mark's parents are reading him the riot act from the way it sounds and looks. If he was hurt, Tommy would have brought him over here to the mobile unit."

"It was easier for him to climb out," Daisy said. "His airbag might not have gone off. But he had to get Jazzi out."

Daisy hurried to the medic who was with Jazzi as she sat inside the vehicle. The medic was dressed in blue scrubs and had a pleasant expression when he told Daisy, "Her vital signs are good. Her pressure and pulse are up a little, but that's understandable. She doesn't have any cuts, but I'm sure she'll have bruises in the morning. She's fortunate they were going the speed limit, which here is about twenty-five."

"It really was a deer, Mom. Honest."

"I believe you, honey. Accidents happen. But I do have one question. Why was Mark driving?"

Jazzi looked down at her espadrilles, then she gazed up at Daisy. "Mark said he'd never driven a PT Cruiser. He asked if he could drive it, and I said he could. I want him to like me, Mom."

At that, Daisy wondered if she'd done her parenting job correctly. She was supposed to be raising Jazzi to be an independent woman. She should be raising Jazzi to believe that a boy should like her just the way she was, not because she gave him something or she did something where she acted in a certain way. On the other hand, who didn't want to be liked?

The medic said to Jazzi, "I think you can go. When you get home, put ice on those bruises. Try to get a good night's sleep. A shake-up like this doesn't always go away overnight. Mom, I think you can keep her home from school tomorrow if you see fit. If she has any symptoms at all like nausea, pain in her body, or a headache, call nine-one-one or take her to urgent care."

Daisy nodded. They were going to have a long talk sometime—if not tonight, then tomorrow. But Jazzi had to know one thing. No matter if she wanted a boy to like her, she had to do what was right. She had to stand up for herself and what she believed in.

When Daisy's doorbell rang, she was happy to see Serena and Bellamy on her phone video monitor. Serena had finally returned her call, and they'd settled on a visit at Daisy's house today.

Jazzi had returned to school, though Daisy had advised her daughter to call her if being at school caused new symptoms to develop. Yesterday, Daisy had taken Jazzi to her family physician to be checked. After a thorough exam, the doctor had advised them to be watchful, but Jazzi could return to school.

"I'm so glad you could come over," Daisy said as she ushered Serena and her dog Bellamy into her house.

Felix looked up at Daisy as if asking if he could greet the visitor. After she said, "Go ahead," Felix went to Bellamy. They communicated nose-to-nose and then went into the kitchen to investigate Felix's bowl.

"She usually stays by my side," Serena said, as if she

were anxious about the fact that Bellamy had gone off with Felix.

"They'll be right back once they figure out Felix's bowl is empty. Would you like tea or coffee? Or something else?"

Serena looked uncertain, as if that were a big decision. Finally, she said, "Tea is fine."

"I made a batch of cranberry pecan scones this morning. Are you interested?"

Serena was still staring after Bellamy. "I don't know." Then she looked at Daisy as if she'd wakened to the fact that she was having tea with a friend. "I haven't had a treat lately. Scones would be great."

"You can pick out what kind of tea you like. I have several canisters for you to choose from."

Daisy had considered how to make Serena feel comfortable. Having tea, brewing it, smelling it, stirring sugar or honey into it, were among the best ways she knew. She was glad Serena had chosen tea for her drink.

Serena followed Daisy into the kitchen. "You're going to a lot of trouble."

"I brew tea at home when I want to relax. It isn't just for the tea garden. Appreciating tea is one of the reasons my aunt and I went into business together. I've always loved tea of all kinds. When I was small, Aunt Iris would invite me over, and we'd have tea together. It was a special time when I could confide in her, or simply tell her what was happening at school."

"That sounds nice." Serena examined the three canisters Daisy had set out on the counter. "My mother and grandmother often made tea at the farmhouse. The kettle was always on the stove, ready to turn on."

Daisy pointed to a red and orange paisley tin. "That's

Darjeeling with apple and vanilla." She pointed to the next one. "That's orange pekoe tea. That last one is oolong tea with a nutty taste."

"Let's go with the Darjeeling and apple." Serena checked on Bellamy, who was now sitting near Felix at the food bowl.

"I think they're trying to tell us something," Daisy said, as she turned on the burner to set the teapot boiling. Then she scooped teaspoons of tea into an infuser that dipped into a Sadler teapot decorated with tiny roses. "I have dog pretzel treats that I picked up at the farmers market. Is it okay if Bellamy has one?"

"Oh, sure," Serena agreed. "I've often bought Edith Armbruster's treats for Bellamy, either at the market or the pet store. She would gobble them all up at one time if she could."

Serena seemed more relaxed now, and Daisy was glad. She wanted this visit to be pleasant. She liked Serena a lot, and she was hoping they could become friends. "See that cookie jar over there?" Daisy pointed to a dog-faced ceramic jar in a corner of the counter. "That has the dog treats in it. Go ahead and take out two."

It seemed as if Serena was making herself more at home as she went to the jar with a smile and took out two pretzel treats.

Crossing to the two dogs, she addressed Bellamy first. "Sit," she said in command.

Bellamy sat, and Serena placed the treat on the floor in front of her. Then she did the same with Felix, and he obeyed, too.

Watching Daisy pour hot water over the tea in the porcelain teapot, Serena decided, "These are two of the sweetest dogs ever. Jonas is so lucky to have found Felix and Felix him."

"We think so, too." Daisy had a plate ready for the scones, and she removed four from a plastic container and set them on the dish. She positioned a large tray with hydrangea flowers painted all over the bottom on the counter and set the plate of scones on that.

"That's a beautiful tray," Serena said.

"It's an antique. I found it at Pirated Treasures, the antique shop on Sage Street. Vi works there part-time."

"I don't think I've ever been in there."

"Otis and a friend of ours, Keith Rebert, run it. It's changed in character over the last year or so. Less Gettysburg memorabilia and more antiques. Keith goes on buying trips through New England."

"I'll have to stop in. I'm still living at home on the farm, but soon I want to find my own place. Noah has already done that. I've always enjoyed the farm and all the animals. It will be hard to leave it." She looked at her dog. "But I'll have Bellamy with me."

A few minutes later, Daisy carried the tray into the living room. The dogs trotted happily behind and soon settled on the rug in front of the sofa. Daisy saw Marjoram and Pepper on the stair landing, peeking down through the slats.

"We have a viewing public," she said to Serena, motioning to the cats.

"How do they like Felix?" Serena asked.

"They tolerate him."

Serena actually laughed. "I've realized animals learn to get along together better than humans do."

"If we sit in here long enough, and the dogs don't

move around too much, Marjoram and Pepper might venture down."

Daisy moved forward on the sofa and poured two cups of tea. The cups were white porcelain with ruffled edges and floral valance-like arcs around the top of the teacups. Pretty green leaves decorated the bottom and the three feet on each cup that were trimmed in silver. They were vintage pieces.

Bellamy sat by Serena's legs, looking up at her adoringly. Serena patted her dog's head as she reached for the teacup. She and Daisy talked for a little while about Jazzi leaving home and going to college.

"I'm going to miss her desperately," Daisy said. "I'm trying not to let that show. I want her to feel that she can leave freely and follow a life of her own. But it's rough to think about and watch as she grows up."

"Do you think she'll come back to Willow Creek after college?"

"I have no idea. She's majoring in social work, and there will be lots of opportunities for that around this area. But she could meet someone at college, and that will take her in a different direction. That's what happened to me. I lived in Florida with my husband while the girls were growing up. After he died, I came back here, and it felt like home again."

Maybe because of Daisy sharing, Serena seemed completely at home as she put a scone on her napkin. She tore off a piece and popped it into her mouth. "These scones are delicious."

"Thank you. Baking is another of my stress-relieving outlets."

Thoughtfully, Serena looked down at Bellamy. "Bellamy is my therapy dog."

"Really?" Daisy was pleased that Serena felt free to share that.

Serena's eyes sparkled with memories as she confided, "Ever since I was a child running around the farm, I had a special dog. They were my constant companions. Back then, I didn't realize that I used them, in a sense, to calm me. If I had a rough day at school, I went to my dog when I came home. If something wasn't going right with a girl-friend, I hugged my dog. I had a mutt who looked like a mix between a schnauzer and a cocker with white ears and a black tail. His name was Boffo. I don't even re-member why, but in some ways, he seemed like a lifeline to the real world. Maybe it's because the farm set us apart in a way. It was a world all of its own. I was happy there. I found school and town and friends were a much harder world to navigate." Serena stopped and took another piece from her scone. "Boffo died when I was in college. I'd been away from dogs while I was there. I missed them and the goats and the chickens, but that was okay."

Shadows began crossing her face as she seemed to re-member those times again. Her eyes became sad, her mouth turned down, and her whole expression changed. She gave a little shrug. "After college, I began having anxiety attacks."

The silence prompted Daisy to ask a question that could coax Serena into sharing more. "Do you know what provoked the attacks?"

Serena looked down at her dog, not at Daisy, her shoulders tense. She bit her lower lip, and Daisy didn't know whether Serena was going to suppress or reveal any more of her history. She soon found out.

"No, I don't know what provoked them." Her voice was strong and firm, but Daisy knew a little about body language. Serena's shoulders were taut with tension, her hands clasped into fists. Body language told Daisy the woman wasn't being honest.

That fact was brought home when Serena changed the subject. "I wouldn't know what to do without Bellamy. I think that's why Noah is considering starting a mobile vet unit. He would travel to people's homes who can't get to his office. For instance, someone who has anxiety attacks and a pet might not venture into the office, even if the pet is sick. The same with elderly clients. I think it would be a great service if Noah started it. Now that the shelter is on its feet, he could."

Daisy could easily see that Serena didn't want to talk any more about her childhood or about her anxiety attacks. That was okay. Maybe if she needed a friend in the future, she would consider Daisy to be one. Daisy hoped that was true. Daisy also hoped that soon Serena could confront the origins of her anxiety. Was it just that Mr. Rumple's murder had taken place at Four Paws Shelter? Or was it something more serious than that?

Later that afternoon, Daisy was walking around her garden when she saw Gavin's car outside of the garage. At least, she thought it was Gavin's car. Maybe Vi had invited him for lunch. However, when she used the code to enter into the garage, she saw that Vi's car wasn't there. Neither was Foster's motor scooter.

She called up the stairs, "Gavin?"

"Hi, Daisy," he said from the top of the stairs. "Come on up. I'm babysitting Sammy. Vi wanted to go into Pirated Treasures for the day, and Foster asked me to babysit."

That was something they should talk about, too, Daisy thought, but she'd see how their conversation proceeded.

Still at the top of the stairs, Gavin opened the secure baby gate so she could go through. "I saw your car," she said. "I thought I'd check out if you were here."

In jeans and a windbreaker to take a walk, she felt a bit grubby. She'd merely secured her hair on top of her head.

"Your day off?" he asked. "I saw you had company when I arrived."

"I did. Serena Langston from Four Paws came over for a visit."

At eleven months, Sammy was almost walking. He crawled almost faster than her cats ran. He was sitting in front of the sofa, pushing a plastic dump truck across the floor. His brown hair was getting longer. Vi was talking about getting him his first haircut. Today, he was wearing red jean overalls and a red-and-white-striped long-sleeved T-shirt. His little feet were bare because he always pulled off his shoes and socks.

"I imagine the Langstons are still shaken up over what happened at Four Paws." Gavin secured the baby gate once more and went over to the sofa. Daisy followed him, and they sat on either side of Sammy.

The little boy looked up at Daisy and grinned, then pulled himself up by the sofa cushion and stood in front of her.

"Happy day to you too!" She picked him up and held him on her lap. He reached for the string on her windbreaker and pulled on it.

She laughed. "Are you trying to tell me to take my jacket off?"

Gavin asked her, "Would you like a cup of coffee? I just made some."

"Sounds good. Pretty soon I'll light the first fire of the season. Nothing's cozier than that."

"Does Jonas like fires, too?" Gavin asked with a wink.

She felt herself blush. "We all do, even the cats. I bet Felix will like to lie in front of it, too."

She gave Sammy another hug, and he wrapped his little arms around her neck. She loved holding him. She was going to miss not being able to drop over here whenever she could if Foster and Vi moved. Another change.

She was holding Sammy tight and looking around the small apartment when Gavin brought her a mug that said BEST SISTER EVER. It was one Jazzi had given to Vi last Christmas. It almost brought tears to Daisy's eyes.

Daisy looked down into the mug that had a slight amount of milk, just the way she liked it. Gavin had been around enough family gatherings to know how she drank her coffee. She knew he always appreciated his black.

"What are you thinking about?" he asked. "You look preoccupied."

"Too much to sort out, I'm afraid. Mainly, that life is one big succession of changes. At my age, you'd think I'd be used to it."

"I'm not sure we're ever used to change."

Sammy began squirming around in her lap, and she let him climb down to the floor. He crawled over to a wash basket that held many of his toys. With great glee, he caught one handle and dumped the whole basket.

Gavin chuckled. "When you can't decide, choose them all."

They both sipped on their coffee while they watched Sammy. Daisy thought about something that had been on her mind. "I want to tell you something, but I don't know if I should."

Gavin looked curious. "Now I'm intrigued."

"First let me ask you—Is Foster always the one who asks you to babysit?"

He thought about her question. "Usually . . . except on rare occasions. I remember one time Vi asked me. She wanted to go with you to a work frolic at Rachel and Levi Fisher's house. I think that was the last time."

"Do you have any idea why she doesn't ask you?" Daisy set down her mug on the coffee table, not knowing if she should be telling Gavin this, but feeling it was the best way to open communication. If he was aware of Violet's feelings, maybe he could help somehow.

"I just thought because I'm Foster's dad, it was easier for him to ask. Why? Is there another reason?"

Daisy bit her lower lip. "Because of her postpartum depression and because she *does* want to work, she's afraid you'll think she's a bad mother."

Gavin looked totally perplexed. "Why would I ever think that? I can't imagine what she went through with the birth and then the postpartum. She's incredibly strong for fighting her way out of that." He was thoughtful for a few moments. "I guess I've never told her that. When I'm around, we talk about Sammy, or I talk to Foster if he's there."

"That's only natural."

Gavin shrugged. "I see the way Jazzi interacts with Jonas. I'd like to have that kind of relationship with Vi. I know I could never take her father's place, but I want her to look on me that way. Do you know what I mean?"

"I do know what you mean. That's why I wanted you to be aware of how she feels. Maybe a conversation or two could help you feel more comfortable with her."

"Does Foster know how she feels? Because he should have told me if he does."

Sammy began making *baa-baa* noises with a stuffed sheep that he'd rescued from the mound of toys.

"She might not have confided that in him."

Gavin shook his head. "If we could all only just say what we think."

"No filter?" Daisy joked. "I'm not sure that would be the best way to communicate, either."

For a while, they talked about the possibility of Vi and Foster moving to Glorie Beck's house. Daisy told Gavin about the tea at the King's farm, and then she mentioned the bucket.

"I imagine lots of places use buckets like that, especially on farms," Gavin reminded her. "What does Jonas think?"

"He thinks the same thing you do. You're both right. I just wondered about it, that's all. It's an odd murder weapon."

"I've seen those buckets. They're heavy enough to crack a skull. I was never on the Rumple property, but I heard about his statues. Some are huge. I like the dog you gave Jonas. Maybe that will be on *your* porch soon."

"Maybe," Daisy said uncertainly.

Seeing that Daisy might be uncomfortable talking about her relationship with Jonas, and what might come next, Gavin skirted the topic. Instead, he continued their conversation about Rumple.

"I always thought Wilhelm Rumple's house was a unique one."

"It's really a cute little house," Daisy said. "But it was completely redone inside. It looked like the original fireplace was kept, but I don't know what else. Wilhelm said he made the millwork himself. It was well-crafted."

"I heard Wilhelm did *all* the work himself."

"Really? How is that possible?"

"He drew up the plans and secured all the permits he needed. Then he worked on it steadily. Word travels, even around the construction business. He called in a plumber to upgrade pipes and an electrician for the wiring. But he did the rest."

"He really was an odd man, wasn't he?" Daisy asked.

Gavin nodded with a grave expression lining his face. "Odd enough to get himself killed."

CHAPTER SIXTEEN

Daisy remembered the first time she'd met Marshall Thompson, a lawyer Jonas had recommended. Her aunt had been in a bit of trouble, and they'd gone to his office. Every time she saw Marshall, she thought about that office with its wood paneling, huge mahogany desk, and oil paintings of Lancaster County farms hanging on the walls. Everything about that office had been quality, just like Marshall himself.

On Friday morning, he was seated in the spillover tea-room with a copy of the *Willow Creek Messenger* on the table before him. He was sipping tea out of a vintage floral teacup but didn't look in the least bit out of place. Tall, at least six foot two, he had thick hair that was snow white and reminded her of classic movie stars from the forties. Today, he was wearing a navy suit that fit him impeccably with a pale blue shirt and a navy pinstripe tie. She approached him with a teapot ready to refill his cup and a plate with a cheese biscuit, a chicken salad triangle, and two snickerdoodles.

He looked up at Daisy, and his eyes widened when he saw the plate. "I don't think I ordered lunch," he said with some amusement.

"We feel indebted to you for all the times you've helped us or our friends."

"Does that mean Iris feels indebted too?" His eyes were twinkling when he asked.

"I don't know. You might have to ask her yourself."

"I might do just that. Word has it that she's free as the proverbial bird."

As Daisy refilled his teacup and set the plate down, she shook her head. "It's hard to believe that everyone cares about our personal lives."

"You and your staff circulate around the public. It's to be expected." He motioned to the fundraising thermometer plaque that was in her front window. "Your business is involved in the community, and you have a reputation for being a sleuth."

"Oh, no. Please do everything you can to squelch that idea."

He chuckled. "Do you have a couple of minutes? You can sit with me while I enjoy these goodies."

The tea garden had emptied out after the morning crowd had enjoyed their breakfasts. She pulled out a chair across from Marshall. "Sure, I can sit with you for a couple of minutes. Is anything particular on your mind?"

"I've heard the police are floundering on this case."

"Too many suspects or not enough?"

"Murky suspects, I think," Marshall said. "Lots of people didn't like Rumple, but I don't think the police can get to the reason why."

"I suppose you heard what happened here with Stanley King."

"Yes, I did. I can always write up an order of protection for you."

"I believe he was letting off steam and didn't know who else to blame."

"You give too many people the benefit of the doubt." Marshall shook his finger at her. "That's going to get you into trouble. You need to be more suspicious."

Daisy couldn't help but grin. "And shelve my idealism? Jonas calls it my Pollyanna attitude, but really, Marshall, you don't want me to suspect the worst of everyone, do you?"

"Seriously, Daisy." He lowered his voice. "What if Stanley King is the man who murdered Rumple? With a temper like his, I can see it happening. If he went after you, imagine if he was really mad at Rumple."

She considered what Marshall had said. "I suppose it's possible he could have gotten in the back door at the dog run, or Rumple could have let him in if he'd known he was coming. He was an investor in King's company, you know."

"I heard that. Still, I don't see why they would have been having a private meeting at the shelter."

"Rumple seemed to have the upper hand with King, at least that's the way he spoke *with* him and *about* him. He could have asked King to meet him there."

"So you believe it was a crime of passion?" Marshall picked up the cheese biscuit and took a bite.

"I believe that to hit someone with a bucket, it almost had to be, don't you think?"

Marshall nodded. "Those are my thoughts." He wiped his hands on the napkin. "Those cheese biscuits are excellent. I might have to take a few of those home with me."

"You can freeze them, too." She considered what she was going to say next. "I know you can't talk about your clients, but Serena Langston told me she consulted with you. I think she's holding something back. I know you can't share what, but do you think she was up-front with you?"

Marshall's face held a troubled expression. "I can't be sure, of course, but like with all my clients, I hope she's not holding back."

"I just hope whatever she's keeping secret isn't a motive for murder," Daisy said.

"So you do have suspicions."

"Not suspicions. I have concerns. Her anxiety is real. She's had a history of it."

Marshall arched his brows.

Daisy waved her hand at him. "I know, you can't talk about what she said. But she *has* spoken with me. I want to help her anyway I can."

Picking up a snickerdoodle, he waved it at her. "That's something else that gets you in trouble. Your willingness to help."

"It takes one to know one," she said succinctly, feeling as if she should shake her finger at him.

"We should form a club. I know several more people who should be in it."

When he finished his snickerdoodle, Daisy stood. "I'd

better get back to work. I have menus to plan, supplies to order, let alone bookwork I haven't finished."

"Doesn't Foster help you with that?"

"Mostly he helps with social media. He's been taking on more outside clients."

"So he can buy a car." Marshall was grinning.

Daisy raised a hand in surrender. "I give up. Everybody in the world knows our business."

"Is Iris very busy?"

"She's usually busy when she's in the kitchen," Daisy teased.

"I'd like to speak with her. Do you think she could take a short break?"

"For you, I'm sure she will. I'll stop in the kitchen on the way to my office."

Daisy was working in her office half an hour later when Iris peeked in. Her aunt's color was high as she entered and said, "Well, I didn't expect that."

"What happened?" Daisy asked, but she thought she knew.

"Marshall asked me out. We're going to have dinner next Wednesday at a restaurant that overlooks a golf course in York. I looked it up online, and it's pretty swanky. I'm going to have to buy a new dress."

"Besides the excitement of going someplace new and buying a dress, how do you feel about the idea of going out with Marshall?"

Iris sank down onto the chair in front of Daisy's desk. "I'm not sure. Isn't it too soon for me to date after Russ?"

Daisy kept a smile from creeping across her lips because she knew her aunt was serious.

"Do you feel as if you're on the rebound? That you're going out with Marshall simply because you broke up with Russ?"

"Russ dumped me," her aunt grumbled. "But, no, that's not the reason I'm going out with Marshall. I like Marshall. I just always felt he was . . . two steps above me."

"Explain." Daisy sat back in her chair.

"Do I really have to point out that he's a lawyer . . . and my schooling was limited?"

"Aunt Iris, you own a business."

"I know, and I did take a few courses at one of those satellite campuses. But I just don't know if I'm . . . sophisticated enough for him, let alone educated enough."

"You are one of the most well-read women I know. I'm sure if Marshall's asking you out, it's because he wants to get to know you better. You weren't this skittish when Russ asked you out the first time, were you?"

"No, but that was different."

"Why was it different?"

"Because I think from when I saw Marshall for the first time, I developed a little crush on him. It just seems unbelievable that he wants to date me."

"I think I'll have to go shopping with you to buy a dress that builds up your confidence. Maybe we can take our breaks together tomorrow and go to the Rainbow Flamingo. We'll make sure you look the best you can."

Iris got to her feet. "I think I'm going to have a spring in my step until my date."

As Aunt Iris left her office, all Daisy could do was smile.

* * *

The following evening was a bit brisk but without the bite of winter. No breeze rustled the leaves on the trees as Daisy and Jonas sat on the swing on her front porch Saturday evening. With his arm around her, Jonas used his foot to gently rock them back and forth.

"I heard a car park at the garage," Daisy said, with questioning in her voice.

"Not a motor scooter?" Jonas teased.

Foster's motor scooter was still the subject of a lot of discussions. Vi and Daisy both were worried about him riding it in the winter. The couple was looking for a used car that they could afford . . . that was in good condition. It wasn't an easy feat.

"I think they were both in for the night. Vi texted me before you arrived."

They heard footsteps on Daisy's front walk. To her surprise, Jazzi and Mark Constantine appeared. Mark, who was senior council president, was tall and lanky. His dark brown hair wasn't gelled tonight but fell across his brow. He was dressed in a hoodie of the school colors, orange and blue. His jeans and high-top sneakers weren't worn, and Daisy wondered if he'd dressed up for Jazzi tonight, and why they were here.

Jazzi was wearing her red and white color-blocked sweatshirt with her jeans. Her black hair flowed straight and loose over her shoulders. Her expression, as well as Mark's, was sober.

Stepping forward, Mark said, "Good evening, Mrs. Swanson, Mr. Groft."

Jazzi intervened, "Mom, Mark wants to talk to you about the accident."

Beside her, Daisy could feel Jonas tense as he stopped

the swing's motion. He started to rise, but she laid her hand on his arm to stop him. "No need for you to leave."

One of his dark brows quirked up. Up until now, she'd handled all of her family affairs on her own. But they were together now. No matter what came up, she wanted his opinion. He seemed to understand that as he relaxed again and leaned back on the swing.

Daisy hadn't seen Mark since the accident. She'd gotten his insurance information, and their insurance companies were negotiating. After all, he hadn't had permission to drive Daisy's car. The body shop and Jonas's mechanic had as much as told Daisy she needed to buy a new car. She'd been using her work van but knew she'd soon have to make a decision and go car shopping.

Mark took something from inside the pocket of his hoodie and held it out to Daisy. She could see that it was a check.

"What is this, Mark?"

"First of all, I want to apologize for the situation I put you and Jazzi in. I never should have asked her to drive your car. I'd never driven a PT Cruiser before, and thought it would be a cool idea."

Daisy attempted to hand the check back to him. "Mark, our insurance companies will be taking care of this."

He vehemently shook his head. "I want you to understand that I like your daughter, and I understand my responsibility in this. I bag groceries, and I'm going to pay you back for anything the insurance won't pay. I can give you my salary from the grocery store every month."

She knew that like Jazzi, Mark was worried about college costs and also the financial help he could accumulate. Scholarship money was probably on his horizon, as it was for Jazzi. But nothing was certain.

Again, Daisy attempted to hand him back the check. "My car was old, and I'm going to replace it. Thank you for taking responsibility. I appreciate it."

Mark looked her straight in the eye. "My guess is that if you were going to buy a new car, you might have given this one to Jazzi to drive. Now it's my fault she won't have one."

Daisy truly did appreciate this commitment on Mark's part. She knew the best thing she could do for him—his pride and sense of responsibility—was to accept the check. Folding it, she inserted it in her sweater pocket. "I think we should come to an agreement on just how much you should pay me back."

The teenager's Adam's apple bobbed as he swallowed hard. "Yes, ma'am."

Jazzi looked worriedly at Daisy, not sure what her mom was going to say.

"How about if we do this. Give me ten percent of your paycheck for the next three months. Then we'll call this even."

He started to sputter, "But that won't even begin to pay for a new car for you."

"*I'll* worry about me finding a new car. You just concern yourself with driving safely, especially if you're with my daughter."

He almost looked as if he was about to lose the emotion he held inside. Then composing himself, he blurted out, "Jazzi told me you'd be fair. I didn't expect you to be *this* fair."

Jonas spoke now for the first time. "Daisy and I think the world of Jazzi. We just want to know that when she's with you, you'll be careful, and she'll be safe."

"I will be careful, sir. I promise." He took Jazzi's hand. "I'll take special care of her."

Jonas gave Mark one of those man-to-boy looks that said he had better take care of her, or he'd have to answer to Jonas. too.

"I'm going to walk Mark down to the garage," Jazzi said. "Then I'll be back."

Considering the fact that Jazzi would be making Mark part of their lives, Daisy made an offer. "I know you might have plans, but I have whoopie pies and hot chocolate inside if you care to join us."

Obviously pleased, Mark gave Jazzi a smile that said that was exactly what he wanted.

"Is it okay if we go inside and start a fire?" Jazzi asked. "There's enough wood and kindling fireside."

"Sure," Daisy agreed, "go ahead. We'll be in in a few minutes."

After the young couple went inside, Jonas asked Daisy, "How long are you going to let them in there alone?"

"Only as much time as it takes to build a fire in the fireplace, nowhere else."

Jonas laughed. "He seems like a nice kid."

"He does, but I want to get to know him better if he's going to be around Jazzi. This will give us a chance to get started."

"Are you playing on their guilt?"

"Just a little. Hanging around with us older folks isn't what they have in mind for an evening, I wouldn't imagine. It will be good for Jazzi to have someone else to talk to and confide in. She has friends, but with Brielle tied up with the new house decisions and taking care of Glorie in between her schoolwork, Jazzi isn't seeing her as much."

"The holidays always mean more if you have someone special around." Jonas's gaze was loving as he said it, and his hand took hold of hers.

Daisy hoped this holiday season would be the happiest that she'd experienced in years.

On Sunday afternoon, Daisy decided to use her free day to pick up cat food at Fur and Feathers. Like many felines, her two were particular. While she was at the pet store, she would buy more treats for Felix, too.

After entering the store, Daisy lifted up one of the royal blue baskets stacked beside the door. She wouldn't need a cart today, since she wasn't buying dog food for Felix. Jonas usually handled the twenty-five-pound bags and the canned food that Felix liked. Daisy was considering cooking Felix food as Edith had suggested.

Today, Edith Armbruster was standing at the pet snacks counter. She waved to Daisy. "Did you try any of those recipes I gave you?" Edith asked, as if she'd read Daisy's mind.

"Not yet. But Felix certainly liked your treats. I see these are the same ones you had at the farmers market."

"Yes, they are. Once in a while I add a new one, but to make them in any quantity, I like to be consistent. The peanut butter and bacon ones always seem to go first, so I make the most of those."

"I'll take three of the dog donuts and two of the ginger pumpkin biscuits."

As Edith bagged those, she said, "I'm afraid you'll have to pay for these separately from the other things you buy here. That's the way I work it with the owner."

"No problem," Daisy said, taking bills from her wallet

purse that she'd dropped into her basket. After she paid Edith and said goodbye, she walked down the main aisle to the pet foods.

When she turned into that row, she stopped cold. Andrew King was standing there, studying the bags of dog food. She was going to ignore him and go look at the pet toys in the next aisle when he spotted her. She was afraid that Andrew was going to accost her like his father had, in spite of what Caroline had said.

However, Andrew called her name. "Daisy?" It had a question mark at the end, as if he was expecting her to run the other way.

Andrew's expression was neutral, his voice . . . polite. "I've needed to talk to you," he said. "But I didn't know if you'd talk to me."

Daisy thought her best course of action was just to stay silent.

Andrew took a few steps closer to her. "I want to apologize to you for my dad. I heard about what happened at the tea garden. I'm so sorry he stormed in like that. All of his reactions lately just seem to be over the top."

Daisy felt her shoulders relax, and relief flooded through her. "I know being questioned by the police is a fearful experience. I'm sorry if I had anything to do with that. But Detective Rappaport and I are honest with each other. I had to tell him what I saw and heard."

"Do you know any more about the investigation than they're telling the rest of us?" Andrew asked.

"I honestly don't," Daisy said. "Are you afraid your dad will be called in again?"

"I'm afraid of more than that. A judge authorized a search warrant to search our grounds. The police concentrated on the stables. Something about a bucket."

Daisy didn't comment on that because that search might have been her fault, too. "Did they find what they were looking for?"

"They took away a few buckets. What did they think, that my dad would leave one out in the open if he'd used it to kill Mr. Rumple? How stupid would that be?"

Often Detective Rappaport had told her, and Jonas, too, that criminals didn't always do the smartest things. Andrew looked so worried, and he was being so honest, that Daisy inquired gently, "You don't think he was involved, do you?"

"I don't know what to think. I truly don't. But I've found out some things in the past few weeks." He shook his head, and his lips thinned as he pressed them together, as if that could keep him from saying more.

"Andrew, I've heard about the pet supplements," Daisy revealed.

Andrew's eyes widened. "I suppose the news will get out all over town, let alone past Willow Creek. Dad was taking shortcuts with his products. I never realized he would do that. He deals with the Chinese on the supplements, and he delegates business matters too freely in areas I know nothing about. I mostly take care of running the farm and raising the horses. We have a good business training and selling them for riding. But now I feel like I have to look into what Dad's been doing. I just want to concentrate on my wedding, not my father's business practices."

Daisy didn't want to ask if the King farm and King's business were in financial trouble. That was pushing their conversation a little too far. But if it was, she wondered if that had anything to do with Wilhelm Rumple's murder.

CHAPTER SEVENTEEN

Sometimes Daisy went bike riding early in the morning for the exercise. On rare occasions, like today, Jazzi joined her. Her daughter seemed to have recovered completely from the accident.

In the garage, Daisy and Jazzi pulled their bikes from the bike rack that Jonas had installed there. Daisy's bike was rose gold, twenty-four inches with enough gears for her to handle competently. Jonas's bike was silver, twenty-six inches, with enough wires on the handlebars to make it overly complicated for her. Jazzi carefully lifted her bike off the rack. It was a blue and purple Schwinn. They walked their bikes down the driveway to the road just as the sun's hot ball was peeking up over the horizon. As they mounted and rode, the sky was pierced with vibrant oranges and pinks that heralded the new day.

They rode silently at first because Daisy knew sometimes it took Jazzi a while to wake up. Her daughter went through the motions until she was fully cognizant. Instead of heading toward town, they turned in the opposite direction, the route Daisy usually took when riding with Jazzi or Jonas. This time of the morning, they might encounter a horse and buggy, but not much else. They pedaled side by side unless they heard a vehicle approaching behind them.

Finally, Jazzi said, "Thanks for the way you handled Mark the other night."

They'd been busy since Saturday night, and she and Jazzi hadn't talked about it. Mark's visit with them had been friendly and fun. Daisy had to admit she liked him. "I like Mark. He was being responsible about what happened. That put him in the plus column in my eyes."

"It's not easy for him to give up part of his paycheck, but that's what he wanted to do. Like he told you, his family's ordinary. His dad does ceramic tile work in bathrooms and kitchens. It's possible Gavin might have even worked with him at some point. His mom's a receptionist for a dentist."

Daisy hadn't wanted to question the teenager too much, so she was thankful Jazzi was supplying some of his background.

"No brothers or sisters?" Daisy asked.

"Nope, and that's probably why he's as independent and self-starting as he is. Last year, I wrote an essay on child order in families. Do you remember that?"

"I do. You're probably right."

They rode along in companionable silence until Daisy felt the side glance that Jazzi gave her.

"What?" Daisy asked, knowing that look from her

daughter. It meant she was thinking about something and didn't know if she should mention it.

"I've been wanting to ask you a question," Jazzi said.

In the few moments of silence that followed Jazzi's statement, Daisy could hear the *clip, clop* of a horse's hooves. The sound was a background noise.

Daisy suggested, "Let's slow up. Then the buggy can pass us."

Rachel's district allowed their faith-goers to ride in automobiles, buses, and trains when necessary. That meant using a driver when distance prohibited using a buggy. Cars were for utilitarian use only. They believed if a person owned a car, they were more likely to go outside of their culture and their faith, and their interactions with Englischers could prevent their community from staying wholly dedicated to God, their faith, and family. Buggies traveled about five to six miles per hour, and because the Amish used them, the keepers of the faith believed their people would most likely stay close to their family and community.

Buggies once made of wood were now fiberglass, and in Lancaster County, the most common color of the top of the buggy was gray. The buggy coming up behind them was powered by a beautiful chestnut horse. Glancing over her shoulder again, Daisy could see that this buggy was a family wagon that could carry five or six family members. Daisy waved as the buggy passed them. Two adults and three children were seated inside. She could see that this one had sliding doors and windows that could open. The windows were open, and the woman waved as the carriage went by.

Jazzi smiled and waved too.

When Daisy had returned to Willow Creek with her

girls from Florida, they had marveled at this different way of life. But Jazzi and Vi had both settled into the more relaxed pace and soon had accepted Amish life as a big part of the way their mom had grown up. They, of course, didn't want to be without electricity, cell phones, or eventually cars. But they'd soon come to understand the philosophy of not having these. Now their lives seemed to be divided between old cultures and new, old friends and new, old ideas and new.

Once the buggy was ahead of them, they picked up speed again, pedaling more leisurely in its wake.

Daisy asked her daughter, "What did you want to ask me?"

Jazzi didn't hesitate now. "When are you and Jonas going to move in together? If you think I'd mind, I wouldn't. Don't hold back because of me."

Daisy felt speechless for a moment, then embarrassed, and then a bit amused. Speaking of new ideas, this was one that Jazzi was apparently embracing. And the truth was, Daisy didn't know how to answer her daughter. She fully believed a committed relationship should evolve into marriage. But how committed and when? At what point was there no turning back? Vows or before that? Should a woman make sure about everything before marriage? Or should trust be the hugest component? If two people loved each other, everything would work out for the best, wouldn't it? She still had so many questions, and she imagined Jonas did, too.

This wasn't just about what she and Jonas did. The situation was also about modeling behavior for her daughters. Just how much did that come into play? Where did happiness fit in? Where did passion fit in? Where did need and practicality fit in? In a way, she wanted to throw up her hands and tell Jazzi it was too complicated to discuss. Yet she'd never done that, and she shouldn't start now.

"Do you know what I believe?" she asked her daughter.

Jazzi pedaled a couple more times. "I think I do. In my case, you'd want me to meet the right guy, date him a year with background checks, meet all of his family, be engaged another year, and not have sex until we're married."

Daisy didn't know whether to laugh or scream. "And what do *you* believe?"

"I'm not sure yet. I know Vi did it all wrong, even though it seems to be turning out right. And me, well, it could be a bit of a trust issue. I figured that out in my sessions with Tara."

Tara had been a psychologist Jazzi had seen when she'd first found her birth mother. Confused, Jazzi had acted out by getting drunk. Daisy had wanted to nip that behavior in the bud. Tara and her cat named Lancelot had been recommended to Daisy by the high school guidance counselor. Jazzi's sessions had been positive and seemed to balance Jazzi's world again.

"Trust issues because you'd been abandoned?"

"Yeah, and also because Dad died. How can I trust that won't happen to somebody else I love? And then there was Colton. I mean, he didn't like me when he first met me."

Colton, Jazzi's birth mother's husband, hadn't known his wife had given up a baby for adoption. It had taken him a while to adjust to the situation, too. "It wasn't that Colton didn't like you. He didn't like the changes in his life."

"I know. If you think what Jonas and you do will affect me eventually, I guess maybe it will. But I think I'm old enough to realize I'm not going to rush into anything. I'm also old enough to know about birth control and what a woman should expect from a man. And none of that at this moment has to do with you and Jonas. What's holding you two back?"

Daisy felt her breath hitch as she thought about it. And that wasn't only from bike riding while she was talking. Physical exertion couldn't prevent her thoughts from running rampant. "I don't know if Jonas is ready to move in with me."

"Because it's your house and your life?"

Wow. Jazzi was more perceptive than Daisy gave her credit for.

"Partly." In a way, she sensed that they were both tired of taking their relationship slow. If they were unsettled by that, wouldn't it affect the way they felt about each other?

"You know, don't you," Jazzi said with obvious exasperation in her tone, "that we're in the twenty-first century. You could ask Jonas to move in. You don't have to wait for him to tell you he wants to."

Was any parent ever ready for a conversation like this? Daisy had always navigated parenthood under the assumption that she was the mom. She was the authority. She was not her daughters' best friend. But now, with Vi and Jazzi becoming more mature, that was changing, too.

Daisy continued to think about her answer to Jazzi's question. Why wait?

They rode up over a small rise, pedaling past a pine forest, until Daisy noted Rumple's Statuary about fifty yards away. However, she didn't just notice Rumple's property. A man was parked in front of it, standing by his car yet looking at the cottage. As Daisy closed the distance, she could see that the man with a baseball cap, flannel shirt, and jeans was Clancy Miller. They couldn't just ride by. That would be rude.

She said to Jazzi, "Let's stop for a minute." Seeing the look in her daughter's eyes, she added, "I know you have to get back in time to dress for school. Just a couple of minutes. I promise."

Jazzi slowed her bike alongside Daisy's. Mr. Miller, who was standing at the edge of the grass at the property, looked their way.

Daisy rode her bike up to his car and then slipped off her seat. "Hello, Mr. Miller. How are you? I had a chance to talk to Caroline at the fundraising tea at the King farm. She looks so happy."

"*That* she is," he said, adjusting his ball cap.

Daisy introduced her daughter.

He pointed to Jazzi. "I've seen you in the store a few times. You come in with your sister, Vi. She likes my croissants."

Jazzi grinned. "Yes, she does, and I do, too. Mom doesn't make those."

He chuckled, then looked back at the house. "I should be at the bakery. I guess you're wondering what I'm doing here."

"That's your business," Daisy said honestly, but she was open to listening if he wanted to talk.

"I was driving by, and I'm just surprised a FOR SALE sign isn't in the yard yet. You'd think all that would be getting settled. The nephew's the only heir."

Daisy supposed that was public knowledge. "Are you thinking about buying it?"

He gave a shrug. "Actually, I was thinking it would be

nice for Caroline and Andrew so they didn't have to live on the King estate."

In-law trouble already? Daisy wondered. Did the Kings and Mr. Miller not see eye-to-eye? Or did he just want his daughter to make her mind up about the life she wanted and not just fit into the King's lifestyle?

Clancy took another look at the cottage and then added, "On the other hand, it's probably not fine enough for them. I imagine Caroline might like it, but I don't know about Andrew."

Would Mr. and Mrs. Andrew King think about moving into a cottage like this? More importantly, was the sale of the cottage with Andrew and Caroline in mind the real reason Clancy was gazing at it now?

Since Iris was closing up the tea garden today, Daisy decided to go out the front entrance and down Market Street to Jonas's store. She was on her way out when she spotted Andrew walking toward her with Duchess. As soon as the dog saw Daisy, she pranced and stretched toward her, sniffing all around her feet.

Andrew said, "Heel," in a commanding voice, but the dog didn't. Her ears flopped as she continued to smell Daisy's legs and then put her paws up on Daisy's knee.

Andrew said again, "Duchess, down," but the dog didn't listen.

He scooped her up and held her in his arms. "It's obvious she's going to need schooling," he admitted with a shake of his head. "We just haven't made arrangements yet. I'm not sure which of us will take her, me or Caroline."

"If you find an evening class, maybe you both can go.

MURDER WITH DARJEELING TEA

Then you'll know what she learns and can back each other up, just like with a child."

Andrew's smile was accepting of the idea. "I never thought of that, but you're right. That probably would be the best thing to do, unless Caroline can get away from her dad's shop for a couple of hours in the afternoon. My schedule isn't as flexible."

"I saw Clancy this morning."

"You mean in the shop?" Andrew asked, looking curious.

"No. I was bike riding with Jazzi, and we saw him standing in front of Rumple's cottage."

"The Mr. Rumple that was killed?"

"Yes, that's the one."

"Did he say what he was doing there?" Andrew wanted to know.

"He said he was looking at the cottage, thinking about if you and Caroline might want to live there if they put it up for sale."

Andrew rubbed Duchess more vigorously. "I don't know how he got that idea. What do you think about the cottage?" Andrew asked. "We haven't started looking yet. I wonder how much land it has. Caroline said she's always wanted to have goats."

Daisy had to smile. "I don't know how much land stretches out behind the house. It certainly has a big yard, and it might even be larger than I expect. Would you consider living there?"

"You mean would we live somewhere that small after living on the grand King estate?"

Daisy felt herself blush. "I didn't exactly mean it that way. I'm sorry."

"No need to apologize. I understand. I think Caroline

and I would like to start out in a small place. It depends if there would be room if we want to have a family. There's no reason I shouldn't take a look, though, when it goes up for sale. Actually, I was hoping to run into you sometime soon. I spoke with my father this week about him coming into the tea garden the way he did."

"I'm sure he didn't appreciate that," Daisy said.

"No, he doesn't like to be questioned about anything. But he did admit he shouldn't have come barging in the way he did. You might expect an apology soon. I don't know, but I just wanted to tell you. He's not going to bother you like that again."

Daisy looked up at Duchess. She gave a little *yip*. It was obvious what she would like. Daisy stepped a little closer to Andrew and petted the pup. "She really is a darling."

"Even my mom loves her now. She gives her the run of the house, which isn't always a good thing. Duchess does better in confined spaces, if you know what I mean."

Daisy laughed. "Yes, I know what you mean. But I bet she's a smart little girl and will learn quickly, especially if you're consistent with her."

"That's what Serena Langston says . . . that consistency is the key."

"Have you been to Four Paws to see Serena since you adopted Duchess?" Daisy couldn't help but ask the question.

"I stopped in briefly to talk to her about my dad's regular supply of vitamins, not the ones for shelters. They stopped using everything of his, but I think I convinced her the regular ones are safe."

"My guess is that Serena would have to see some proof."

Andrew looked surprised at that. "You mean she won't just take my word?"

"Not after some of her dogs were made sick. I know the line's not the same, but animal lovers are fiercely protective."

Andrew looked down at Duchess, took one of her ears into his hand, and fingered it gently. "I suppose that's true . . . very much like kids."

"Wouldn't you say your horses are like big kids?"

Andrew gave a shrug and a wry smile. "Billy has more to do with them than I do. He does care, though, as you said. He watches every pattern of their hooves, the look in their eyes, the swish of their tails. I guess I never realized that before."

Duchess began squiggling in Andrew's arms, just like a baby might. He seemed to patiently accept the fact that she had a personality of her own, and he was going to have to learn to deal with her in the best way possible. He sat her on the ground, and she wound her leash around his leg.

Laughing, he unwound himself. "I better be going."

Daisy waved as he walked down the street and away from the tea garden. She, on the other hand, headed to Woods.

She passed Wisps and Wicks. Betty Furhman was standing in the window, arranging her handmade candles that had beautiful natural scents. She waved when she saw Daisy. Next, Daisy passed an insurance office and a store that sold hand-sewn purses and travel bags in colorful prints—flowers, plaids, and even animals. When the weather was nice, the shopkeeper put a display rack outside so that anybody passing by could see their quality. The store, Pretty Things, also sold a selection of suncatchers that gleamed with blue, gold, and red glass in the window.

Arden Botterill's shop, Vinegar and Spice, was next in the line. The tea garden bought flavored vinegars, olive oils, and various spices from Arden. She and Arden had had a go-around about PR on the homeless shelter not so long ago. But that hadn't affected them doing business together.

Offices for an accountant and a lawyer with rentals available on the second and third floors didn't catch her attention. But Woods did.

Jonas had rearranged the front window again. Maybe he'd sold the pieces that had been highlighted there. A blue, distressed farmhouse jelly cupboard stood front and center. Beside it sat a dark pine cobbler's bench that gleamed in the rays of sunlight. Those two pieces were accompanied by a reclaimed wood dry sink with a black granite counter. All three pieces were stars in the furniture realm and showcased beautifully what Woods carried inside. The large, white ironstone porcelain pitcher and washbasin bowl in the indented portion of the dry sink reflected what early Americans used it for.

After Daisy opened the door to Woods and stepped inside, she expected to see Jonas or Elijah either conversing or helping with customers. Instead, however, she spotted Elijah and heard him arguing with another Amish man. She heard Elijah warn, "You have to tell what you know."

The two men were so involved in their discussion that they hadn't seen Daisy walk in. Now they noticed her. They both looked awkward. Whomever Elijah was speaking with had a beard and black felt hat similar to his. They both looked as if they had been caught in a discussion they shouldn't be having here. The man Elijah had been speaking with raised a hand in farewell and darted past Daisy and out the door.

With his face reddened, Elijah regained his composure. "Hello, Daisy. I'm sorry my cousin Zebediah was so rude. He's not usually like that."

"He seemed upset about something."

"Zebediah is a farrier. I think a horse must have stepped on his foot recently, or kicked him somewhere else." Elijah tapped the side of his head. "He's not thinking clear."

Daisy could easily see that Elijah was upset about his cousin. "Is there anything I can do to help?"

After looking as if he might answer her, Elijah blew out a breath. "No, Daisy, but thank you for asking. I can't talk about it with anyone. Zebediah has to come to terms with his past."

Daisy couldn't imagine exactly what that meant.

Two hours later, Jonas stood at Daisy's stove where a large Dutch oven sat on the burner. "This is one of the recipes that Edith gave you that seemed to be the easiest to cook. It makes enough that Felix could have several meals from it."

"Edith said not to switch to food like this all at once. When it's cooked, we can mix it with his kibble or even mix some with his wet food. We don't want him to have digestive problems."

At her island, Daisy spent a few moments simply appreciating Jonas in her kitchen. In his black T-shirt and indigo jeans, he looked at home. She liked having him here . . . in her life . . . and in her house. "Are you sure you don't want an apron?" she joked.

"Do you think I need one?" he asked with a mock scowl. "I'm a very neat cooker."

"I think the word you want is *chef*."

"For dog food," he said wryly. "That would be great on my résumé."

He'd placed cups of water in the Dutch oven. He opened a package of ground turkey that Daisy had bought from a butcher and dumped that into the pot.

"These ingredients are easy to have on hand," Daisy noted. "I raised the dried rosemary."

"Yeah, I was kind of surprised that was in the recipe. But why not, right?"

They'd had all the ingredients ready to go. Next, he poured in the brown rice.

Going to the freezer, Daisy removed frozen broccoli, frozen carrots, and frozen cauliflower. It was a combination pack that worked well for this. She snipped open the top with scissors and then poured half of the package into a bowl on the counter. Saving the rest for another time, she put a twisty on the package and then put it into a zip-lock bag to keep it fresh, stowing it back into the freezer. "What would *you* like to eat tonight?"

"This needs to come to a boil and then simmer for about twenty-five minutes. After that, we add the frozen vegetables and cook another five to ten minutes. It will have to cool before we give it to Felix."

"So what are you hungry for?" she asked again. "I have leftover chicken. I can make chicken chili. We can have cheese biscuits with it."

"And a salad?" he asked.

"That sounds good." Going to the refrigerator, she removed the container with the leftover chicken.

After the dog food was set to simmer and chili slow-cooked in a Dutch oven, Daisy stood at the counter, making dough for the biscuits.

"Do you want me to help?" Jonas asked.

"No. Why don't you make a pot of tea? We can have that while we wait for the dog food to cook."

"Will Jazzi be here for supper tonight?" Jonas asked.

"No, she's staying overnight with Brielle. Something about using her laptop and an app to do a computer simulation for Brielle's room at the new house. I think Brielle's excited about it."

"That's good. I'm sure they'll enjoy working with Gavin."

After the biscuits were baking in the oven, Daisy sat with Jonas at the island. He'd poured cups of tea for the two of them. From her cupboard, he'd chosen a transferware scalloped cup and saucer set. They'd been crafted in England by Jones, George & Sons. They were a beautiful blue, and she had a jelly jar to go with them. She sat beside Jonas, and her arm brushed his as she leaned forward to pick up her teacup.

He looked at her as if he wanted to kiss her, but instead he said, "Tell me again what Elijah said to Zebediah."

"I couldn't hear most of it, but I did hear one thing loud and clear. Elijah told him, *You have to tell what you know.*"

Jonas shook his head. "I don't understand. I suppose it could be about anything."

"I believe Elijah was on the verge of telling me what it was about, but then he decided not to. And you know how the Amish hate gossip. They think it's a sin. When Elijah said that Zebediah has to come to terms with his past, it felt like something personal. Elijah knows what it is, but I have a feeling not many people do."

"So you think it's a secret Elijah is keeping for Zebediah?"

"It could be. Or a personal problem that Elijah wants to keep in the family."

The timer Jonas had set went off. He stood, crossed to the Dutch oven again, gave the mixture a stir, and then raised his brows at Daisy. "It seems done to me. I'll just take the lid off and let it cool."

As soon as Jonas took the lid off the Dutch oven, Felix came trotting in from the living room, where he had been snoozing with the cats. Standing before the stove, he lifted his nose and sniffed.

Jonas asked, "How do you think it smells, Felix?"

The dog gave a bark.

"We have to let it cool and then you can try it." Jonas stirred the mixture again and took it from the burner. Felix went to Daisy and sat beside her. She petted his head.

Jonas crossed one foot over the other and leaned against the counter. "You know you have to decide soon whether you're going to get a new car or get the PT Cruiser fixed. They're calling it totaled, but that's because it's old."

Daisy had been thinking about this dilemma since the night of Jazzi's accident. "I think I'd like to buy something new. Well, not new, but pre-owned. There's no reason I need a new car. I just want something solid and safe to use to drive Jazzi to college, wherever she goes."

"Do you know where you want to look?"

"I know exactly where I want to look. Wilhelm Rumple's brother is a used car salesman. York will be the perfect place to shop."

CHAPTER EIGHTEEN

Herman Rumple's pre-owned vehicle lot was located at the east end of York near the Galleria Mall. As Daisy and Jonas drove there, she was excited about more than one thing. First, about having a car again. She'd purchased her purple PT Cruiser in Florida. It had been a good car, but now, all these years later, even without the accident, it needed more work than she was willing to put into it. If it could be fixed for Jazzi, and only if it could be repaired safely, would she consider letting her use it. Maybe Jazzi and Foster could share it. Daisy needed something reliable to haul people, tea supplies, and sometimes a dog."

Do you have anything special in mind?" Jonas asked her.

"You mean the perfect car that I've always wanted?"

He glanced at her with a raised brow. "I don't think you dream about cars."

"You're right, I don't. But I am concerned with color, comfort, and how much it will carry."

"You want a specific color?"

"Nope. But I don't want red, white, or black."

Jonas laughed. "I think you're in luck. Colors in cars are a trend."

"I do want something pre-owned. I'm not going to spend money I don't have and pay money to a bank again."

"Are you willing to haggle?"

"That depends. Let's just see what kind of a sales-person Herman Rumple is."

"And you know he's working this evening."

"He is. I called to check. We should be getting here when his supper break is over."

"Who did you talk to?"

"A friendly receptionist. She was very informative."

Stealing another look at Daisy, Jonas grinned. "I still think you should be one of Rappaport's investigators. You coax more information out of people than he does, and he knows it."

"Is that why he's so grumpy with me?"

"He's grumpy with you because he likes you. He's be-ginning to look at you as a fond niece or even a daughter. He left his family behind, though I don't know why. I'm glad he's finally making friends in Willow Creek."

As they arrived at Colonial Motors, Daisy could see Rumple's pre-owned car lot was like most other car lots she'd been to. In the area in front of the building were spaces for customers to park. On the right side stood garages. Over to the left was a whole area with sparkly, shiny, clean vehicles.

Jonas pulled into one of the customer spots. "Do you think you can trust a car salesman you've just met?"

"I hope so. I checked his reviews. He has good ones. Oh, a couple of people complained, but you always have that with reviews. Most consider him honest and fair. What more can I ask?"

"And you want to bring your car up here to be serviced?"

"It's not that far, really. I can always walk to the shopping center."

"All right, then. Let's do this."

Jonas exited the driver's side at the same time Daisy exited the passenger side. They met on the sidewalk. Before they even set foot in the showroom, Herman Rumple came out to greet them. She'd intended to ask for him, but now she could let things proceed naturally.

From Herman Rumple's picture on the website, she'd realized he looked nothing like his brother. He was tall and slim, handsome with a pleasant face. He had russet-brown hair parted to the side, a long nose, and cheekbones that were a little sunken. Dressed in a suit and tie, he looked crisp, even though it was the end of the day. He shook hands with them as they all introduced themselves.

Daisy decided she didn't want to start out with a false façade. She explained, "We're from Willow Creek."

Jonas said, "I volunteered at the shelter where your brother was killed. We're so sorry."

Herman's face was totally impassive. Daisy could find no grief on it, nor any other emotion. "I spoke with your son at Mr. Rumple's funeral. I also met Hans, your brother's dog. It looks like he and Dustan are going to make a good match."

"Dustan loves dogs, almost as much as Wilhelm did," Herman stated factually. "Did Dustan know you needed a car?"

"Not exactly. But he did tell me you sold pre-owned cars. My daughter was in an accident recently in my car. The insurance company says it's totaled. I'm still trying to decide whether I'm going to have it repaired or not. Even if I do, I'm looking for a new vehicle."

She told him what she was looking for, the same way she'd told Jonas.

Herman thought about it and then said, "Let me go inside and get the key fobs. There are a few vehicles I think you might like."

After Herman had gone inside, Jonas asked Daisy, "What do you think?"

"Too soon to tell. We'll have to look at some cars, and I'll see if he's a slick salesman or if he's really trying to sell me what I need."

Half an hour later, Daisy had examined three different cars. She'd kind of settled on a blue Journey with low mileage. It seemed perfect for what she wanted. While she examined the hood, she heard Jonas and Herman at the back. Jonas somehow had gotten him talking about his brother.

She heard Herman say, "My brother and I were very different."

Daisy came around the side of the vehicle and stood there, listening.

"You know, when someone believes something, and you can't convince them otherwise?" Herman asked.

Jonas nodded. "I'm a former detective. I've seen it all. So, yes, I know exactly what you're talking about."

When Daisy peeked around the car, she saw that Herman looked dejected. "Wilhelm always felt that me and our parents looked down on him, because he was short, and his features were very different from ours. The doctor explained genes mutate, and anything can happen. I really know so little about all that. But I think Wilhelm always felt like an outsider. He almost felt like he'd been adopted and was a different strain from the rest of us. But he was wrong. No one could tell him so, though."

"Once a kid has an idea in his head, it's hard to shake it out," Jonas suggested. "I worked with teenagers in Philadelphia when I was on the force. It was hard to convince them that they could find a new life. They had to believe it. They had to leave their old friends behind."

"Yeah, and what makes it worse is our father left. When he did, Wilhelm blamed himself. I never thought of blaming myself. I always thought Mom and Dad had problems, and it's just the way it was. But not Wilhelm. He lacked self-confidence. I tried to help him, but I never could."

Since she'd been listening, Daisy didn't pretend that she hadn't been. Joining the men, she said, "I suppose you and your brother pursued different interests."

"Oh, we did," Herman readily agreed. "I liked sports, but Wilhelm . . . he was the studious one. All he wanted to do was to be on his computer playing video games. But what really did it—" Herman shook his head. "You don't want to hear about my old stuff."

"The truth is," Daisy said, "we'd like to learn more about your brother. Now and then, I help the police collect information. I'm not sure they have a direction on this investigation. Anything that you could tell us might help."

"I talked with them," Herman admitted. "But they didn't seem to want to know history. They wanted to know things like when I saw my brother last, if we'd argued recently, what was his relationship with me and my son. I told them the truth. We didn't have a relationship."

"Did they ask why?" Jonas obviously wanted to know.

"No. Not the specifics. The detective I spoke with was more interested in filling in a timeline before Wilhelm was killed." Herman studied Daisy for a few moments, then revealed, "Wilhelm and I went our separate ways when he hacked into my credit card account and ran up purchases on it. And then, when my mother died, he wouldn't help with any of the funeral expenses. That was the last straw. That was it. We didn't speak afterwards. Once trust is broken, what's the point of having a relationship when you know nothing is ever going to change?"

"It *is* hard for people to change," Jonas admitted. He looked at Daisy and reached across to hold her hand.

"Thank you for telling us what you did," she said.

Herman patted the rear of the car that Daisy had been examining. She knew his conversation with them about his brother was over.

Jonas knew it, too. He asked Daisy, "What do you think?"

"I think I want to drive this car. Can I take it out?" she asked Herman.

"That's what I'm here for. Come inside, and I'll make a copy of your license. You and Mr. Groft can take it for a spin."

As Daisy and Jonas followed Herman inside, Jonas leaned close to her and asked, "What did you get from all of that?"

"It's easy to see that Wilhelm was a loner, and it looks like he was a hacker, too. I think you and I should talk to Zeke about that, don't you?"

Jonas gave her hand a squeeze, and she knew he agreed.

It was a done deal . . . at least, last night it had been. Daisy and Jonas had taken the blue Journey for an hour-long drive. Daisy had driven the car on bumpy roads and on smooth roads. The seat fit her well, so if she made a long drive, she wouldn't be uncomfortable. There was also plenty of room for suitcases and boxes if she took Jazzi to college. The car still had a partial warranty, and that was important to her, too.

Now, this evening, Jonas had driven the car, too, to try it out, and he agreed that it handled nicely. As Daisy had taken the driver's seat again, they discussed what they'd learned last evening.

Daisy kept her hands on the wheel and her eyes on the road, but she took back roads she knew well. "Do you believe Wilhelm stopped his hacking after he split with his brother?"

"I don't know, Daisy. Once a hacker, always a hacker, wouldn't you think?"

"That means that you believe a man can't change."

"I don't know about changing, but hacking is a skill that not a lot of people have, at least not ordinary people. I can see him using it to get ahead, can't you?"

Daisy thought about it as she followed the road. "I think this is important enough to call Zeke, don't you?"

"You can call him right from here, now that you're all hooked up with your phone in your car."

"All right. His name is on my contact list." Then she said clearly, "Call Zeke."

She'd called Zeke's personal cell phone, and he answered after the first ring. "Daisy?"

"I'm in my new car. Well, it's a pre-owned car, and I'm trying out the phone system."

"That's why you called?" Zeke asked, sounding amused.

"No, that's only partly the reason. I wanted to talk to you about Wilhelm Rumple."

Zeke went quiet for a few seconds. "Daisy, I can't talk to you about the investigation."

Jonas chimed in, "She doesn't need information, she wants to give *you* some information. Are you open to that?"

"I should have known you were involved," Zeke said to Jonas. "Go ahead, Daisy. Tell me what you've got."

"It started when I bought my new pre-owned car from Herman Rumple, Wilhelm's brother."

She heard Zeke's deep groan.

"Now don't do that," she protested. "I really needed a car. Why not go to his car lot? It made perfect sense to me."

"Oh, I suppose it did," Zeke said with sarcasm. "And I don't suppose Jonas stopped you."

"He wanted to make sure I picked out the right car for me." She could almost see Zeke shaking his head, or maybe rolling his eyes, as Detective Rappaport often did.

"Let me ask you a couple of questions so I know where I should start from," Daisy said.

"Go ahead. I might not answer."

"I suppose you've talked to Wilhelm Rumple's brother."

"Is that a question?" Zeke asked.

"Yes, it is. Let's not go around in circles, or I'll be driving all night."

Zeke gave a short grunt. "Yes, I talked to the brother. But they were estranged. I didn't get much."

"They were estranged for a reason," Daisy confided. "Do you know what that reason was?"

"I was more interested in their recent history. If this brother had nothing to do with Wilhelm Rumple now, if he hadn't seen him, and we checked that out as thoroughly as we could, then he wasn't a suspect."

"There might be more than one reason to talk to his brother, don't you think?" Daisy asked.

"And what should I talk to his brother about?"

"These brothers had a history."

"I didn't care about their childhood, Daisy. If they hadn't been around each other for years, what point was there in talking about it?"

Daisy took a deep breath and slid a sideways glance at Jonas. She decided to take a different tack. "Even if brothers aren't close, they know things about each other. In this case, Herman experienced something you might want to know about his brother. Wilhelm hacked into Herman's credit card account and ran up purchases. Then he wouldn't help with funeral costs for their mother. That was the last straw between them."

"And how does that help me now?" Zeke asked.

"If Wilhelm didn't leave hacking behind, maybe he hacked into something that got him into trouble."

"She could be right about that, Zeke," Jonas said. "What if he hacked into a company's secrets? What if he found out the vitamins that King was selling could be harmful to pets? What if he found proof of it?"

"Are you telling me you think Stanley King murdered Rumple?" Zeke asked.

"No," Daisy was quick to say. "I'm not saying that, and I don't think Jonas is, either. But you can't overlook the possibility that Rumple's hacking skills got him into trouble."

After a minute or so of silence when Daisy wondered if she'd lost the connection, Zeke admitted, "I find the whole thing weird."

"Weird how?" Jonas asked.

"We didn't find a computer at Wilhelm Rumple's. All we found was a burner phone, which was no help at all."

"A burner phone because he didn't want his phone calls traced?"

"Possibly," Zeke said warily. "But I don't want you thinking too hard about that. If Wilhelm was a hacker, he needed a computer. Because of what you told me, I don't think I need to question the brother again. But I do think I need to question the nephew."

"Do you think he has Rumple's computer?" Jonas asked.

"I think it's a possibility. Rumple was a businessman. I can't imagine he didn't have a computer. If we could find it, it could give us the clues as to why he was murdered. But I don't want the two of you searching for it."

"I'm not searching for anything," Daisy assured him

innocently. "I just thought Herman's story was information you should have. Speaking of stories, I have a Storybook Tea on Saturday to get ready for. Would you like to buy a ticket?"

Zeke ended the call with a word Daisy couldn't make out.

"You get his goat," Jonas said.

"Half the time I don't even try to."

"That's what makes it so enjoyable to watch."

Daisy cut a glance to Jonas. "I really am going to concentrate on the Storybook Tea preparations. I don't have time for other distractions."

"Pull over," Jonas said.

"What?"

"Pull over. I'd like to give you a distraction other than your Storybook Tea."

Daisy was storing sealed containers of chocolate chip cookie dough into the walk-in Thursday morning when Iris came into the kitchen. Her hair was bouncy, her cheeks were flushed, and her smile was wide.

Daisy closed the door to the walk-in and turned to her aunt. "How was your date with Marshall last night?" she asked coyly.

Iris fluttered her hand, smiled even broader, and looked like a teenager who had gone on her first date. "I like him, Daisy. I always have. Marshall was a perfect gentleman and treated me as if I were worth a million bucks."

"You are," Daisy quipped, looking over her aunt's shoulder at Tessa, who was also grinning.

"I'm not as educated as he is," Iris mentioned, not for the first time.

"I don't think Marshall is looking for someone with a PhD," Tessa advised.

"Tessa's right, as she usually is," Daisy said with a wink. "My guess is Marshall, like most men, is looking for someone to be companionable with, to care about the same things he does, just to simply . . . care."

"We do care about many of the same things. He talked about his niece Olivia a lot. Remember, she's his receptionist?"

"I remember," Daisy said.

"And we talked about the homeless shelter and the tea we both like. He's very knowledgeable about that."

"Did you feel attracted to him?" Tessa asked, always the one to be blunt, even as she poured carrot-grape salad into a tray for the refrigerated case.

Iris turned beet red now, from her neck up to her forehead. "Tessa."

Tessa merely gave a shrug. "It's important, don't you think? What do you like best about him?"

Iris grew a little dreamy. "I like the way his silver hair gleams under the lights, the way his aftershave smells spicy. His white shirt collar was so starched, I asked him how he stands it."

Daisy and Tessa laughed. Snickerdoodles were cooling on a rack on the counter and, using a cookie lifter, Daisy began layering them into a pan for the case. "I'm so glad you had a good time."

"There is a problem, though," Iris said as she went to the sink to scrub her hands before she started working.

"What's that?" Daisy asked.

"What if Detective Rappaport *does* ask me out? What am I supposed to say?"

"What do you *want* to say?" Tessa inquired, with an amused look in her eyes.

"I like the detective," Iris admitted. "I have no idea what he'd be like on a date."

Daisy lifted the last of the cookies into the pan. "Then if he asks, go out with him."

"I can't date two men at once," Iris protested.

"Actually, you can," Tessa said. "After all, how else are you going to decide which one you'd like to end up with?"

Iris looked stunned, as if that idea hadn't even entered her head.

A few minutes later, Daisy left the kitchen and went to the sales counter to put the cookie pan in the case. Eva, Tamlyn, and Foster soon arrived and set to work, readying the tearoom for opening. Daisy crossed to the front door, unlocked it, and turned the CLOSED sign to OPEN.

To her surprise, Elijah Beiler was already standing there.

She motioned for him to come in. He did, looking uncomfortable. He wasn't one of her regular customers.

She said, "Hello, Elijah. I can give you the best table in the house."

He quickly shook his head. "*Nee. Guder mariye.* I do not need a table."

Elijah looked so serious that Daisy asked, "What do you need?"

He pulled on one of his suspenders, indecision crossing his face. Then, as if he had no choice, he asked, "Can you meet me and my cousin Zebediah at Levi Fisher's house tonight about seven?" He looked around the tea garden, where servers were readying tables. "I don't want to talk here, and it is not right for us to talk to a woman alone. Rachel will be at the house tonight."

"Do you want Jonas there?"

"Jonas will learn in time what we have to say. Only you . . . for now."

Daisy didn't ask any more questions. This meeting was serious, and she hoped she could bring to it whatever Elijah needed.

CHAPTER NINETEEN

When Daisy arrived at the Fishers' farm that evening, she parked and caught sight of Luke unhitching a horse from a buggy.

He waved and called, "Mr. Beiler and Deacon Beiler are inside with *Mamm* and *Daed*."

Deacon Beiler? Zebediah? She hadn't known that was his title, but then she guessed there was no need for her to know that.

Rachel came to the door. The expression on her face was sober.

A breeze ruffled the edge of Daisy's sweater and the ends of her hair. Dusk was falling, and soon it would be Standard Time. Then darkness would fall over Willow Creek around five p.m. Fall to winter and seasons changing. What was tonight about?

Rachel motioned Daisy to come inside, her black apron flapping as she swiveled into the mud room. "Let's stay here," she said. "The men are in the kitchen. It wouldn't be right for you to be alone in the house with them."

"So what's the plan?" Daisy asked, ready to comply with whatever Rachel dictated.

"Levi is in the barn doing chores. He knows this is to be a private conversation. I'm going to go to the far corner of the kitchen, but I'm not going to be listening. If you and the men keep your voices low, I won't hear."

"So you have no idea what we're going to talk about?"

"None. Zebediah has always been a man of few words, especially since he became a deacon."

"So he ministers to the Amish in your district."

"That is true. Elijah has convinced Zebediah to speak with you, though he doesn't want to. If you can keep that in mind, it will help."

"I *will* keep that in mind, but now you're beginning to worry me. Maybe the police should be involved."

Rachel vehemently shook her head. "If you mention the police, Zebediah will leave. He's already told us that."

"I feel as if this is a huge responsibility you're placing on my shoulders."

"You are trusted," Rachel said simply.

At this moment, Daisy didn't know if that was a good thing. "All right. I'll be respectful to Zebediah, but I might have to ask questions."

"Just because you ask, doesn't mean he'll answer."

With a reluctant nod, Daisy consented. "Let's do this."

Elijah and Zebediah were still wearing their hats when they entered the mudroom. They looked like brothers in their blue shirts, black broadcloth pants, and suspenders.

Their beards were about the same length. But Zebediah's eyes glanced here and there rather than at Daisy. His shoulders were slumped, and Daisy thought he looked like a man that the world had worn down.

Elijah introduced Daisy to his cousin. Broaching any subject with a strange Amish man was awkward, but this terrifically so.

Daisy started bluntly. "Elijah asked me to meet with you here, but I have no idea why. Can one of you tell me why I'm the person you wanted to talk to?"

"This is about Mr. Rumple," Elijah explained plainly. He nudged his cousin with his elbow.

Zebediah looked Daisy up and down, seeming to assess her. "You and Jonas Groft are courting, *nee*?"

Daisy supposed in Amish terms that is exactly what she and Jonas were doing. "Yes, we are. Jonas can be trusted, too, you know, if you don't want to talk with me."

Zebediah exchanged a look with Elijah. "Like you said, she's not prideful."

"No, she is not. She has helped the police many times. She needs this information you have."

"I do not want any part of the police," Zebediah maintained.

"Daisy understands that. Right, Daisy?"

"Deacon Beiler," she said. "I don't know what you have to tell me, but if it will lead to Mr. Rumple's murderer, I might have to discuss it with the police. I can't promise you I won't."

"I don't have direct knowledge," the deacon revealed in a low voice. "But my experience could be someone else's."

That was as puzzling as this meeting. Finally, Zebediah seemed to make a decision. He shifted on his feet, and then he began. "My sins caught up with me. This ghost has followed me for twenty years."

Daisy didn't even know if Wilhelm Rumple had been around Willow Creek twenty years ago, but she was here to listen. "Go on," she encouraged.

"I married when I was nineteen. I was starting my blacksmithing business and still helping on the family farm. *Kinner* came fast. Ella birthed three in five years. She turned away from me, because she was tired all the time and had babies hanging on her."

Elijah gave his cousin a look. Zebediah rubbed his hand down over his face and beard. "No excuse. No excuse," he repeated, looking pale now above his beard.

Daisy wasn't sure what to say or do. She didn't want to upset the balance of this conversation. She wanted Elijah and Zebediah to give her as much information as they could to help with the investigation of Rumple's murder. Shoving her hands into her sweater pockets, she waited.

"I had a . . . fling with an Englischer. She became . . . with child. I provided for her in another town while she was pregnant. We gave up the baby for adoption."

Someone could have knocked Daisy over with the proverbial feather. She tried not to show surprise or shock. In many ways, the Amish weren't different from anyone else. Yet in many other ways, they were.

Zebediah didn't seem to be able to go on as he clasped his hands together and took deep breaths.

With a bit of a shrug, Elijah turned toward his cousin as if in sympathy. "I'm the only one who knew about this . . . the only one."

"Not true," Zebediah said with a sigh. "The midwife knew. The adoption people knew."

"But no one in the community," Elijah reiterated. "If the word had gotten out, Zebediah's life would have been destroyed. He repented on his own and became the *gut* man that he is now . . . the *gut* father . . . the *gut* husband. If he had gone to the bishop and confessed, all would have been lost. If he had let his history come out later, he would have lost his standing in the community . . . and maybe his marriage. No one would trust him for advice or counsel."

Daisy had always considered that a person's past deeds predicted the future. In many cases, they did. But if God and community came together to change a man, how could *she* say it wouldn't happen? Unfortunately, she could predict what they were going to say next.

"Tell me the rest," she said quietly.

"Zebediah makes sculptures out of horseshoes and the like," Elijah explained.

"Jonas mentioned that," Daisy said.

"Mr. Rumple sold them for me," Zebediah confirmed. "He took a percentage. After the first few months we were doing business together, he revealed he knew about my past. It was as if my life was an open book to him. How could that be?"

That question was easy for Daisy to answer. "If there had been an adoption, there are records. There had to be a birth certificate."

"But how could Wilhelm find out about all of that?" It was obvious Zebediah's world was still swimming.

"Elijah, you know about the Internet from working with Jonas, right?" Daisy inquired.

"Sure. I know Jonas finds things on there. Somehow, he used it to help find Jazzi's birth *mudder*, ain't so?"

"Exactly. I've learned that Mr. Rumple had hacking skills. That means he could infiltrate databases, records, that kind of thing, whether he was legally able to or not."

"He was blackmailing me," Zebediah admitted. "But I had nothing to do with the man's murder. You've got to believe that."

Even though Daisy had just met this man, she *could* believe that. She couldn't see him going into the Four Paws dog run and using a bucket to smash Wilhelm's head.

"I understand why you told me this. If he was blackmailing you, he could have been blackmailing someone else . . . someone else who got angry enough to commit murder."

Daisy immediately thought of Serena and her panic attacks. Could Wilhelm Rumple have been blackmailing her, too?

Daisy sat in her new car, thought about everything she'd learned for about a minute, and then activated her hands-free phone in her car. "Call Serena," she requested.

Serena's phone rang a few times before she picked up. "Hi, Daisy."

"I know it's getting late," Daisy said, seeing that it was almost eight o'clock. "But I'd really like to meet with you. Are you at home?"

There were several seconds of hesitation. "No, I'm not. I'm at Four Paws. This is really necessary tonight?"

"I think it is. Do you want me to come there?"

Again, that hesitation. "You can come here. Hetta is with me tonight. I was going to leave in a little while, but I'll wait for you."

"I'll be there in five to ten minutes."

"Do you want to tell me what this is about?"

"I'd rather wait until I see you." Daisy needed to see Serena's face when she asked her questions. She wanted to gauge the woman's mood when she responded. She wanted to finally find out the motivation behind Wilhelm Rumple's murder.

Ten minutes later, Daisy parked at Four Paws and walked in the main door, not knowing what she would find. The lights were lower than usual. On a timer, they cut back at night. The hallway past the dogs' kennels was dimly lit, but Daisy could see a shadowy figure there. It must be Hetta.

She suddenly shivered. Was it wise coming here at night? Was it wise pursuing this? Yet she didn't feel she could tell the detectives exactly what Zebediah had confided in her. She'd promised she'd keep it secret if she could. Speaking with Serena was one way to do that.

Daisy should have seen all the signs more clearly much sooner. Everything had seemed so muddled, and now she guessed why. People who knew Wilhelm Rumple had a reason not to like him—a very good reason, one that could be a motive for murder, if Daisy was guessing correctly.

Daisy was about to ring the little bell on the desk when Serena appeared from the hall, Bellamy beside her. Daisy tried to keep her demeanor relaxed. Serena, if not Bellamy, would pick up any nervousness if she showed it.

"Hi, Daisy," Serena said. "You sounded so serious. What's wrong?"

"That's what I've come to ask you. Can we go somewhere private to talk?"

Serena motioned down the hall to the kennels. "As I

mentioned, only Hetta's here tonight. We can talk anywhere you'd like."

"How about we go back to your office, just the two of us?"

"Sure. You don't mind if Bellamy comes along?"

"No, of course not," Daisy said, with a little laugh that she hoped kept her voice light.

When she rounded the butcher-block-topped counter, Bellamy came over to nose her. Daisy petted the dog's head. "You're a sweet girl, and I know you're good for your mistress."

"Yes, she is," Serena said. "Come on, there are two chairs down here. Let's sit."

They walked down the hall to a small office. They went inside, but Serena left the door open.

Bellamy went behind the desk with Serena and sat beside her. Daisy took the chair in front of the desk. To her surprise, Four Paws gave her the creeps at night. All the lights were dimmer, and there was a hollow sound about the place. Every once in a while, she heard a dog bark—a yip from a small dog or a bigger bark from a large dog. It was an odd feeling being here, but she knew she had to do this.

"I'd like to know what happened when you were in college that caused the anxiety attacks."

Serena nervously ran her fingers around her braid on the top of her head. Then she looked Daisy steadily in the eyes. "I don't think that's any of your business."

"No, it might not be my business, but then again, it could be, if it has anything to do with what happened to Mr. Rumple."

Serena's face drained of color. She reached for the

drawer beside the desk and pulled it open. Daisy's heart beat so fast, she didn't know what she was going to do. What if Serena had a gun in that drawer, or a knife, or another kind of weapon? Maybe this was why she should have asked Jonas to come along.

As Daisy tried to keep her pulse at a decent rate, Serena pulled a pack of tissues from the drawer. She set them on the desk. "Daisy, I really don't want to talk about this." Her voice was already thick and a bit choked.

"I think you have to talk about it, Serena. Was Wilhelm Rumple blackmailing you?"

Serena's mouth dropped open. Her eyes became wide and glistening, and a tear rolled down her cheek. "How did you know?"

"I didn't know for certain, but I guessed. I don't think you're the only one. So how about if you tell me what happened?"

Serena stooped to Bellamy, gave her flanks a rub, and then her neck, and then her face. Daisy suspected Serena needed that fur under her hands. She needed the warmth of the dog near her to be able to face whatever she was going to reveal.

"I was in college," Serena said. "And I'd been doing really well. But then I went to a frat party, and I went home with the wrong guy. The situation could have been a lot worse. He basically pushed me up against a wall and tried to do more than I wanted. But I got away, and I left the frat house. The thing was—I started having anxiety attacks. I didn't want to tell anybody what happened. After all, I should have been able to handle it. It's not like I was raped."

"Serena, you were assaulted."

"I've come to realize that now, but then, I was young and naïve. The thing is—I wasn't too naïve about college life, not when it came to how to cheat on a final paper."

This, Daisy had never suspected. "What do you mean, you *cheated*?"

"I couldn't keep my mind on my studies after what happened. I guess it was a form of PTSD. I didn't have a therapy dog then. I just tried to make do . . . tried to get through each day . . . tried not to startle easily . . . tried to concentrate on my work. But I couldn't, and I knew I was going to fail if I didn't hand a paper in. I had to turn in a paper and get a decent grade. So I bought one on the Internet. This girl said she often wrote papers for students, and it was no big deal. My professor thought it *was* a big deal. Someone had turned in that exact same paper two semesters before. He caught me cheating. He gave me an F. I had to make up that one class to graduate. I left that school and transferred to an online school. I made up the credits and I earned my degree. Noah doesn't know."

"But Mr. Rumple found out," Daisy guessed.

"I have no idea how he found out."

No one was around, yet Daisy felt her skin crawling. Because she was alone with Serena? No, Bellamy was perfectly relaxed. It shouldn't have anything to do with that. Nobody else was nearby, right?

Serena looked as nervous as Daisy felt. Because she was guilty of murder? Or simply because of anxiety? There was nothing simple about this.

"Serena, I need you to tell me the truth about something."

Serena wouldn't look at her. She looked everywhere but at Daisy. The woman's gaze settled on Bellamy, and she again petted the dog as if her life depended on it. "I always try to be honest." There was a quaver in her voice, and Daisy heard it.

"I believe that Wilhelm Rumple was blackmailing several people in Willow Creek. You aren't the only one."

Serena's head snapped up, her eyes met Daisy's, and they soon filled with tears. She ran her hand down Bellamy's head again and clutched at her fur.

"Can you tell me about your experience with Rumple? Your story might help other people."

"I didn't kill him!"

It was a vehement denial, and Daisy didn't know whether to believe her or not.

"You had means, opportunity, and maybe a motive, right?"

"Yes," Serena admitted softly. "But I didn't kill him. I wasn't here that night. I had already left."

"Tell me what happened with Rumple. Please."

Her soft inquiry seemed to convince Serena. She shook her head as if warding off all the thoughts. "I didn't know what to do. I really didn't know what to do. Noah still doesn't know about college . . . about the blackmail."

"Noah didn't know why you changed schools?"

"No, I just told him I needed a change. I told him I could finish up on my own terms. He accepted that. He knew I had anxiety as a child. He didn't question me. He should have, but he didn't."

"So what was your experience with Rumple?"

Canvassing the small room with her gaze, Serena looked as if she wanted to escape. But there was no place to go. "He started working here. He loved the dogs, so I thought he was a good person."

"Most dog people usually are."

"I know, right? But about six months after he was volunteering here, he came to me one night. I was here late, and nobody else was around. He told me he knew about my college *experience*. He even knew the name of the paper I had bought. I realized then that he either had someone investigating for him, or he was an expert hacker. He asked for a sum of money every month, and I paid him."

"Did you pay it out of the shelter funds?"

"Oh, no. As you know, Noah and I pay ourselves a minimum salary. Noah makes a lot more because of his vet business. Since I still live at home, I don't have many expenses. So I paid Rumple every month. I would go to the bank and cash a check for miscellaneous expenses, and then I would give him the cash. There's no record of it. At least, I don't think there is."

Daisy reached out and touched Serena's arm. "Serena, you have to go to the police."

"I can't. They'll think I murdered him."

"You said you left that night before he was murdered. Can you prove that? Do you have an alibi?"

She shook her head sadly. "No. I spent time in the barn with new lambs before I went into the house that night. I was out there a long time. My parents didn't know I was home. What should I do?"

"Make an appointment with Marshall Thompson for tomorrow. Talk to him about it. Listen to his advice. My guess is he'll want you to go to the detectives. I don't think yours is the only story about blackmail that they're going to be hearing."

"You know other people who were blackmailed?"

"I do, maybe even Stanley King. I'm going to do a bit

more fishing. You have to keep hope strong that the truth will come out. It will, you know. It always does."

"Noah and my parents will be so hurt."

"Maybe. But they love you. They'll get over it."

"I've been a nervous wreck since before Rumple died and afterward, too. I don't know who killed him, but I wasn't sorry they did."

"I don't think you're the only one who feels that way. It seems Wilhelm Rumple was a complicated person. Yes, he loved dogs, but he was also a crook."

Both women stood. Without hesitating, Daisy gave Serena an encouraging hug. Whether she was right or wrong, she believed that Serena hadn't killed Rumple. But who did?

Bellamy and Serena walked Daisy to the lobby. She waved at them as she left, giving Serena a hopeful smile.

However, as she went out the front door, she again experienced the feeling of caterpillars crawling up her spine. Could someone be watching her? Hetta, maybe? She hadn't seen her as she'd left.

In the parking lot, Daisy heard a car engine start up around the side of the building. Who would be in the parking lot now? She didn't want to find out. Quickly using her key fob to unlock her car, she hopped in, then closed and locked the doors. Seconds later, she started the engine, backed up, and zoomed out of the parking lot.

Daisy kept her eye on her rearview mirror as she drove home. No one followed her. She was safe.

The following morning, Daisy started out on her bike. The sky looked like a steel-gray cover overhead. Clouds swirled, and she wondered if rain would fall before she finished her ride. She followed her usual route as leaves rustled about her. Trees were dropping them swiftly, readying for the new season. Dampness soaked the air, not quite a mist. Not yet, anyway. These bike rides allowed Daisy time to think . . . time to process . . . time to sweep cobwebs from her brain. She considered her conversation with Serena last night, and what she should do about it. Should she herself go to the detectives? And what about Zebediah? Could she keep his secrets?

Daisy expected that Serena would call her today, either after she talked to Marshall or after she spoke with the detectives. Daisy decided to just wait to see what happened next. After all, the Storybook Tea would be happening tomorrow, and her attention should be focused on that.

The breeze picked up into a wind, and Daisy found herself riding into it . . . against it. She pedaled harder, wishing now that she'd forgone this bike ride this morning, exercise or no exercise. Her thigh muscles felt as if they were going to cramp.

To her relief, she saw the Rumple property up ahead. Once she passed that, she knew her ride would be more downhill than uphill. She found she enjoyed riding best when Jazzi or Jonas accompanied her. Maybe it was the company, or maybe it was the bits of conversation. It seemed natural. Daisy remembered when Jonas had bought their bikes, and then they'd gone together to buy one for Jazzi at Wheels. Since then, the three of them had grown ever closer.

Daisy hadn't been aware of any cars on the road before. Nevertheless, now she heard the hum of an engine. The vehicle was coming up behind her, and it was coming fast. Before she could even think about riding off the road onto the narrow shoulder, the silver pickup truck skimmed by her so close that it knocked Daisy and her bike sideways.

Before she could blink, Daisy was lying in a heap on the side of the road, her bicycle on top of her. Her first thought was—had that hit been an accident? She remembered the sound of the vehicle in the parking lot at Four Paws last night.

Had she just tangled with a murderer?

CHAPTER TWENTY

Daisy's knee was still bothering her as the Storybook Tea flowed around her. She was lucky that was all that was bothering her. Fortunately, the October day was sunny, and the temperature was in the sixties, so they could still serve out on the patio. She'd been scrambling along with the rest of her staff to keep up ever since ticket holders had begun pouring in.

Jonas had arrived early with her staff, eager to help if he could. She'd called him last night after the bike riding incident, and he, of course, had called Detective Rappaport. They'd both arrived, ready to take her to urgent care, but she'd insisted she didn't need that. She needed a stiff drink and a bandage, and she'd be fine. Today, however, she was still sore, and her slim, gray corduroy-knit pantlegs rubbed against the large bandage on her knee.

But she could block that out with adrenalin, especially when they were this busy.

Daisy concentrated on the smiles on peoples' faces. Children had brought their favorite books along. Parents wore name tags with their favorite books written on them. Daisy noticed *Ramona the Pest*, Roald Dahl's *Charlie and the Chocolate Factory* and *James and the Giant Peach*, and of course, many Dr. Seuss books—*The Cat in the Hat* and *How the Grinch Stole Christmas!* among them. One little girl carried *Charlotte's Web*, and a four-year-old boy, *Goodnight Moon*. The story of Ferdinand was represented, along with *The Polar Express*. One of the moms had printed *The Giving Tree* on her label, and her son carried *The Little Engine That Could*.

Gavin grinned as he gave his ticket to Foster. He'd printed *The Wind in the Willows* on his tag, and his teenage daughter Emily carried *Corduroy*, a beat-up version that she must have loved since she was small. Daisy herself wore a name tag that was printed with *Anne of Green Gables*. Everyone was talking to each other about their favorite books and the children's favorite stories. There were some dads here today as well as moms. She heard one gentleman say to the man next to him, "I can never understand the allure of *Grimm's Fairy Tales*. Some of them were downright grim, though my favorite was 'Rumpelstiltskin.' After all, Rumpelstiltskin got his due, didn't he?"

Daisy didn't have much time to think about the comment, when Ned Pachenko began talking to his audience in the main tearoom. Ned introduced himself and then began with, "I made up a few songs with your favorite book titles. I watched the books you carried as you came in, and the ones your mom and dad printed on their labels. I'm going to start with mine, *The Black Stallion*, and then we'll add to that. If I ask you to shout out your book title, do it loud and clear."

Soon, Ned was singing, the audience was participating, and everyone seemed to be enjoying Daisy's Fall Surprise tea blend, whether they were drinking it hot or iced. She felt relieved and suddenly wished she could sit for a few moments. She headed to the kitchen to see how everything was going there, but Jonas and Detective Rappaport caught up with her and snagged her arm. Jonas's hand was at the small of her back as he guided her to her office. It was as if he'd read her mind.

"Why don't you sit for a few minutes? Morris and I want to talk to you."

Uh-oh, now what? On the other hand, maybe Detective Rappaport had found out something about the person who had shoved her off the road.

Daisy could hear shouting and laughter and the music from the tea garden. She knew she couldn't stay here long. She looked from Detective Rappaport to Jonas. "I only have a couple of minutes. What do you want to tell me?"

Jonas nodded to the detective.

Detective Rappaport crossed his arms over his chest and looked down his nose at Daisy. "As usual, you've stirred up a hornets' nest."

"I was bike riding, detective. That's all."

"Bike riding, my ankle. You've been talking to too many people about the Rumple murder."

"Not many," she protested. "And some of them have come to me."

"Are you going to tell me who they are?"

"Not particularly. Not yet. I do know Serena Langston or her lawyer will be calling you."

"Thompson already did. I listened to her story early this morning. My guess is you believe more people than Serena have been blackmailed by Wilhelm Rumple."

"It makes sense, doesn't it?"

"Yes, it truly does. We're going to bring Stanley King in again to talk about it. I wouldn't be discussing this with you if you hadn't almost been run over."

"Do you think Mr. King had something to do with it? And the murder?"

"Let's just say I've looked into silver pickup trucks."

"Who owns them?" Daisy asked, almost jumping up out of her chair.

Jonas laid his hand on her shoulder. "Easy now. Andrew King has a silver pickup, and so does Clancy Miller. I believe they're on the detective's list to question. Right, Morris?"

Daisy should have remembered Clancy's silver pickup truck. He'd parked it in front of Rumple's house the day she and Jazzi had stopped to talk to him.

"They are on my list to question. We'll get to the bottom of this, Daisy. Just stay cool, serve tea, and don't get in my way."

"That sounds more like a threat than a warning," she muttered.

The detective grimaced. "I'm glad to see you're too busy here to get into trouble today. I'll be buying some of those cookies decorated with the Cinderella castle, as well as a few gingerbread men. I might even buy one of the Nancy Drew cupcakes, though the Hardy Boys were my favorite."

She had to smile at that, in spite of his warning. "I thought you were on a diet."

"There are times when a man needs a little sugar, and this is one of those days." He looked at Jonas. "Keep her safe."

"Do you think I haven't tried?"

With an overblown sigh, the detective shook his head. "If I find out who ran you off the road, I will let you know. Your bike had a paint scrape on it, and we've sent it off to be analyzed. I should know the make and model of the truck soon."

After Rappaport left her office, Daisy stayed sitting, thinking about the last few weeks—Rumple, his brother, his nephew, his dog, and everything that had happened.

"Uh-oh," Jonas said. "Your brain is working much too fast."

"So much has happened, and so many people are involved. I'm just trying to fit it all together."

"That's Morris's job."

"I suppose, and maybe the paint analysis on the truck will pay off. But whoever the killer is seems impulsive to me. Who knows what he or she is going to do next. It's more than worrisome."

Jonas held his hand out to Daisy. She took it. "Go back to Woods," she said. "I'm safe here. I'm going to get into the mood of the tea and simply enjoy myself."

"Noah and Serena asked me to come over tonight to talk about everything that's been happening with them. Do you mind?"

"No, of course not. After today, I'll just go home and chill. Jazzi will probably be with Mark tonight, so I'll have a quiet evening. Noah and Serena need your support right now."

Jonas wrapped his arm around Daisy's waist as he walked her back into the tea garden. As he left, she waved. He gave her one of those smiles that was meant just for her.

After Jonas had gone, Daisy joined in the celebration of the Storybook Tea. Still . . . in her mind, she began putting together all the clues that had surfaced regarding Rumple. She considered the statues in his backyard and the statues in that secure safe. Uppermost in her mind was the oddity that there hadn't been a computer or evidence of his bookwork.

She poured tea. She distributed cookies shaped like horses to represent *The Black Stallion* and *Misty of Chincoteague*. Peanut butter and jelly triangles were a hit with the kids. Blueberry-lemon and cinnamon scones with jams were a hit with the adults.

Through tea service, Daisy considered Rumple's Plott hound and the security system on the man's property. After spending a few more minutes listening to Ned and watching the children and adults interacting and having a good time, Daisy went outside to see how her servers and customers were faring there. The music drifted out.

Spotting the man who had mentioned *Grimm's Fairy Tales*, she went over to his table. "Too noisy inside?"

"A little. I came out here for a break. That's all right, isn't it?"

"Sure, it is. You mentioned *Grimm's Fairy Tales*. Have you read them all?"

"I got my kids one of those volumes with many of them, a hardback with beautiful illustrations of each fairy tale. They were seven or eight till we started reading the stories, though. My daughter always thought 'Hansel and Gretel' was scary. 'Little Red Riding Hood' doesn't end the best way, either, depending on which version you read. She loved 'Sleeping Beauty' and 'Cinderella.' But then there was 'Rumpelstiltskin,' with a king, a queen, a father and daughter, a silly little man, and a secret room. That could almost be a story for a present day."

"Yes, it could," Daisy said, as her mind began spinning very fast. "Is there anything else I can get you?" she asked, even though Foster was the server. But Foster was busy at another table right now, and there wasn't any reason why she shouldn't help.

"I saw someone had a plate of little sandwiches. Could I have one of those?"

"Sure, you can. With that service, adults receive a chicken salad triangle, prosciutto-wrapped cantaloupe, avocado on rye, and bruschetta with goat cheese and tomato."

"That sounds perfect."

Spotting Foster, she made eye contact with him. He crossed to her and asked, "What do you need?"

"How about one of the adult sandwich plates and a warm-up on this gentleman's tea?"

"Right away," Foster said and left for the kitchen.

After exchanging a few more words with the man at the table, her thoughts ran around and around until she settled on what she wanted to do. She hoped Gavin was still in the tearoom.

Emily was involved with a girl about her own age. They had their heads together over a book, and they were animatedly talking. Daisy motioned Gavin to her office. He nodded and met her there.

"What's up?" he asked, after she'd gone inside and closed the door.

"I have a question for you."

"Go ahead," he said.

"You told me that when someone builds a house, or extensively renovates, their plans are filed in the mayor's office."

"They are. The plans are all online now. Why?"

"Do you have access to them?"

"I do," he said warily. "What do you want to see?"

"I'd like to see the house plans for Wilhelm Rumple's cottage."

After Daisy closed the tea garden for the day, Gavin met her at her house. They sat at her kitchen island. Gavin had stopped at his office to access the database with the plans for Rumple's house. He'd printed them out and brought them along. Marjoram sat on one stool, watching them, her golden eyes following Gavin's hands as he smoothed out the paper. Pepper, always the practical feline, sat at her dish, waiting for a treat.

Daisy asked her, "Didn't Jazzi already give you a few treats today?"

Pepper looked back at her and blinked, then raised a paw to dab at her whisker.

Daisy went to the cupboard, found the little bag, and took out two of the green treats. Then she dropped them into Pepper's dish. Marjoram didn't seem interested right now. Her gaze was still on the sheet of paper Gavin had placed on the island.

Daisy went to the chair next to his, pulled it out, and sat.

Gavin's forehead had multiple creases, and he squinted at the plans.

"What do you see?"

Gavin's forefinger was following a few lines.

That motion had caught Marjoram's attention.

Taking a small calculator from his pocket, Gavin tapped in numbers. Daisy could see the dimensions printed next to the walls on the plan.

"This doesn't make sense," he grumbled.

"What do you mean it doesn't make sense?"

"Something is off. The numbers don't add up. I do this for a living, Daisy."

Daisy wasn't sure what Gavin was seeing or calculating, but she mused, "I wish we could get into that house and look around."

With a sly grin, Gavin reached into his pocket again and took out a Post-it note. "I didn't just stop at my office for the plans. I also made a call to the real estate agent. Rumple's house is unofficially for sale now."

She peered over his arm at the slip of paper. "That doesn't have a name on it. It has numbers. What are they?"

"It's the code to the lock box. Do you want to take a look inside his house?"

"We can do that legally?"

"We sure can. Aren't you considering buying the house?" His eyes twinkled with mischief.

"Why, maybe I am," she drawled. "Let's go."

As Gavin drove, the darkness, the pines looming above them, and the rural road made Daisy shiver. Every once in a while, she peered through the back window of Gavin's truck. Were those headlights? Was someone following them? The lights disappeared. Her imagination was in overdrive.

She picked up her phone. "I'm going to text Jonas, so he knows where we are and what we're doing."

"Are you nervous about going into the house?" Gavin asked.

"Detective Rappaport told me to be careful. He doesn't think my accident was really an accident . . . that somebody tried to run me off the road."

"Daisy, you didn't tell me that."

"I didn't want everyone to worry. But I think we should be careful tonight. That's why I'm texting Jonas."

"Maybe we shouldn't do this."

"We're almost there, Gavin. I don't want to turn back now. But maybe we shouldn't be so visible."

"There are plenty of woods around Rumple's place," Gavin responded. I can park the truck behind some trees, and nobody will see us." He looked sideways over Daisy's outfit. "You're dressed for trekking."

She'd worn a flannel jacket, jeans, and trainers. After all, she might like to take another look at the statues at the back of the property, unless someone had carted them all away by now. But she doubted that. Moving them would be a major undertaking that she probably would have heard about at the tea garden.

Gavin's truck was a four-wheel drive. Near Rumple's cottage, he easily went off the road and found a gap in the tall pines.

After he parked, he switched off the engine and studied Daisy. "I think you should stay here. Let me go and have a look around first. Did Jonas text you back?"

"Not yet. If he's having a serious discussion with Serena and Noah, he might have switched off his ringer. Do you have a flashlight?" she asked.

"I have a couple in the back. I'll take the mag light. I'll

be fine, Daisy. I have my phone, too. I'll text you if I find anything unusual, or if it's safe for you to come. No one should know yet about the house going on the market. It's a pocket listing."

"What does that mean?"

"It means that Dustan Rumple has a contract with my friend to sell the house. It won't be listed on the MLS, the multiple listing system. There's potential for a faster deal when the listing agent has clients who might be interested in the property . . . and fewer showings to strangers."

"Unless the agent has someone who wants to look at it under the cover of night," she murmured. "I'm going to keep the windows down so I can hear anything around the truck."

"I don't know, Daisy. I'd feel better if you were protected in the truck, doors locked, windows up."

"I have pepper spray in my pocket. I'll be fine."

"Famous last words," Gavin grumbled. Reaching over the seat, he rooted around on the floor in the back, then turned around again with the mag light in his hand. He handed her a smaller flashlight. "Just in case."

Daisy lowered her window, letting in the scent of pine, damp leaves, and fall. After Gavin closed the driver's side truck door, she sat nervously in her seat and waited. It seemed she heard every sound—the whisper of the branches, the pine needles falling, the leaves skittering across the ground, a soft hoot of an owl, maybe a squirrel scrambling. It was enough to make her almost crazy.

After three minutes, she studied her watch. She looked at it again after five. Next, she picked up her phone. Jonas hadn't texted back. Gavin hadn't texted.

She listened, almost sticking her head out the window.

She could hear nothing. Could she? That wasn't a car engine, was it?

A branch broke. Then another. Was someone trekking through the woods?

Silence. Silence so still, it made her nerves itch. Was that possible for nerves to itch, or did they have to tingle or hurt?

Thoughts whirled in her mind—suspects, one after the other, Jonas's smile, Jazzi's laughter, Sammy's giggles, the way Vi and Foster looked at each other.

No, her life wasn't passing in front of her eyes.

Another three minutes gone. He'd been gone thirteen minutes now, or was it fifteen?

At twenty minutes, she knew Gavin had been gone too long . . . way too long.

Opening the truck door, she tried not to make a sound. Still, it was hard to close a truck door without clanging it. She had to close it, or the battery would die from leaving the light on.

Her flashlight turned on, her phone in one pocket, pepper spray in the other, she rounded the hood of the truck. She listened again and didn't hear a sound. So much for listening. She was going to move.

Hunching a bit, she ran toward the house, keeping close to the woods. She was sure the lock box would have been on the front door, so she had to aim that way. Jogging across the front yard, she was afraid someone would see her. She turned off her flashlight. No motion-detector light switched on now. The whole system was probably turned off.

At the stone cottage's door, she looked around and didn't see or hear anybody, not even Gavin. It was a thick, heavy, arched door, and maybe he was inside snooping . . . checking things out . . . searching.

She hoped so.

The padlock for the lock box was dangling open. She turned the knob on the door. The heavy door creaked as she opened it and slipped inside. Shutting it behind her, she stood frozen . . . listening. Maybe the dark was playing tricks on her. She thought she heard something.

Switching on her flashlight, she shone it around. She was standing in a small foyer. Hurrying, she rushed down the hallway to Rumple's office. Outside the doorway, she stopped and listened again. There was a thump. Was that a muffled shout?

Rushing into the room, she flipped the switch on the wall, which turned on the small Tiffany lamp on the desk. It didn't glow much farther than the top of the desk.

She heard the thumping again. She called, "Gavin?"

The knocking was harder now, and she thought she heard her name. It was coming from behind the wall! She was sure of it. How could Gavin be anywhere there?

Gavin had said the house plans didn't make sense because the dimensions didn't add up. That meant one thing. He'd suspected there was a secret closet or something like that. There were decorative wall panels around this room. She went toward the wall behind the desk that was facing forward into the room. Molding had created the decorative rectangles. The pounding was definitely coming from behind there somewhere. So was the sound of her name . . . muffled, but she could hear it.

Placing her flashlight on the desk so it was aimed directly at the wall she was focused on, she ran her fingers over the rectangles . . . then the wood trim surrounding them. She could hardly reach the top of the panel toward her left. Swinging around the desk chair, she climbed up on it, holding onto its ladder back. As her fingers searched across the molding, she thought she felt a divot. Climbing down from the chair, she picked up her flashlight and took it up with her when she climbed up again. She spied the mark that could be a hinge.

Running her hand to the left along the decorative molding, she wiggled it up and down. Finally, she realized the molding strip itself could be a lever. Shoving up the end of it, she felt it shift.

She yelled, "Gavin, I'm coming. Hold on."

Grabbing the chair, she went to the panel on the right and climbed up. Knowing what to do now, she found the edge of the molding strip and lifted that one, too. The action released a lower panel, molding and all. It popped open, impeded by the chair.

She quickly jumped down. Gavin was already shoving his way out of the enclosure, and he was angry.

His words tumbled over each other. "My phone had no bars in there. We've got to get out of here. A woman came in behind me. She hit me in the back of the knees and over the head with the chair. Somehow, she shoved me in and shut the door. We have to call the police."

Before they did, though, Daisy wanted to see what was in the hidden closet.

Actually, it was more than a closet. As she quickly glanced around, she could see a sophisticated computer setup. She spotted three monitors, a tower hard drive, and several external hard drives.

"Once you're in, how do you get out again?" she asked.

Gavin shrugged and winced. "My guess is, the door won't open from the inside without an unlocking mechanism triggered with the computer. I don't know. Come on."

Before they could exit the small room, however, someone tried to close the door on them. Daisy saw it closing. She pushed her hands out in front of her and rammed the door open. Gavin helped her, and they pushed until it gave way. Daisy saw a flash of brown hair. She couldn't tell for sure, but she thought their adversary who had pushed back was a woman.

As they ducked out of the small room, Gavin was limping badly.

Stopping, Daisy asked, "Gavin, are you all right?"

"I'll be fine. I'm going to call the police." He already had his phone in hand, ready to punch in 9-1-1.

"I'm going to see who locked you in," Daisy said, and ran out of the den toward the kitchen. She doubted if the woman would go out the front and risk crossing the front yard. Daisy headed for the back door.

"Daisy, don't go out there," Gavin called. "At least wait for me."

She didn't wait. She ran, pepper spray in hand. If Gavin called the police, they'd be here in a couple of minutes. She wanted to know who the murderer was *now*.

Through the kitchen window and the back door's plate glass, Daisy saw the motion-detector light in the backyard unexpectedly flash on. Had Dustan kept those working on purpose because of the statues?

She turned the back doorknob and found it unlocked. Rushing outside, she ran down the steps and heard a voice she recognized.

"Daisy," Jonas called. "What's going on?"

"The murderer is here. She tried to lock us in the secret office."

Seeing a flash of red under one of the lights, brown hair brushing across the back of it, Daisy sprinted. "It's Edith," she called to Jonas. "Edith Armbruster."

Edith was weaving in and out of the concrete statues. Suddenly, she picked up a small bunny and tossed it toward Daisy. It grazed her arm, but she kept sprinting.

Edith tried to run, too, but there were so many statues . . . so many blocked paths. Dustan must have been back here rearranging and sorting. Edith tripped over a miniature concrete garden bench. That was the chance Daisy was waiting for.

Before Edith could crawl to her knees, Daisy flattened and sat on her. Suddenly, Jonas was at her side. Leaning over the woman, he nudged Daisy away and pulled Edith's arms behind her back, keeping the woman secure.

The fight seemed to go out of her.

Edith sobbed, "I didn't mean to kill him. He just made me so mad. He drained Mom's savings, all because she made a mistake when she was a kid. I didn't mean to hurt *you*. I just wanted you to stop poking around."

Breathless, Daisy asked, "Why did you follow me tonight?"

Edith let out a cry of anguish. "I just wanted to find the info he had on my mom. I tried to break in before, but the alarm went off."

Daisy sank onto the ground and turned toward the house. Gavin was limping out the back door. Sirens broke the silence. Red, blue, and white lights flashed. Zeke and two patrol officers ran toward them.

Jonas let go of Edith's arms, sank down beside Daisy, and wrapped his arm around her.

EPILOGUE

Four Paws Animal Shelter was busy today. Jonas had asked Daisy to meet him at the shelter so they could talk with Bart Cosner, who was adopting a dog. She'd quickly agreed, knowing they'd hear something about what had happened to Edith and the rest of the Rumple case.

After a hug and a smile, Serena told them Bart and a dog were making friends in one of the runs. Daisy and Jonas headed that way. Immediately, Daisy could see that the pup was a cutie. About thirty pounds, he was long and a bit pudgy with short legs. He was definitely mostly basset hound. His coat was brown with tan spots, and he had a white nose with a black spot right in the center. Bart was hunkered down on his knees with him. He had given the dog a chew toy. The hound settled with it between his paws, looking up at Bart adoringly.

"I think he's chosen you," Jonas said.

Bart glanced at them over his shoulder. "And I've chosen him," Bart assured them. "I just have to sign the paperwork. The kids are going to love him. Marjorie, too. In fact, she'll probably spoil him rotten."

Daisy had met Marjorie, who was a loving wife and mother. Daisy was convinced she'd give the dog plenty of attention.

"But you didn't come here to see my bonding with a basset hound, did you?" Bart's smile was wide and teasing.

"Of course, we did," Daisy responded. "If you have anything to tell us, we're here for that, too."

The patrol officer aimed his attention at Daisy. "You're asking *me* instead of the detectives because you know they'd give you another scolding."

Detective Rappaport and Zeke had read Daisy the riot act. "Gavin and I just went to look at a vacant house. We didn't expect the murderer to follow us."

"You seem to attract them," Bart quipped, standing and putting his hands on his hips. He wasn't as imposing in jeans as he was in his uniform. "We think Edith had been following you for a while. She seemed to think you could find the information she wanted."

"I'd like the whole story," Daisy said. "*Before* Trevor Lundquist exposes it in the *Willow Creek Messenger*. I think I deserve a little more consideration than he does."

Bart studied her, then Jonas, and nodded. "I suppose that's true. That secret room you found was a trove of all the information we needed about Wilhelm Rumple. It had super-fast Internet and every bell and whistle imaginable. Our tech guy had a fine time exploring it."

"I wonder how much of his time Rumple spent in there," Jonas mused.

"From the files he had on citizens of Willow Creek, and farther afield, he spent hours and days in there."

"How many people was he blackmailing?" Daisy asked.

"Too many to count," Bart responded. "We're still sifting through everything. He turned hacking into gold by collecting an income from his victims."

True to her word, Daisy had kept quiet about Zebediah Beiler, who had gone to his wife and bishop and confessed. But to Daisy's knowledge, no one else knew about Rumple blackmailing him.

"I'm glad Serena came to you about her experience. That probably helped you blow the whole case open," Jonas said.

"It did . . . because then we knew what to look for."

In the week that had passed since the fateful night when the killer had tried to run from Daisy and Gavin, she'd wondered about Edith and her motives. Rumors had flown around town, but Daisy didn't know what was true. "Can you tell us what drove Edith to murder? The night we caught her, she said something about her mom."

"Since it's going to be a public record, I can tell you about it," Bart said. "Edith confessed to us, and Hetta Armbruster answered all of our questions. When Hetta was a juvenile, she was involved with a convenience-store theft by her boyfriend. She drove the getaway car. Her father hired a good lawyer, and her record was sealed. If her brush with the law ever got out, she was afraid she would lose her job and her reputation. It was possible she couldn't volunteer here at the shelter anymore, either. She loved the life she'd made and didn't want it to change. I think Serena is talking to her about what happened and working through it with her. Dogs are everything to Hetta, as they were to Edith."

"I suppose Edith saw what was happening?" Jonas guessed.

"Yes," Bart answered succinctly. "Apparently, Hetta's life savings went to Rumple's blackmail. She won't be able to retire, ever. She'd been helping Edith stay afloat, too. Edith's dog biscuit business was just getting off the ground. Before that, she relied on her mother for basic necessities. Edith couldn't stand on her own, and she saw her mother's security dribbling away. That was enough to make her confront Rumple that night in the dog run."

"So it was an impulsive crime of passion," Daisy said. "Did Edith tell you where she hid the bucket?"

"We found the bucket at Hetta's. She didn't even know it was there. It was one of the reasons Edith made a full confession. She didn't want her mother to be blamed. Edith had put the bucket in Hetta's backyard by the woodpile and filled it with kindling after she cleaned it. But she missed traces of Rumple's blood, and we managed to lift some partial prints of hers."

"What are the charges?" Jonas inquired.

Staring down at the pup, who was still enjoying his chew toy, Bart answered. "My guess is the public defender will try to negotiate a manslaughter plea for Rumple's murder. Edith has also been charged with counts of assault for going after you and Gavin."

"Did you prove her truck ran Daisy off the road when she was bike riding?" Jonas asked.

"The analysis hasn't come through yet on that. That could add another charge."

"I can't help but feel a bit sorry for her," Daisy said. "I

don't think she planned for any of it to happen. Was Stanley King also being blackmailed?"

Bart dug his hand into his jeans pocket as if considering whether he could answer Daisy's question. "As you probably guessed, some of Stanley King's business dealings were underhanded. He knew about the vitamin D problem long before it came to light, and so did Wilhelm Rumple, who had done his research. It wasn't just about the vitamins, though. Rumple's blackmail included a plan to ruin Andrew and Caroline's romance by bringing King's questionable business dealings to light, going to the press, ruining his reputation and Andrew's. King was trying to protect all of that by paying Rumple monthly installments."

"What about Mr. Miller?" Daisy asked. Putting the pieces together from what Ruth Zook had told her about Miller's business woes, the way he suddenly had money for the rehearsal dinner after Rumple was killed, Daisy suspected he was being blackmailed, too. After Edith had been apprehended, Caroline had come to the tea garden to unburden herself and confided to Daisy that her dad had taken an interest-free loan from Stanley King to keep his business afloat. But the blackmail had put more pressure on his finances that neither King nor Caroline had known anything about.

"Clancy Miller's story is an old one," Bart said, deciding to apprise Daisy and Jonas of the baker's situation, too. "He'd been in business with his brother in Pittsburgh. After his wife died, he began drinking and gambling. He embezzled money from his brother. When his brother found out, he didn't press charges. Clancy moved to Willow Creek with Caroline, hoping for a new start.

He never expected Rumple to dive into his past. It was almost as if Rumple read the phone book listing everybody living in Willow Creek and then Googled them. Actually, he more than Googled them. He concentrated on business owners, but if he got a whiff of anything in anybody's past that was a secret, he went with it."

Jonas looked pensive when he said, "Hopefully, everybody who Rumple blackmailed will have clear consciences now from confessing their secrets. I understand Andrew and Caroline are still planning their wedding."

"At least *they* have a happy ending," Bart said. "And so do I." Bart crouched down again near the mild-mannered basset hound. He stroked the canine's long velvety ears and then ran his thumb over the dog's wrinkled brow. "Basset hounds are supposed to be loyal, and they track scents well."

Daisy realized it was as if Bart needed a few concrete reasons for falling in love with the dog. "Are you going to name him or let your kids do it?" Daisy asked.

"Oh, they've all seen videos of him already. My youngest wants to name him Scout. Actually, I think that might be the perfect name. What do you think, Scout?"

The dog looked up at him with liquid, dark brown, expressive eyes and barked.

Daisy and Jonas both laughed.

After goodbyes all around, Bart left with his newfound family member.

Jonas and Daisy turned to each other. Jonas's green gaze stayed on her a few moments, and she thought she saw something unsteady in his expression. She was feeling unsteady herself because of all the thoughts about him and their life together zinging through her.

Jonas hesitated, then said, "We'd better go get Felix. He could get into trouble with Bellamy if given enough time."

She wanted to say, *Wait. Not yet.* But in that instant, her courage left her. "Yes, we should go get him," she agreed, yet she didn't move. Neither did Jonas. It was as if their hearts were communicating, even though their words weren't.

As they stared into each other's eyes, Jonas breathed, "I don't ever want to lose you."

Daisy's hands were sweaty, because she had something important to ask Jonas. Now wasn't exactly the right time, but when would be? Her courage rose up, and she took hold of it. "I don't want to lose *you*, either."

"Zeke and Tessa have advised me if I don't make a move soon, you're not going to know how much I love you," Jonas confessed, the tension in him obvious from the set of his jaw and the squaring of his shoulders.

In unison, they asked each other, "Do you want to live together?"

At the same moment, they answered each other's question. "Yes!"

"Tonight?" Jonas hopefully suggested, as if he still wasn't sure what important step they'd both taken.

"Tonight." Daisy wrapped her arms around Jonas's neck, eager to start a life with him . . . day and night . . . forever and ever.

Then Jonas did something totally unexpected. He leaned away from Daisy and got down on one knee. "Will you marry me, Daisy Swanson?"

Nodding and crying now, she knew whatever family they created together would be perfect for them.

ORIGINAL RECIPES

CHICKEN CHILI

2 tablespoons olive oil
½ large, sweet onion, chopped (about a cup)
½ cup grated carrots
5 tablespoons flour
½ tablespoon chili powder
½ tablespoon ground cumin
2 cans chicken broth (14.5-ounce cans)
2 cans great northern beans (about 15 ounces)
1 can black beans (about 15 ounces)
1½ cups cut up cooked chicken

Toppings can be sour cream, cheddar cheese, or chopped tomato.

Using a high-sided skillet, slightly heat the olive oil on medium, then drop in onions and grated carrots. Stir until the onion is translucent. The carrots will steam further in the cooking process. I mix flour, chili powder, and cumin (you can add more of the spices if you like it spicier) and then sprinkle that mixture over the onions and carrots. Stir for a minute or two until the flour and spices are worked in.

Once you have a paste, pour in one can of chicken broth. Stir until gravy-like, and then add the other can. Cook on medium to medium high for about two minutes, constantly stirring to thicken. Add beans. I use canned beans to make this a quick recipe, but I rinse them with water to cut sodium. Stir in chicken.

There are two ways you can cook further. Leave the chili on the stove and simmer for about 20 minutes, or use the method I like—just put the chili into a Crock-Pot

(I spray mine with cooking spray) and turn on low for about three hours. The beans soften more, the spices have more zest, and the chili is ready whenever you want it!

There are so many variations on this. You can chop peppers and add them instead of the carrots. You can mix in chopped tomatoes with the chicken. I try to keep it as low salt as possible by rinsing the beans and not adding any additional salt. But salt to taste. It tastes even better the next day!

CHEESE BISCUITS

2 cups flour
¼ cup shortening (I use Crisco)
3 tablespoons baking powder
2 cups shredded cheddar
½ cup milk
½ cup sour cream
½ teaspoon salt

Mix ingredients together with electric mixer. Form dough into six balls and place in a nine-inch round non-stick cake pan.

Bake at 400 degrees for 15–17 minutes.

Let sit for 10 minutes before serving.

MILD PEACH SALSA

3 peaches (diced)
1 large tomato
$\frac{1}{4}$ green bell pepper
1 tablespoon sugar
Juice of one lemon
$\frac{1}{2}$ cup chopped sweet onion
$\frac{1}{8}$ tablespoon pepper
$\frac{1}{4}$ teaspoon salt
3-4 crushed red pepper flakes

Gently mix all ingredients in a medium bowl and serve cold. I also use the salsa over a pork loin.

Visit us online at
KensingtonBooks.com
to read more from your favorite authors,
see books by series, view reading
group guides, and more!

Visit us online for sneak peeks, exclusive
giveaways, special discounts, author content,
and engaging discussions with your fellow readers.

Betweenthechapters.net

Sign up for our newsletters and be the first
to get exciting news and announcements about
your favorite authors!
Kensingtonbooks.com/newsletter